Ivy threw her arms around Cam and squeezed. "I think that's the nicest thing you ever said to me."

"Mom?" Eight-year-old R.J. opened the pantry door. "You know the lock doesn't work. Why would you close this door?"

Ivy elbowed Cam out of the way. "It was Cam. He was trying to show me where he put everything."

R.J. stood staring at Cam with his hand on the doorknob. "What was Mom looking for?"

"A pineapple slicer." Cam said the first thing that popped into his head. He walked out of the pantry.

Sarah and two other customers stood in the diner, frowning.

"But..." R.J. dogged his heels. "We don't have any pineapple."

"I know." Cam wasn't giving up on this ruse. "I told her she shouldn't buy any until she had one."

R.J. stopped in the middle of the kitchen. "But... I'm confused."

So was Cam. But it wasn't pineapple and pineapple slicers that confounded him.

It was Ivy.

Dear Reader,

Ivy Parker has been a key figure in the Mountain Monroes series. A single mom, she runs the Bent Nickel diner, which is the only place to eat in Second Chance. She's not an overachiever. In fact, she's a little scared that the Monroes will change Second Chance into a thriving metropolis and make it that much harder for her to run a business and raise her two young sons. Status quo is the way to go!

And along comes overachiever chef Camden Monroe. He's got a Michelin star and several opportunities in the mix, including licensing his own food line and a shot at television stardom. But only if he continues to uphold his stellar reputation. That's hard to do when the only place he can cook is a diner in the Idaho mountains with a woman who thinks frying an egg is haute cuisine!

I'm pleased to add Ivy and Cam's kitchen romance to the series. I hope you come to love the Mountain Monroes as much as I do. Each book is connected but also stands alone. Happy reading!

Melinda

HEARTWARMING

Charmed by the Cook's Kids

———

USA TODAY Bestselling Author

Melinda Curtis

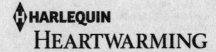

HARLEQUIN
HEARTWARMING

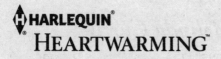

ISBN-13: 978-1-335-88973-7

Charmed by the Cook's Kids

Harlequin Enterprises ULC
22 Adelaide St. West, 40th Floor
Toronto, Ontario M5H 4E3, Canada
www.Harlequin.com

Printed in U.S.A.

Recycling programs
for this product may
not exist in your area.

Prior to writing romance, award-winning *USA TODAY* bestselling author **Melinda Curtis** was a junior manager for a Fortune 500 company, which meant when she flew on the private jet she was relegated to the jump seat...otherwise known as the potty—seriously, the commode had a seat belt. After grabbing her pen—and a parachute—she made the jump to full-time writer. Melinda's Harlequin Heartwarming book *Dandelion Wishes* will soon be a TV movie!

Brenda Novak says *Season of Change* "found a place on my keeper shelf."

Jayne Ann Krentz says *Fool For Love* is "wonderfully entertaining."

Sheila Roberts says *Can't Hurry Love* is "a page turner filled with wit and charm."

Books by Melinda Curtis

Harlequin Heartwarming

The Mountain Monroes

Kissed by the Country Doc
Snowed in with the Single Dad
Rescued by the Perfect Cowboy
Lassoed by the Would-Be Rancher
Enchanted by the Rodeo Queen

Return of the Blackwell Brothers

The Rancher's Redemption

Visit the Author Profile page
at Harlequin.com for more titles.

THE MOUNTAIN MONROES FAMILY TREE

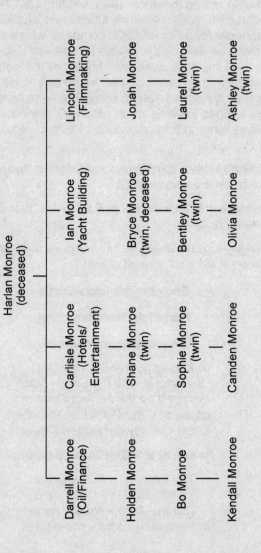

Harlan Monroe
(deceased)

Darrell Monroe
(Oil/Finance)

Holden Monroe

Bo Monroe

Kendall Monroe

Carlisle Monroe
(Hotels/
Entertainment)

Shane Monroe
(twin)

Sophie Monroe
(twin)

Camden Monroe

Ian Monroe
(Yacht Building)

Bryce Monroe
(twin, deceased)

Bentley Monroe
(twin)

Olivia Monroe

Lincoln Monroe
(Filmmaking)

Jonah Monroe

Laurel Monroe
(twin)

Ashley Monroe
(twin)

PROLOGUE

"NO ONE ATE my chef's surprise." Eight-year-old Camden Monroe sat alone on top of a picnic table at a Pennsylvania lakeside campground.

"Well…" Rather than point out that benches were made for sitting and tables for eating, Grandpa Harlan joined him. He smelled of sweet coffee and cigar smoke, aromas Cam associated with adventure and laughter. "You must have some idea why they couldn't stomach your breakfast."

"No." Cam glared at the green gas cookstove and the large frying pan caked with burned eggs.

"*Ca-a-a-m…*" Grandpa Harlan stretched out his name in a way that expected truths, not excuses.

"The eggs might have been dry," Cam allowed, gaze still caught on the frying pan.

"*Ca-a-a-m…*"

"Or overdone in parts." Code for burned. Cam snuck a glance at his grandfather.

The old man raised a white, bushy eyebrow.

"I thought the extra cheese and salt would make it taste good." Cam picked at a carved heart in the wood tabletop, but it refused to flake. It was harder than his burned eggs. "Better even."

He'd thought his two siblings and nine cousins would lick their paper plates clean. If they had, he'd have said, *"Surprise!"* and admitted the eggs weren't perfect, but he'd have spoken proudly because he'd also have fixed his mistake.

Wasn't that what Grandpa Harlan was always preaching? Fix your errors? Take pride in your work?

But nothing could fix those eggs. Or ease the taint of failure, a stink that was going to cling to Cam like the smell from a skunk. And he'd been so hopeful when everyone had scooped large portions from the frying pan.

Because his cousin Holden was oldest, he'd shouldered his way to the front of the line and had been first to take a bite of Cam's egg-and-potato scramble. He'd shouted a warning— *"Abort! Abort! Abort!"*—and then run to the trash can and tossed in his plate. It had landed with a thud as loud as thunder.

Ten more jokes and thuds had followed.

Only Grandpa Harlan had tried to finish his breakfast.

Cam's stomach turned in mortification.

And he hadn't even eaten his own cooking!

"This is a lesson, Cam." Grandpa Harlan drew him closer, lowering his voice as if his eleven other grandchildren were near and hadn't run off to the diner down by the lake for breakfast. "You can't cover up your mistakes. Do you understand?"

Cam nodded. "Monroes always do their best." It was something his father and grandfather preached.

Cam had to be perfect.

Or be the butt of Holden's teasing forever.

CHAPTER ONE

"I'M NOT GOING to cook in a diner." Top chef Camden Monroe crossed his arms over his chest and glowered.

When he was in his restaurant kitchen, this stance and stare usually brought those in his employ back in line. Pronto.

But Cam wasn't in his kitchen or even in a restaurant. He stood on creaky floorboards in the Lodgepole Inn in the center of remote Second Chance, Idaho. He stared at his older brother, Shane, and one of his younger cousins, Laurel, neither of whom backed off or even looked to be considering his statement as ending their discussion.

"I'm serious," Cam reiterated, holding his ground.

"You usually are." Shane had been in Second Chance for months. Since January. And in that time, he'd changed. Gone was the power suit, the crisp haircut, the Italian dress shoes. In their place? Khakis, a navy polo, penny loafers. Had his sharp ambition and drive for perfection been dulled, too?

Cam silently vowed that wouldn't happen to him. "Even if I did cook in the diner, my vote wouldn't change." Meaning his vote to sell Second Chance, a town they'd inherited from their grandfather. The town with the diner in question.

"This isn't about the vote," Shane muttered unconvincingly. He led those in the family who were keen to keep ownership of their grandfather's hometown.

"We're not asking you to change your opinion." Laurel twisted her long red hair over one shoulder, and then rested her palm on her pregnant belly. She'd been in Second Chance just as long as Shane. Both were engaged. Both looked more relaxed than Cam had felt in years. "And we're not asking you to open a restaurant here," she said.

Right. But Shane had asked him to contribute to the town before casting his final vote. *Gee, as a chef, what could that contribution be?*

Cam's scowl deepened. He imagined the expression was making permanent grooves in his face. "So the only thing you're asking me to do is cook in a *diner.* Me. You know I've got—"

"A Michelin star." Shane's gaze flickered upward as if he was considering rolling his eyes. "Never fear, bro. Everyone knows chef Camden Monroe is both talented and creative."

"Able to make exquisite meals out of nothing." Laurel continued the flattery. She'd been doing that ever since Cam had grumpily entered the inn's communal space this morning.

And why wouldn't he grumble? There was no espresso machine. He'd had to make coffee using one of those pod brewers. And drink it from a paper cup!

He understood his relatives were mellowing as they settled down in Second Chance, but he'd thought they'd retain their standards for good coffee. He hoped they hadn't lost their taste for good food.

"Cam, your talent is why I want you to cater my wedding," Laurel said soothingly. But her smile wavered, and her hands seemed to seek comfort as they cradled her large baby bump.

Cam's resolve broke, loosening the foundation of his scowl.

"Who wouldn't miss your cooking?" Shane drew Cam down from his proverbial pedestal, and they walked toward the Lodgepole Inn's manager apartment and its small, antiquated kitchen. "But you need space to work your magic."

"Especially for more than a hundred guests." Laurel followed closely behind them. "Thanks to my mother, what was going to be a quiet, private ceremony has become an event to include Hollywood's movers and shakers. I'd never ask you to cater something like this from my kitchen."

Which was a good thing, since Cam would never agree to it, either.

There might have been four feet of counter space in the inn's main-floor apartment, not counting the small table barely big enough for four. The stove looked older than he was. The microwave only had one setting. There was a battered Crock-Pot on the chipped Formica counter, a testament to the quality of meals prepared there. The kitchen was more appropriate for a college student than a wedding caterer.

Prepare appetizers and a main course here? Cam shuddered.

Maybe they're right. Maybe Cam needed the diner.

But there were obstacles to their plan. To satisfy more than one hundred people, he'd require at least a dozen feet of prep space. Assistants and servers. Adequate cold storage. Larger oven space. And those were just the obvious needs on his list.

His gut knotted. All those wedding guests. All his family, including his impossible-to-please cousin Holden. The pressure to live up to high expectations—to constantly reinvent, to be the perfect chef, to make every plate a work of art—continued to mount. Knots tightened. Time slowed. Monroes always contributed to the bottom line.

Contribution or no, it was a mistake coming here.

But he'd given Laurel his word.

"The kitchen at the Bent Nickel Diner is so much larger," Shane said, oblivious to Cam's near panic attack. "There'll be plenty of room to bring in the tools of your trade."

"Yes." Laurel slid her arm around Cam's waist and rested her head against his shoulder. "And when Ivy tastes the breathtaking dishes you make in that kitchen, the Bent Nickel's menu is sure to change. Ivy's a smart businesswoman. She'll recognize the profit potential in a menu upgrade."

Cam scoffed. Not only did they want him to cook for the wedding as if he had access to a gourmet kitchen, but they also hoped he could bring about change to the local diner's menu?

Impossible.

The woman who ran the Bent Nickel Diner was the queen of kitchen shortcuts. He'd eaten there once on a previous visit, told her what he thought of her food, and she'd banned him for life. Ivy wouldn't welcome him in her domain. She wouldn't…

Cam breathed deeply, his stomach unclenching.

Here's my out.

"Aren't you forgetting one thing?" Cam looked at Laurel and Shane in turn, the tension inside of him easing. "Aren't you forgetting Ivy hates me?"

IVY PARKER MARCHED across the Bent Nickel Diner, arm raised, finger pointing toward the restaurant's main entrance. "Get out!"

Chef Camden Monroe, the offending would-be patron, gave her a smile that burned her chest like jalapeño-induced heartburn.

How does such a handsome man still affect me so?

"Out!" Ivy repeated, fully aware her audience included her customers and her two impressionable young kids. But she was fuming.

Honestly, if not for Nick and R.J., she'd have added an unflattering description of what she thought of Cam.

Get out, you heartless, talentless food snob!

"Nobody criticizes my food and comes back for more." Ivy blocked the aisle and waved her hand as if she could erase Cam's presence. His dark-haired, dark-eyed, all-too-handsome presence.

"So…" Cam had a grin that might have made Ivy's heart pound if he'd made eye contact. He was that gallingly good-looking. Thank heavens for his huge ego. He stared at the back wall as if she was beneath him. "Are there no second chances in Second Chance?"

He thought this was a joke?

"*Out!*" Heat radiated from Ivy's chest, up her neck and into her face.

"Now, Ivy." Laurel Monroe stepped in Ivy's path, pregnant belly first. "Hear us out."

"No. This is my place." Ivy paused. It wasn't exactly her place. She'd sold it to Harlan Monroe, Cam's grandfather, several years ago and had been leasing the Bent Nickel back from him for the enviable rate of one dollar a year. But Harlan was dead, and her lease was up at the end of the year. Whether or not those generous terms were renewed was up to Harlan's twelve grandchildren, including Chef High-and-Mighty Monroe.

Heaven help me.

Cam huffed. His gaze, black as a moonless night, met Ivy's with a jolt. It sent a warning— *let me in if you want your lease renewed.*

Ivy's heart stuttered. She'd thought her divorce had done away with power struggles in the diner.

Cam was big and bad in the food world. One of those hoity-toity, much-revered chefs who charged a hundred dollars or more for a meal—a small, pretty serving on a delicate white plate, a meal that didn't fill bellies. Cam wasn't setting foot in the Bent Nickel again, no matter how long he stood there huffing and puffing.

Ivy lifted her head high, swallowing back unwelcome awareness of the man and unwanted doubts. "I reserve the right to refuse service." She wouldn't look at Cam again. She wouldn't take in those chiseled cheekbones. She wouldn't stare at that obstinately curling hair. She wouldn't—

She looked.

Cam had resumed smiling, as if he knew she'd been backed into a corner and he could waltz right in.

"Out!" Ivy's arm popped up once more, narrowly missing Laurel's belly.

"Ivy." Laurel drew back a few steps. She was pregnant with twins and yet somehow managed to look delicate and stylish.

Both times Ivy had been pregnant, she'd been as huge as a whale and had worn her then husband's T-shirts and sweatpants.

"I know Cam needs a mouth filter, but…" Laurel's smile was pleading. "My wedding is in a few weeks and Cam will be catering."

"Bully for him." That didn't mean Ivy had to put up with a peer who despised her food. "He can eat at the inn until the big day." Because the last time he'd been in, he hadn't just cut apart and cut down her scrambled eggs, he'd tried to eviscerate *her*!

Shades of my ex.

"Mom." Ivy's five-year-old son, Nick, slid next to her and wrapped his arms around her waist. He smelled of hot chocolate and boy. "Are you mad?"

"Yes." Ivy drew her youngest closer.

"What did that man do?" Nick stared up at Cam. "Did he try to steal the cash register?"

"No," Ivy said, albeit reluctantly. She'd love to attribute Cam with dastardly deeds.

"Did he ask for a second order of French

fries?" Nick asked. Seconds of sides was a no-no.

Cam smiled at Nick in what someone else might have called a kindly way—someone more gullible than Ivy.

"He did not order seconds on fries," Ivy said through gritted teeth.

"Did he try to sit in Shane's spot?" Her oldest son, R.J., appeared at Ivy's opposite side and pointed toward a booth with a Reserved sign on it. R.J. was eight, accelerated in reading books and people. "Big tippers get saved seats."

"A wise practice," Cam murmured, scanning the half-filled diner, then added, "If unnecessary."

Ivy swallowed a frustrated growl. Mondays were always slow.

"Then what did he do?" R.J. leaned against Ivy's side and stared up at her.

"Yeah, Mom." Nick swung her hand. "Why is the big man bad?"

Ivy pressed her lips closed. Chef Camden Monroe upset her on too many levels. He made her want to try again—at life, at love and in the kitchen—but for all the wrong reasons. She had to stay in her lane and forget about impractical dreams.

The intruding Monroe lifted his black gaze to hers, stifling her breath as he crossed his arms over his broad chest. All the while, he continued with that smug smile, as if he'd snuck in past her defenses like a Monroe Trojan horse.

He's not in yet.

She could still refuse him entry. After all, Shane and Laurel weren't escorting him past her. No matter how tenuous Ivy's position, they still respected her rights to the Bent Nickel. But Chef High-and-Mighty stared down at her as if he'd never worked in a restaurant until he was of legal voting age, never had to listen to a spouse tell you how worthless you were in and out of the kitchen, never held a baby in one arm and a toddler in the other and wondered how to keep a restaurant's doors open.

He's been coddled.

And like coddled eggs, he was soft.

Except his arms. They were strong enough to heft a sixteen-quart pot filled with pasta.

Ivy sucked in air and the desire to curse. Her attraction to Camden Monroe and her envy of his accolades were both pretty high, as disconcerting as his pretty low opinion of her and her food was. She couldn't have him in her diner.

Not for a meal today. Not for all the meals between now and Laurel's wedding.

Family was important. Family, not her ability to make exquisite food. She drew her boys closer.

"Ivy, please." Laurel had the good grace to look guilty. "I need a caterer and Cam needs a place to cook." Her gaze moved toward the rear of the diner. Toward Ivy's kitchen.

Chef Big Guns wasn't here for breakfast. He was here to—

Oh, heck no.

Without looking at Cam, Ivy shook her head. "He can use yours."

Laurel was marrying Mitch, who ran the Lodgepole Inn, although she wasn't carrying Mitch's babies. Not that Mitch let that bother him. He had a heart as big as Ivy's. He was going to love Laurel's twins as if they were his own. But, still, Laurel was heading toward her wedding day with a lot of loose ends, all of which were causing her stress.

What would Harlan want me to do?

Ivy's resolve would have wavered if Chef Big-and-Bad hadn't huffed once more.

He'd want me to stay in my lane.

"I can't work at the Lodgepole Inn." Cam's voice was rough, no doubt worn from snarling orders to underlings. "We believe your kitchen—"

"You haven't been in my kitchen," Ivy said mutinously, holding her boys protectively at her side.

"Can we just look?" Laurel smiled softly.

"You want to look? Like the Health Police?" R.J. was just finishing third grade and had recently become interested in the comings and goings at the diner.

"He's not the Health Police." Nick scoffed, tugged his ear and then pointed at the would-be invading Monroe. "He smiles."

"That I do." Smiling, Cam bent lower to speak directly to her boys. "I'm not the Health Police. I'm a friend, a chef who wants to borrow your mom's kitchen."

A friend?

Ivy made a strangled noise that earned her a shoulder pat from Laurel.

"Are you a real chef?" R.J. asked, as if he'd never seen one before.

Ivy stiffened.

Laurel's shoulder pat became a shoulder rub.

Cam nodded. "I went to chef school and everything."

Ivy's stiff shoulders spasmed.

"Cool." R.J. ran to the back of the diner,

where his friends were congregating. "Hey, guys! Guess what?"

"He's a chef! Just like my dad!" Nick skipped after his older brother, leaving Ivy feeling lesser than a certain handsome male chef.

Before Ivy had a chance to get all maudlin, Laurel took Ivy's hand and gave it a squeeze. "It would mean so much to me. Please?"

Chef Food Snob straightened and stared at the kitchen, ignoring kids and cooks and reasons for menu choices. He looked every inch the high-powered, well-respected chef who thought the Bent Nickel and its clientele were beneath him.

More than anything, Ivy wanted to refuse.

But Laurel was one of her favorite Monroes. And there was that lease…

CHAPTER TWO

"THIS DOESN'T INSPIRE ME." Cam glanced around the large, outdated kitchen at the Bent Nickel. Forget his contribution to the small town to appease Shane. He wanted to turn around and head back to Las Vegas. "It's inspiration-free." Like the rest of Second Chance.

"Good." Ivy harrumphed.

Cam was used to entry-level kitchen staff being insecure when he was near. He was used to chilly greetings and shade cast his way by older, more experienced chefs. For his own survival, he'd learned to put the lesser-skilled and less renowned in their place. In fact, he'd tried to reinforce his position as top dog when he'd eaten here previously, and he'd only experienced a smidgen of remorse for his scathing review of Ivy's breakfast, which wasn't as inedible as much as plain.

What he wasn't used to was Ivy's reaction. She hadn't crumpled. She hadn't backed away in shamefaced silence. She'd defended her plainness—as if it was okay to be average.

And she was doing it again today.

Cam watched Ivy out of the corner of his eye. She had her hands on her hips and her gaze on him.

"Are you done?" she growled.

Without answering, Cam surveyed the kitchen once more.

The workspace wasn't laid out efficiently— too many steps between the sink and the food-prep area, too many steps from the sink to the refrigerator. The grill was too large and the oven too small. There wasn't enough storage. He opened a drawer and poked through various utensils, grudgingly acknowledging they were of good quality, if not out and at the ready. A peek beneath the prep counter revealed a gleaming set of stainless-steel cookware. The butcher knife in the block was sharp enough to slice tomatoes with precision.

Overall, the kitchen was poorly laid out, but well equipped. So why had the meal Ivy had prepared for him been average? And why was she so defensive of just meeting the bar in terms of culinary effort? The diner had that 1950s charm—checked linoleum, chrome-and-pleather barstools, a sparkly white Formica dining counter. Clean but comfortably worn. Quaint but without any standout features. A roadside dive. The ideal setting to find surprisingly good food.

His gaze returned to Ivy, squarely this time.

Like her kitchen, on first glance Ivy didn't shine, either. Her hair wasn't bright enough to be blond or dark enough to match the walnut brown of his hair. She was neither too short nor too tall. Her features were unremarkable, and her figure was hidden beneath a man's shapeless, beige T-shirt that proclaimed, Life Is Hard. Eat Dessert First. Like the kitchen and her cooking, she was just average.

Unless you took note of her expressive eyes. They were the color of aged bourbon and they gave away every emotion she was feeling. Anger. Annoyance. And, surprisingly, vulnerability. As if she was afraid.

Not of Cam, certainly. But of something.

"You may go now," she said testily.

Having taken multiple vacations and holidays with eleven cousins and siblings, Cam was used to letting testy words flow over him and used to taking note of nuances—either on someone's face or in a bite of food. If she'd been a Monroe, he'd be scrounging up ingredients to make something quick, sweet and decadent to soothe her prickly mood and draw out her concerns.

But Ivy wasn't a Monroe. She was one of the many Second Chance residents benefitting from his grandfather's whimsical approach to business. He should give her no quarter.

Yet for all Ivy's adequateness, for all the vulnerability in her eyes, she spoke regally, as if confident she was the superior cook in the kitchen.

Ivy's tone made Cam give her a longer, deeper look. He took in those beautiful eyes and the hint of worry lines around her mouth—lines that deepened as soon as she realized he was staring at her.

She needed a serving of molten-lava cake. Possibly two.

Not ready to give in to her demand that he leave, or his impulse to bake for her, Cam opened the refrigerator, and began investigating.

Ugh. It was filled with prepackaged food. Cheese individually wrapped in plastic. Bags of precut lettuce. A tub of margarine. Cam wanted to slam the door and say *No*.

No to cooking in this kitchen.

No to Second Chance.

No to rejection and failure. Not that he'd

been able to control rejection or failure, even as recently as last week.

He slid a sideways glance at Ivy.

Her chin was up, nose in the air. "I'll happily break the news to Laurel that my kitchen doesn't inspire you."

Cam glanced out the kitchen at Laurel, who was sitting in a booth talking to a pair of grizzled old men. She was always trying to keep the peace in the family. She deserved a special wedding day—a perfect celebration with exquisite food her guests could find no fault with. He was unable to say no to Laurel. Truth be told, he was unable to say no to any of his siblings and cousins when they needed help. His generation of Monroes had shared adventures with Grandpa Harlan. They had history, shared a bond. Plus, his siblings and cousins had been the first ones to rave about Cam's cooking when he'd finally learned enough to make edible food, which had built his confidence enough to pursue a career in the culinary world when his parents had wanted him to follow Shane's footsteps in business.

Say no to Laurel? He couldn't do it. He was going to cater her wedding.

But he was sure he couldn't live up to Monroe standards of perfection in this diner.

The refrigerator door slammed shut. Ivy moved between it and him, and crossed her arms, her brow pinching, as all traces of wariness were buried beneath a cold veneer of anger.

Cam wanted to pacify the situation, backtrack for overstepping, not fight. But he wasn't here to offer an olive branch. He took Ivy by the arms and gently but firmly moved her out of the way of the freezer. But not out of his grip. Her skin was soft and warm, tempting his hands to linger.

"You can't just walk into my kitchen and then…"

Cam opened the narrow side-by-side freezer door and stilled. He'd never seen so many bags of chicken nuggets, tater tots and French fries, all jammed around boxes of frozen pizza. This took average fare to the extreme.

He dragged his gaze from Culinary Hackville to Ivy.

Her brow was no longer furrowed. However, her cheeks were the deep pink of a ripe peach. The longer he was with her, the more he saw beyond her averageness. Those eyes… The delicate curve of her chin… She was beautiful.

What did that say about her food?

Nothing.

"Say something," she whispered, clearly pained. She wasn't a Monroe, but she called to him nonetheless.

Cam opened his mouth to put her at ease before he recognized the opportunity for what it was—a chance to goad Ivy into kicking him out of the kitchen. He pressed his lips together.

If Ivy refused Cam the use of her diner to cater Laurel's reception, so much the better. He could retreat to Boise and make arrangements to rent a professional-grade, gourmet kitchen and transport everything to Second Chance on Laurel's wedding day. He could escape Shane's hidden agenda (he always had one), deliver on Laurel's right to a perfect wedding (baby-daddy complications notwithstanding), and avoid this unusual, unwanted attraction to Ivy (her appeal was growing).

Decision made, Cam cleared his throat, determined to prod Ivy until she kicked him out permanently. "Why don't you want me to cook here? Are you afraid I'll steal your secret recipes?" He gestured toward the frozen food, welcoming the cold blast of air from the open freezer. "A real chef would never work in a kitchen like this, with food like this."

Amazingly, Ivy didn't wither and have a meltdown.

Quite the opposite. Her back stiffened. Her chin rose. Her eyes blazed with a fire he didn't understand.

She was a cook in a diner, and a poor one at that. Why did his attack give her strength?

"There are no chefs in *this* kitchen." She snatched a menu from a clip on the fridge and held it in front of her chest. "This is a diner. Short-order cooks only."

Where was her pride? Where was her indignation?

Where is my out?

Cam tried again. "Short-order cooks are fine for Idaho hillbillies and carloads of families looking for cheerful, forgettable meals when they stop to use your bathroom." He lowered her arm. "But given you aren't banning me for life, I'll be creating flawless food here for my cousin's wedding reception."

How much bigger of an opening did she need to toss him out?

Instead of giving him the boot, Ivy laughed. *At him!*

Deep down inside, in a place where Cam hid his insecurities, something shuddered and whispered, *She knows.*

She knew that his success had been orchestrated by his wealthy, influential family. She knew that he wasn't perfect in the kitchen. She knew that his Michelin star had been a fluke.

A fluke?

Cam frowned so hard his entire body tensed, suppressing insecurities, squashing doubts, locking fears of imperfection deep inside, where they belonged.

I earned that star. Me, myself and I.

"I've changed my mind." Nose in the air, Ivy flounced toward the dining room, shoulders squared, hips swaying. "I'd like to see you try and cook five-star meals in here. You can start practicing tomorrow."

"Practicing?" he choked out.

No one walked away from chef Camden Monroe, much less challenged his abilities before doing so.

Cam waited for his stomach to knot. He waited for stress to lock his chest in a sweaty embrace.

He waited, but nothing happened.

IVY'S EXIT WOULD have been perfect, if not for Eli Garland, Second Chance's independent-study teacher, standing in her path. Every child in the rural county had to meet with Eli at least one hour a week during the school year.

Compared to Cam's dangerous good looks,

Eli was safely attractive, blond and blue-eyed with an easygoing demeanor that didn't make Ivy's skin feel tight or her heart pound. Eli was also a great tutor for the kids.

Her gaze tried to shift from Eli to Cam, as if Cam was the last uneaten cookie on a plate and she was on a bender from a strict diet. "What can I help you with, Eli?" Because there was always something.

Notebook paper from the stock supply she kept in the pantry? Antibacterial wipes? Tape to hold artwork on the wall? She was the homeschool room mother. And she liked it. She truly did. She knew every child in Second Chance, was like a second mother to them all. But it was rewarding and exhausting at the same time. And she'd brought it on herself, insisting years ago, after Robert left her, that Eli meet with his students in the diner. She'd been gracious but adamant. Big-hearted but secretly selfish. With her kids in school at the diner, she never had to close the Bent Nickel to drive them to and from Eli's cliffside cabin. For Eli's part, a central location in Second Chance meant no one ever complained that they had to make the drive to his remote residence. Once Eli was on board, they'd settled into a routine that everyone appreciated.

Oh, there'd been bumps in the road. Kids could be messy, loud and rambunctious. The bathrooms required more cleaning. Back then, kids sometimes brought food from home, which caused a ruckus among those without a snack. At first, Ivy couldn't afford to feed them, not with the fancy food on her menu. Not with homemade hot chocolate and made-from-scratch muffins, which she charged a premium for. But she couldn't stand to see kids stare longingly at paying patrons' plates or at the baked goods in her counter display. So she'd bought prepackaged oatmeal and hot chocolate—just for the kids. And then frozen nuggets, tater tots and French fries—just for the kids. Gallon tubs of vanilla ice cream for milkshakes—just for the kids. And she didn't charge the children because they'd become an extended part of her family.

Having the town kids in the diner had paid dividends. The Bent Nickel became a place the locals hung out. Her business for breakfast and lunch increased, and demands on her time multiplied. Between caring for her boys and the schoolkids, and an uptick in business, she'd needed a shortcut regarding her menu. Her first *aha* moment was the community coffeepot. Folks got their own coffee and paid on the honor system. No more running around refilling mugs. She'd held out on downgrading her menu for a year after her divorce. But there was no denying the bottom line—plain, no-frills food was what people ordered most often. The two-egg breakfast. Pancakes. Burgers. Chicken nuggets. Grilled cheese. Four years ago, she'd revamped the menu to optimize inventory management. And then, everything fell into place.

The kids, not just her own, knew the rules and routine. Eli knew the rules and routine. The residents knew the rules and routine. Was the menu overly simplified and plain? Yes. But no one in town complained. Was it the culinary success she'd dreamed of? No. But no one left the Bent Nickel hungry. Was it a challenge raising children in a restaurant? Yes. But she knew that, having been raised in one herself.

"What do you need, Eli?" Ivy asked again.

The teacher gave Cam an inquisitive look, as if he didn't want to interrupt. Finally, he sighed and said, "It's about refreshments for this year's graduation."

At the end of every school year, Eli highlighted accomplishments, big and small, for all his students. This year, Adam Clark and her son Nick were graduating from kindergarten, so they'd be featured in the special ceremony.

"I'll make a chocolate cake," Ivy promised. Nick's favorite.

"From a box, most likely," Chef Pain-in-the-Butt murmured from behind her. "I can make appetizers. When is this graduation?"

Ivy snorted. He'd most likely make something kids would never eat, like escargot.

"Graduation is this Saturday at noon." Eli beamed at Cam, sucking up to the Monroe in the room. He was a smart man when it came to schoolwork, but not the brightest tool when it came to his social network. Cam couldn't help him long-term.

"We'll stick with cake," Ivy said firmly, trying to remind Eli with her raised eyebrows who buttered his bread. "And punch."

"I thought you said I could practice cooking in your kitchen." Cam moved next to Ivy until their shoulders nearly touched. "Come on. It'll be fun."

Nothing with Chef Michelin Star would be fun. "What if you find out tomorrow you can't make anything in this kitchen? You said it didn't inspire you."

Cam glanced around. "Shortcomings aside,

I can make anything, anywhere. Inspired or not."

"Can you?" Ivy glanced out to the picky eaters working their way through math worksheets. "It's almost time for morning snack."

Cam gave her refrigerator the side-eye. "I can do that, too. After a trip to the store." And without another word, he headed toward the door.

"A snack prepared by a chef." Eli smiled. "The kids are in for a treat."

Ha! Ivy bit her lip as Eli returned to his students. They were in for something, all right. Michelin-star chefs didn't do kid-friendly cuisine.

"Thank you." Laurel appeared in the kitchen doorway and gave Ivy a hug. "Thank you for letting Cam in. He seemed more excited just now than he's been in a long time."

Ivy turned on the oven and then took out a bag of tater tots from the freezer. "Really?"

Laurel nodded. "Shane and I have been worried about him. Cam hasn't laughed much since Grandpa Harlan died. This change of venue will be good for him." Laurel moved closer, lowering her voice. "You'll be gentle with him, won't you?"

"Gentle?" *Ha!* Had the three little pigs been gentle with the big bad wolf? She thought not.

"Cam could use a little kindness." Laurel hugged Ivy once more. Thanked her again. Assumed Ivy was going to do what she asked—be gentle with Camden Monroe.

Ha! Not even if her lease depended on it.

CHAPTER THREE

"Wow. Ivy LET you in." Shane accompanied Cam to the general store, which was conveniently located between the diner and the inn. "Honestly? I didn't think you had it in you."

"I don't need your vote of confidence." Cam wandered the aisles in the small store, seeking inspiration for a snack for kids, and feeling a spark of interest he hadn't felt in a long time. Food lining the aisles called to him, everything a potential ingredient. Ladyfingers. Heavy cream. A small basket of strawberries. "Of course, Ivy had to say yes. You're her landlord."

"You're her landlord, too," Shane pointed out. "Your ownership of this town is equal to mine."

"I don't want to be her landlord. I want to sell Second Chance so I can start my own restaurant," Cam said, suddenly lacking in sparks. He paused before a colorful display of locally made preserves and jellies. He couldn't think of what to do with them. Nothing perfect, anyway. Spreading them on white bread wouldn't excite anyone.

Where was the creativity he prided himself on? The intuitive feel for blending flavors that had earned him that Michelin star? He blamed Shane. And Ivy.

Practice? *Michelin-star chefs don't practice.* They dabbled. They experimented. They explored. They created edible art for discerning tastes.

"In the meantime—" Shane picked up a jar of apricot jelly, tracing the quill image on the handwritten label "—whether you want to sell or not, you have to agree that we need to increase the town's economic potential. And changing Ivy's menu will help do that. More travelers and locals will eat at the Bent Nickel, and subsequently, more will spend time in our stores."

Cam frowned. "That's a lot of pressure to put on a restaurant." On Ivy and her averageness.

Shane dismissed Cam's observation with a nod of his head. "The town is hosting an Old West festival after Laurel's wedding. We hope to have hundreds attend."

"And you believe once visitors have a taste

of Second Chance they'll be hooked?" Why had Shane picked up apricot jelly? Why not the diced-apple preserves? "Do you really believe that Second Chance will become the next great undiscovered pit stop along America's highways and byways?"

"Yes." Shane sidled closer. "Listen," he said, lowering his voice with a glance toward the woman at the checkout counter. "I doubt Ivy has the skill to upgrade the menu by herself. Why don't you give her some tips? I'm not asking for the moon here. I like Ivy, but I bet she's never heard of Dijon mustard or aioli sauce."

"Ivy's not going to listen to a word I say." Nor should she. It was her restaurant. Cam took the apricot jelly from his brother, determined to recall a recipe or come up with a stunning idea of how to use it. "I have no sway over Ivy. She hates me." Her animosity was actually freeing. Just thinking about Ivy now cleared his culinary vision. Apricot jelly was perfect with waffles. "She hates everything about me."

"Everybody hates you at first, Cam." Shane wielded his older-brother humor, unwelcome as always.

"Everyone hates you at first, too, bro," Cam responded, clapping back. "And you don't have any superpowers, like cooking, to win them over." Not that Cam had won anyone over lately.

In February, he'd been hired to bring culinary excellence to La Trilogie in Las Vegas. The kitchen there had been a chef's dream, the menu in need of only a few upgrades and adjustments. There had been fanfare and press releases when Cam took over operations. It was only natural that he, as the executive chef, would evaluate the work of his kitchen staff and request they meet a higher standard—*his*. So what if he was resented as the outsider, the man who rocked the boat in calm waters? He'd been hired to bring La Trilogie a Michelin star. That required precision and sacrifice.

Too bad the only thing sacrificed was me.

Shane hadn't taken the bait to exchange insults with him. Instead, he was peering at Cam's face. "What's wrong?" his brother asked.

"Nothing." Cam put what he hoped was a more neutral expression on his face. It was bad enough their father had fired him. But to be fired by La Trilogie… "I'm just annoyed that you've been here nearly six months and you still have no business plan for this little town other than a festival and a menu change."

"Who says I…?" Shane shook his head, still staring at Cam. "Don't try to distract me. You're burned out. I can see it in your eyes. You need a vacation."

"That's why I'm here." What a lie. If he hadn't been fired, he'd still be in Vegas. If he hadn't been fired, he wouldn't be sending his agent's calls to voice mail. All those opportunities his agent had been lining up? Guest spots on television, meetings with companies interested in licensing his name or obtaining his product endorsement. None of it was possible without Cam's name associated with a high-end restaurant, so why answer the phone?

"Step away from the ingredients aisle." Shane took Cam's arm. "Ivy's got kid snack time down."

"French fries and chicken nuggets?" A guess, but Cam grimaced in disgust nonetheless. "I can make something better. I can outcook anyone." With the right resources.

While Cam pretended great interest in the apricot-jelly label—made locally by Quill Canners—Shane stood silently for so long that the woman at the register asked them if they needed any help finding something. Both Monroes politely declined.

"You know," Shane began gently, "when I

ran the family's luxury hotels, I used to believe I could handle anything the family threw at me. My work was everything. It defined me. And then Grandpa Harlan died and Dad fired me and I had no idea who I was."

Cam didn't want to admit that being fired twice in six months had shaken his confidence.

In January, their father had fired them all— Shane, who'd run the hotels, Cam, who'd run the restaurants inside those hotels, and Sophie, who'd managed the vast Monroe art collection. Grandpa Harlan had made their termination a condition of his will—Dad and his brothers couldn't inherit a dime unless they fired every family member. Their cousins were no longer Monroe employees, either.

And then last week, the owner of La Trilogie had let him go. Him. Chef Camden Monroe.

So much for a Michelin star equating to job security.

"I found myself here," Shane said, breaking into his thoughts.

"You sound like you no longer hold a grudge against Grandpa Harlan or Dad," Cam said, clinging to his. His ability to contribute—his importance to the Monroe bottom line—had been questioned after being terminated by his family in January. "That black mark on my résumé is a hard thing to get past."

"It took me a long time to forgive," Shane admitted. "I had to realize Grandpa Harlan wanted us to slow down and find something we're passionate about." He tapped a spot over his heart. "Something we weren't pushed into for the good of the Monroe Holding Company."

"I love to cook." Cam thrust out his chin, channeling Ivy. "Food is my passion." That wasn't going to change, no matter how many times he was fired.

Please let that be the last time I'm fired.

"You're good at making food," Shane said in an even, reasonable voice, as if he pitied Cam. "No one can take that away from you."

But they had. His failures had undercut his confidence in the kitchen. He was second-guessing everything from the acidity level in guacamole to the amount of salt in his signature red sauce.

Cam rolled his shoulders out of the defeat position and told himself none of that was permanent. "Cut to the chase, Shane. What's your game plan for me and Second Chance? Force Ivy out at the Bent Nickel and install me in her place? I promised to contribute to Second

Chance as an investment, but I see it as an anchor around my neck. I'm not staying."

"Other than motivating Ivy to change her menu…" Shane laid a hand on Cam's rigid shoulder. "I want what Grandpa Harlan wanted for you, Cam. Happiness. What do you want?"

Perfection. There was nothing else. "I want to be my own boss. Open a restaurant in a city that appreciates fine cuisine, like San Francisco." Break into television. Introduce a line of his own sauces or cookware. He had dreams, and the need for a big nest egg since job security was an issue.

"That's a good goal." Shane nodded slowly, considering him. "In the meantime, take time here to breathe the mountain air."

Cam scoffed. "I'll be too busy to laze around. I need to test out the wedding menu and make snacks for schoolkids." Cam resumed his perusal of the store. "If only there was a decent store in town."

"I can order whatever you need," said Mackenzie, the eavesdropping salesclerk of the only grocery store in Second Chance. The young brunette's smile was as polished and confident as a concierge at a Monroe luxury hotel.

"Thanks, Mack." Shane turned his back

on her. "Why don't you make chocolate pancakes?" He grabbed a bag of chocolate baking chips. "Or breakfast parfait? Egg burritos? Toast and jelly? It's toast and jelly you've got in mind, isn't it? You're still holding that jar."

Cam hadn't really considered why the apricot jelly was still in his hand. But suddenly, he remembered his earlier thought. "Waffles."

"Waffles?" Shane pointed toward the frozen case and boxes of premade waffles. "Frozen?"

"Not frozen." That's what Ivy would do. "Homemade waffles with apricot glaze and blue-cheese crumbles." The recipe was clear to him now, redeeming in its harmonious, multilayered simplicity. Not to mention it was a proven Monroe favorite.

"Oh." Shane glanced at the box of frozen waffles once more. "But—"

"No *buts*." Cam grabbed a bag of wheat flour, white and brown sugar and then moved toward the small selection of vanilla extract. "You used to love it."

"Yes, but…" Shane fidgeted. "There's something you should keep in mind. I love your waffles, but my boys—"

"The ones you're adopting when you marry Franny?" Cam mentally reviewed his ingredient list. Vanilla extract. Baking powder. Baking soda. Blue cheese? Cam hurried to the cheese section, frowning when he saw how limited the choices were.

"Yeah. I'm adopting Adam, Charlie and Davey." Shane followed Cam at a much slower pace. "They've been raised on the basics. Peanut butter and jelly. Jarred spaghetti sauce. As far as I can tell, the only homemade things they eat are cookies."

"You don't give kids enough credit. They'll love this." And so would Ivy. He could just imagine the astonished look on her face when she tried a bite. He dumped his ingredients on the checkout counter.

"Blue cheese is an acquired taste, Cam. Not to mention apricot…" Shane eyed Cam's purchases. "The boundary of culinary adventure in Second Chance stops at strawberries. Trust me. A little sweetened yogurt and you could wow them with a strawberry parfait."

"I know what I'm doing."

"But—"

"Shane, I don't meddle in your business." Which currently involved opening a summer camp for disadvantaged kids up the road. "Don't meddle in my kitchen."

Shane raised his hands. "Don't say I didn't warn you."

"The only thing I'll need—" Cam sent the woman behind the counter a significant look "—is a better selection of cheese."

Mack grinned. "Give me a list and consider it done."

When Cam returned to the Bent Nickel's kitchen, Ivy was closing the oven door. She set the timer and then smirked at Cam. "It's only fair that I wish you luck. These kids are more brutal than any New York food critic."

"Thanks for the heads-up." Cam didn't give her comment any credence. His apricot-and-blue-cheese waffles were a winner. He found the waffle iron, plugged it in and got to work, barely aware of Ivy darting in and out.

A warm, comforting aroma arose from the oven. She was making French fries or tater tots.

When the timer went off, Ivy returned. She opened the oven and removed a tray full of tater tots. She sprinkled bacon bits and cheese on top, and then slid it back in, setting the timer for five more minutes. While Cam plated waffle squares, drizzling them with warm apricot glaze and dotting them with blue cheese crumbles, she washed and chopped cherry tomatoes and chives. The timer chimed. She took out her tater tots, slid them into a large serving dish, topped them with tomatoes and onion and then took a plastic bottle—Cam gasped!—of sour cream and drizzled it on top.

With a derogatory sniff toward Cam, Ivy picked up her lowbrow snack. "Do you always take this long to make a simple dish?"

"No." That was a resentful *no*. Since his father had fired him, his need to be precise had slowed him down considerably. But normally? No.

No matter. Kids didn't judge food on speed. Tater tots versus waffles? No contest.

Smiling, Cam took in his handiwork. Without a strainer, the glaze was a little lumpy, but it was practically perfect. Good enough for this crowd. "Order out."

No one came running to whisk his plates to hungry, eager customers.

Chuckling, Cam picked up two of his dishes and brought them to the tables where the kids were. Many had cheesy tater tots on individual serving plates in front of them. Some were dipping tots into salsa.

Jarred salsa, Cam bet, smirking.

Tater tots and store-bought salsa versus chef Camden Monroe's waffles? Ivy was going down.

"What's that?" Ivy's older boy peered at one

of Cam's waffles. "Did your syrup go bad? It's not brown."

"That's apricot glaze." Cam continued smiling. As a kid, his siblings and cousins had been skeptical of his creations at first, too. But he'd eventually won them over—with these waffles, no less. Experience was on his side.

Ivy's younger boy pointed at a blue-cheese crumble. "Are those boogers?"

Laughter ensued. And it wasn't only at the kids' table.

Some old guy wearing blue coveralls was filling a coffee cup from a large urn. He chuckled.

"That's cheese." Cam's smile felt strained. He'd forgotten these were Ivy's customers, used to her minimalistic style of cooking. And yet, he wasn't ready to believe Shane was right.

"Mom says when cheese turns white, we shouldn't eat it." Her oldest son spoke solemnly, as if Ivy's words were the gastronomic gospel and he a devout disciple.

"This is a different kind of cheese. A white cheese." Even to his own ears, Cam sounded defensive. He lifted the corners of his smile higher. "It used to be my sister Sophie's favorite breakfast." He looked around for his sister, but although his nephews were present, his sister was not. "I used to make it for Alexander and Andrew when they came to visit." Granted, his now five-year-old nephews hadn't been to visit him in at least half a year, but still, they'd remember, wouldn't they?

At the mention of their names, Alexander and Andrew came over to peer at his work. They were identical twins and had identical reactions, as they drew back and intoned, *"Ewww"* at the same time.

"Really?" Ivy had gotten to them, too? Cam couldn't help but huff. "You've had this before. And you loved it."

The tiny traitors giggled and scurried back to their seats.

"Boys," Shane said from his reserved booth on the other side of the room. "Try one of your uncle Cam's waffles."

Three young cowboys slunk in their chairs and murmured, "No, thanks."

Their teacher gave Cam a sympathetic glance.

This was… Cam felt unable to move beneath the crushing weight of humiliation.

He couldn't win over this crowd? Maybe he deserved to be fired.

"I'm Roy, the town handyman." The old man teetered up to Cam. "I'll try one of those booger waffles. I'm always up for the scary stuff."

Since there were no other takers, Cam handed the thin old man a plate, hope rekindling.

Roy set down his coffee mug. He pushed the blue-cheese crumbles off his waffle with one finger, and then nibbled on one corner, chewing slowly. Finally, his thin, pale face brightened. "Do you know what would make this taste better?"

"Nothing?" Cam asked, watching Ivy cheerfully take someone's order at a booth near the door.

"Turkey." Roy handed the plate back to Cam. "You know them turkey sandwiches with cranberry sauce on top? That's what it reminds me of."

"You can finish that one, Roy." Cam glanced around to see if he had any more takers. Not a child lifted their head. "And have seconds."

"No. Thank you." Roy reached for a spare plate on the kids table. "I prefer nacho tater tots."

Defeated, Cam returned to the kitchen.

How had this happened? Booger waffles was his go-to kid pleaser.

His phone rang. It was Brian, his agent. He sent it to voice mail.

Ivy marched into the kitchen, triumph in every sneakered step. She tsked. "Rule number one of restaurant management. Know your audience."

Her attitude prodded Cam out of his funk. "First rule of chefdom—exceed customer expectations." He took a bite of waffle, savoring the layers of flavor. "Those kids are missing out."

Ivy watched Cam closely. Then, with a brisk nod, she moved to the sink. "Don't take it personally. I warned you they can be a tough crowd." She scraped plates clean and then loaded them into the dishwasher. "And they have groupthink. If one kid hesitates, they all hesitate."

Cam frowned, putting a hand to his forehead. Was this a truce? If it was pity-induced, he'd rather remain at odds with the short-order cook. He pushed a plate across the prep counter toward her. "Are you part of that groupthink, too? Or are you brave enough to try something new?"

She cast him a gaze brimming with annoyance. "What makes you think I haven't had apricot-glazed waffles before?" She turned her back on him, reaching for detergent. "You didn't even strain your glaze. It's lumpy."

Cam paused, amazed she'd noticed the one flaw in his dish. "I couldn't find your strainer."

"It's where you'd expect to find it. With the colanders in the pantry." She huffed. "You could have asked. I would've told you."

"But you don't like me." Why would she help him? He'd taken every opportunity to pound out their differences, to be cruel.

"I may not like you, but I don't like to see anyone do a public face-plant." She scrubbed the grill, pausing when an older couple entered the diner. She called out, "Sit anywhere. The menus are on the table and the bathrooms are in the back."

She was a cook who didn't want to see her competition fail?

The knots in Cam's gut eased. They shouldn't have, but they did.

CHAPTER FOUR

"Whatcha bakin', Mom?" Nick climbed on top of a barstool in the apartment above the Bent Nickel after it was closed.

"Molten-lava cake," Ivy said.

There were equalizers that helped Ivy sustain her one-woman show in the Bent Nickel—dessert (ideally chocolate), working in a gourmet kitchen (upstairs), and moving at her own pace (not a paying customer's). Her nightly rituals helped her be a loving single mom, and a hopeful member of the community.

Hopeful. Something Camden Monroe was not. He'd reached the pinnacle in the culinary world and it still didn't seem to make him happy.

A man with looks like that...

If he smiled at her...

Lucky for Ivy, he was tall, dark and sullen. *Totally not my type.*

Not that she had time for a type, what with

twelve-hour days at the diner. And about that many days until her ex-husband showed up for his biannual visit with the boys, which felt more like his biannual opportunity to make Ivy feel worthless and insignificant. Robert would mount a verbal campaign and show no hint of a crack in his veneer of perfection. Unlike Cam.

Chef Hoi Polloi wasn't invincible and that made him less intimidating.

She'd developed callouses where powerful men were concerned, but that toughened skin needed to stay strong. Ivy had less than twelve hours to recharge so she could face the kitchen invader and grind through another day.

Thankfully, Cam wasn't invading *this* kitchen. Her inner sanctuary. Few in town had seen her personal paradise.

Ivy stirred melting butter and chocolate on a double boiler in her gourmet kitchen. The white Shaker cabinets and Carrara marble countertops were aesthetically pleasing. But it was the functionality that satisfied her culinary sensibilities—a triple-wide stainless-steel sink and a large, dual-fuel range with six burners and two ovens, one of which was convection. It was a joy to cook here. *Truly in-*

spiring. Ivy chuckled, thinking of Cam's reaction to the diner's kitchen.

"Chocolate cake makes me laugh, too." R.J. shot up from the couch and hurried into the kitchen. In the midst of a growth spurt, he was beanpole-thin and interested in everything, most recently cooking, a pursuit she encouraged carefully, always with fun in mind. "Can I help?" he asked. Without waiting for permission, R.J. dragged a stepping stool closer, climbed up, claimed the whisk and took over stirring duties.

"It smells yummy-yums." Nick rubbed his tummy. "But so did that man's waffles today. Hot jelly and cheese. Mmm-good."

"I know." R.J. sighed dreamily. "I almost stole the blue cheese Roy picked off his waffle."

Ivy stopped measuring her dry ingredients into a bowl. "Hang on. You liked them? But you told Cam…"

"He made you mad." Nick lifted and lowered his shoulders.

"Yeah." R.J. nodded, speaking in that voice that was too old for his young years. "That's why I told the kids not to touch his waffles. But Charlie was so hungry. I thought he'd take a plate."

"Good thing he had nacho tots first." Nick giggled.

"And then you called them cheese boogers!" R.J. chortled, nearly falling off the stool.

Ivy was about to tell them that submarining Cam hadn't been nice, but her laughter mingled with theirs. How much better did life get than this?

A bolt of fear pierced Ivy's happiness. She could lose this safe place if she didn't get that lease renewed with good terms.

Stay in your lane, Ivy, and you'll be just fine.

Harlan hadn't realized her lane dead-ended when he died.

Ivy separated eggs and combined them in a bowl with the sugar and salt. She used the mixer on high until everything was pale and smooth. And then she added R.J.'s butter-chocolate mixture and flour, folding them together quickly. Just not quickly enough to whisk away her fears about a lost lease and what that might mean to their way of life.

"I think we need to talk about the possibility of moving away from Second Chance." How could she even consider such a thing? Outside of Second Chance, Robert would consider it open season on Ivy. Fear lanced through her.

Both boys gaped at her. Second Chance was the only home they'd ever known.

Nick was first to crack. "I don't wanna move," he wailed.

"Why would we leave, Mom?" R.J. sat on the kitchen stepping stool he'd been standing on.

"The Monroes have let us live here a long time, but that may change." It was time Ivy faced facts and considered changing lanes. She'd been foolish to assume Harlan's benefits and protections would last forever.

The land in Second Chance was worth more than any of its struggling businesses. And it was owned by twelve Monroes who couldn't agree on anything—five wanted to keep it and seven wanted to sell, including Cam. Other mountain towns had disappeared to make way for luxury homes and vacation destinations, all in the name of profit. She couldn't ignore the warning signs forever. Still...

Stay in your lane.

She felt safe here.

"Mom," R.J. said in his solemn voice. "The Monroes love us. They eat here every day."

"Uh-huh." Nick nodded his head vigorously.

Ivy wanted to point out that the Monroes weren't terribly fond of her food, that their lease could be revoked at any time and that the town had been without a doctor for five months, but those seemed like heavy topics for two young boys. "We could move closer to your uncle Elliot." Her brother, who owned a restaurant in Falcon Creek, Montana.

Ivy poured the batter into several lightly floured ramekins, and then slid them into the oven.

"I vote no moving." R.J. put the kitchen stool back in the corner.

"Me, too." Nick returned to the couch, where he rubbed his head against the pillow until he was comfortable.

"Knock, knock." Mackenzie appeared at the slider of their second story back porch. She ran the gas station and general store, both of which closed and opened at seven, like the Bent Nickel.

The boys greeted Mack without taking their gaze from the television screen.

Ivy welcomed adult conversation. And since Mack was in the same boat as Ivy when it came to her lease, misery loved company. "How'd your day go?"

"Good. A steady flow of customers and brisk sales." Mack carried a bottled smoothie and a bag of barbecue potato chips. She may have turned thirty, but she still ate like a teenager. She took a seat at the island. "I heard you went five rounds with that new Monroe."

Ivy filled the sink with soapy water. *"Chef Monroe."* That man was a piece of work. So confident. Still, she'd felt a shock when he'd taken her arms and shifted her out of his way, a jolt like the first tart taste of lemon in a finely made meringue.

"Cam." Mack nodded. "He came in my store today and pooh-poohed my selection of cheese." Mack huffed. "What does he expect being way up in the mountains?"

"The world. He expects the world." If he'd only go back to where he'd come from, he'd probably get it. "I'm worried, Mack. What if the Monroes want to change things here?" Ivy lowered her voice, as if saying it softly might keep it from coming true. "What if they want *him* to turn the diner into something fancier? You know, one of those cafés like they have in resort towns."

"You mean the ones that charge a fortune for a sandwich?" Mack didn't hide her sarcasm. "Locals can't afford that. The Bent Nickel would go out of business in a month."

"Maybe not a month," Ivy allowed, dunking dirty pots and bowls in the sink to soak. "But if they kick out Eli and the schoolkids, sales will dwindle. What about you? What if they wanted you to offer trendier, more expensive merchandise?"

"I'm continuously updating my stock," Mack said with a shrug. "I sell wine Shane likes, which isn't cheap. I stock premium crackers and brie. And you… You brought in chopped salad and specialty teas for Laurel. It's not like we're sitting on our tails doing nothing new. They have to see we're trying."

Ivy sighed. "Maybe I'm overreacting because Chef Monroe is going to cater Laurel's wedding reception from my kitchen and no one else has cooked with me for years." Not since she'd handed Robert divorce papers.

"Your kitchen?" Mack glanced around. "I love your kitchen."

"Not this kitchen." Not her joyous refuge. "He's going to be cooking downstairs."

"Oh…" Mack smiled slowly. "He's going to suffer a little."

"Not near as much as we've suffered wondering about our fate." Ivy scrubbed the double boiler. "For all the changes the Monroes talk about making, we still don't have a clue as to what's going to happen when our leases run out. And we don't have a town doctor. They're contractually obligated to provide the town with one." And she, as a single mom, had a responsibility to be near health care.

Mack rolled up the ends of her chip bag. "Now that I think about it… Three Monroes have opened businesses in town—Laurel and Sophie have their shops, and now Shane has his summer camp for kids. Cam could open his own restaurant here. The closed bakery is available and sandwiched between two touristy shops that just reopened for the season."

"Cam would never open a restaurant here." A man like that had too much pride to run a restaurant at a crossroads of two remote mountain highways. A man like that couldn't see how important the people in his life were. Instead, he'd be too busy slaving away in the kitchen on a quest for fame and adoration.

Ivy's parents owned a high-end restaurant. It was their life's calling. Unlike Ivy, they didn't allow the local home-study teacher to hang out at the back tables with his students. Unlike Ivy, they hadn't respected the need for a child to be a child. To them, a family business meant everyone worked, no matter how young or small. Unlike Cam—or any chef chasing a Michelin star—they weren't interested in world renown. Like Cam, they were interested in perfection in and out of the kitchen. To them, Ivy was a failure.

"What's that smell?" Mack sniffed. "Something's burning."

"It's not my cake. And it can't be Chef High-and-Mighty." Ivy removed the molten-lava cakes from the oven. "His kind never burn anything."

Mack turned, grinning. "Unless he's trying to cook on the stove at the Lodgepole Inn."

"Mitch said his main burner was unreliable." Ivy grinned back.

The two women looked at each other and laughed.

THE FLANK STEAK was smoking.

Cam hadn't realized the burner on the inn's stove wasn't calibrated correctly. He'd been dicing potatoes and onions, thinking about Ivy and wondering if she knew how to use the chef's knife in her kitchen, wondering how to broach the topic of upgrading her menu, wondering how a woman like her came to be in a place like this.

He turned the flank steak over in the pan and poked it with a fork, checking for doneness. It wasn't the best cut of meat to begin with, but now it had the consistency of shoe leather. Cam shut off the burner.

"Where's the fire?" Shane entered the Lodgepole Inn's kitchen.

Cam turned on the stove's ventilation fan, which chugged ineffectively, seemingly clogged with grease. "I'm off my game." No wonder he'd been let go. Cam opened the kitchen's side door and then waved a tea towel to clear the smoke. "And this kitchen needs a working smoke alarm."

"True on both counts." Shane sat at one of two chairs in the small eat-in kitchen. "I just want to go on record and say I'm here for you, bro."

"Like there was ever any doubt." His older brother was as loyal as they came. Cam removed the steak from the pan, then put it gently on the cutting board to rest. Or die, like his career. He poked around Laurel's refrigerator, hoping to find something to salvage that charred cut of meat. But there was no chance of another chef surprise.

Shane watched Cam closely in that way of his that indicated more than a passing interest. As loyal as he was, Shane was always butting in where he wasn't wanted. "Now I would never presume to know what should go on one of your fancy wedding menus, but—"

"Fancy food isn't in your wheelhouse. Why don't you tell me what you'd like to see on Ivy's menu?" Because Shane always had an opinion and Cam would rather his opinion be about Ivy's trajectory than his. He shut the refrigerator and prodded the steak. It was now officially DOA. "If you've got wishes, they don't count unless you say them out loud." That was one of their grandfather's sayings.

"I wish you were happy." Shane remained watchful. "Can I make you a peanut-butter-and-jelly sandwich?"

"No. You can invite me to that ranch your fiancée owns." Cam speared his ruined dinner with a fork and dumped it in the trash. "They raise bulls, so I'm assuming they have steak and a working grill."

"The Clarks keep rancher hours. By now, they've already eaten dinner and are winding down for the night." Shane paused, continuing to peer at Cam's face. "Why don't you tell me what's really bothering you?"

"Pass." It wasn't like Shane could find him a new job or repair his bruised ego. Cam drew in a breath. "I'll whip up something chocolate for now." Laurel probably had chocolate chips or powder around. Chocolate was a balm for the soul. Chocolate made him think of Ivy and that vulnerable look in her eyes.

"Sorry about the stove. Dad says we need a new one but he's too busy commuting every day in his quest to earn Second Chance historical significance status." Gabby, Mitch's daughter, poked her head out of a bedroom, raising her fist as if she was part of a political movement. She had pigtails, a retainer and a tendency toward horning in on conversations she wasn't a part of. "I like chocolate, too. But I prefer cheesecake." She crossed the kitchen and hugged Shane—two meddling peas in a pod. "You'll tell me when Wyatt Halford is going to arrive, won't you, Shane?"

Cam frowned. "Wyatt Halford? The actor?"

"Yes. He's supposed to come to the wedding." Shane grinned at the preteen. "You planning on going all fangirl, Gabby?"

Gabby jumped up and down, clapping, and grinned right back.

"Wyatt Halford?" Cam murmured. Aunt Genevieve really was delivering on A-list wedding guests. He needed to put serious thought into Laurel's wedding menu.

"Gabs, you need to practice your speechlessness," Shane teased. "If you run at the mouth when you're introduced to Wyatt, it's going to be meme-worthy."

"Why is Wyatt Halford on the guest list?" If Cam knew more about said list, he'd have more success designing the dishes.

Shane and Gabby exchanged a glance that seemed to say *Should we tell him?*

"Yes, tell me," Cam commanded, this being a kitchen and him used to being in charge and obeyed.

Shane shrugged, donning a serious poker player's expression. "We've invited Wyatt to Second Chance to entice him to play a role in cousin Jonah's film script. You know, the one about the stagecoach robber. We're hoping the location and atmosphere will sway him." He exchanged another glance with the preteen. "And cousin Ashley has asked him to be her wedding date, since she's producing the film and went out with him previously."

"*Shane*…your brother should know the truth." Gabby rolled her eyes as she faced Cam. "Wyatt went out with your cousin *Laurel*, who was pretending to be Ashley. Those twins she's gonna have are Wyatt's but he doesn't know it yet. And since my dad is marrying Laurel and wants to adopt her babies, he wants to tell Wyatt the truth face-to-face and ask him if he'll let go of his parental rights."

Cam forgot his kitchen fail for a moment and stared at them in shock. He'd known Mitch wasn't the biological father of Laurel's babies. He'd heard rumblings that things were complicated, but this… He pointed at Gabby. "Should you know all this?" *Should I?* Or anyone in Second Chance? His cousin Ashley, Laurel's twin sister, had a career in Hollywood and a reputation to protect. This was the stuff of gossip magazines. Scandals like this got in the way of business dealings.

"Should I know? Ha! Laurel's gonna be my stepmom. What do you think?" Gabby opened cupboards and then the refrigerator. "By the way, there's nothing in the house to make chocolate anything or cheesecake, for that matter. Laurel has a stash of Chunky Monkey ice cream, but that's about it in the sweet department. If you're hungry, there's leftover lasagna in the blue plastic tub."

Shane shuddered and mumbled, *"Monday lasagna,"* as if it was as unappetizing to him as booger waffles had been to Roy.

"Pass." Cam took his cue from Shane and started cleaning the kitchen instead.

Gabby drifted out to the common room.

"I said it earlier but I'm going to say it again." Shane stood. "You need a vacation. If you aren't going to tell me what's bothering you, why don't you sit on the back porch and take in the view. The sun sets early out here and the silence is helpful in gaining perspective."

"Sure. What else am I going to do?" Cam breathed in deeply, imagining he smelled chocolate.

Shane put a hand on Cam's shoulder. "Take time to slow down and the answers you're looking for will come."

Cam wasn't interested in answers. He wanted his magic in the kitchen to return—his speed, his confidence. But Cam suspected it was going to take more than two weeks in the Idaho mountains to get his mojo back.

Laughter from outside drifted through the open door.

Laughter and the smell of warm chocolate.

"Is that chocolate cake?"

Ivy bolted upright and nearly spilled her yet-to-be-eaten dessert in her lap.

She swung her feet around to the side of the lounger she was in and faced the man coming up her second-story porch stairs. "Chef Trespasser. What are you doing here?"

"That's the Cake Police to you." Cam paused at the top of the stairs, suddenly looking appealingly unsure. "I saw you from the inn's back porch and… I'm sorry. Nobody has fenced backyards here. I should go. I just…" He ran a hand through his short, dark hair the way Shane often did. Cam's hair was the same color and cut as Shane's, but his hair was thicker, curlier, and his chin more stubborn. "I just burned a steak—something I haven't done since I was ten—and I think it threw me off balance. And then I smelled your cake…" He pressed his lips together but that didn't stop him as he repeated, "I should go."

Since she'd first met Cam, Ivy had recognized his caustic pride as being similar to Robert's and had pushed back against it, defending her hard-won independence. If Cam had intruded on her sunset yesterday, she'd have sent him away without a qualm. But for all Cam's swagger, he wasn't Robert. Today, she'd witnessed his waffle rejection, handled with aplomb. And now, Cam was admitting a kitchen fail without so much as a temper tantrum. The chef inside of her could sympathize and her feminine instinct wasn't putting up walls.

Cam turned to go.

"Wait." She extended her plate with the minicake. "Chef Michelin Star burned steak for the first time in forever. That requires comfort food."

He hesitated. "Are you sure?"

"Yes." Although a part of her wanted to say no. He was still a very good-looking chef and a danger to the lane she'd chosen. Ivy stretched her hand farther toward him anyway.

He hadn't moved from the top of the stairs. "That's not the kindergarten graduation cake, is it? I wouldn't want to be party to disappointing young tykes."

"I won't make that cake until Saturday morning." She wobbled the plate in the air. "Last call."

He approached the spare lounger and sat down so that he was facing her. His gaze searched Ivy's for a heart-pounding moment before he accepted her cake. And then his attention turned to her work. "Molten-lava cake." He tested the dessert's texture with his fork and then took a bite. "It's good."

"You don't have to act so surprised." And make her regret her invitation.

"Why not? You surprise me." He took another bite, drawing all the chocolate from the fork.

"It's just cake." But he was devouring every last crumb. She excused herself and went inside to grab another serving and water for them both. She made sure the drapes were drawn shut on the slider so their conversation would be muffled and not wake the boys. Plus, she didn't want him to see her kitchen. "Lucky for you, I made extra. And by the way, you shouldn't say things like a woman surprised you unless you qualify it."

Am I searching for compliments?

She was. Inwardly, she recoiled. She didn't need validation from him. Outwardly, she held her ground, because it had been a long time since a peer had complimented her work.

He tapped his fork against his plate, like the best man about to make a toast. "Okay. You're not what I was expecting based on your agreement with my grandfather."

There were no compliments in his revised statement, nothing about her food at all. Ivy set down her fork and let anger lift her words. "You think I took advantage of Harlan?"

Cam shrugged.

Annoyance skittered across her skin like

the cool evening breeze. "I admit. I was young and foolish when my husband and I bought the Bent Nickel. We took out a loan and set up what we thought was our dream business. Put fancy sandwiches on the menu. Baked fresh goods every morning. Rotated in daily and seasonal specials. And a year later, we could barely pay the mortgage, much less our food bill." Credit. How Ivy despised it. She tapped her fork against her plate. "When your grandfather showed up, he was like Shane, so full of ideas it made my head spin." Not that Robert had wanted her to listen. "But no one in Second Chance could afford to buy in to his plans. We were all just scraping by. So he bought us out."

"An angel investor." Cam nodded.

"It wasn't an investment. It was a sale. But Harlan let most of us run the businesses as we pleased." She understood why Cam would be suspicious of those who'd taken Harlan's deal. Some had accepted the millionaire's money and retired early, leaving town. Others became snowbirds, returning for the summer. But for a few, like Ivy, the combination of Harlan's friendship and his financial backing had changed their lives.

"Was the sale the wake-up call you needed?

Was that why you changed your menu?" Oh, he was curious, but there was also a jaded note in his tone.

She'd like to think he was wondering about Harlan's intentions rather than judging her character, but she deserved to be judged.

"We made no change in the year after the sale." How Ivy hated to admit that. "We paid off our debt and kept right on going for a while, thinking Harlan's Midas touch was going to kick in at any time." It hadn't. "There wasn't much left after we paid off all our debts." After they'd remodeled the kitchen upstairs. "When it became clear Robert wasn't going to get what he needed here, he left." She lifted her chin as she delivered the half truth.

Cam set his empty plate on the side table that separated the pair of loungers. "The chef left, and the menu changed to fit the short-order cook."

Ivy didn't correct his assumption about who she was or the reason for the eventual menu change. It was easier to let people think what they would. It gave Ivy a freedom of sorts when it came to the Bent Nickel.

"My grandfather would be proud of you," Cam said with his usual gravitas. "Running the Bent Nickel alone."

"I like to think so, too."

The sky changed color, casting the Sawtooth Mountains to the east in a deep purple-gray.

"The best part of sunset is about to happen." Ivy regretted inviting Cam to stay now. This was her time, a bit of stillness before she collapsed in bed. "Don't talk. Just watch the sunset."

"And breathe, I assume." He glanced over his shoulder to the west, where the sun was going down. And then he looked at her with a quirk in his brow. "You're not facing the sunset."

"Sometimes the best views are behind the scenes." Ivy pointed to the Sawtooth Mountains with her fork and began eating.

The Sawtooth Range changed slowly from purple-gray to a dark blue-black, before giving way to shadow against the faintly emerging stars. And through it all, Cam sat silent and still next to her, as if he belonged there.

Robert had never let Ivy sit outside alone. There was always a game on television he needed her to see, a dream he blamed her for blocking, a criticism he had to make about the diner's daily performance. She had been his right-hand man. His appendage. And appendages weren't allowed to have their own thoughts, interests, or opinions.

But those days are over.

Ivy set her empty plate on the tray, wanting to just as firmly set aside her attraction to Cam and everything he represented. "Why did you burn your steak? Other than the fact that Mitch's stove is older than dirt."

"His burners are for burning. Literally." Cam delivered his observation as evenly as if he was reporting on the weather during a dry, sunny spell.

Ivy chuckled. Cam may lack the overwhelming charisma of his grandfather, but he'd inherited Harlan's wit and humor.

Cam's stomach growled. "Sorry. I'm going to have to scrounge something from Mitch and Laurel's kitchen when I get back. It's inconvenient that the town rolls up its sidewalks at seven p.m. every day."

"But it's smart business sense given the lack of customer traffic." Ivy resisted the polite compulsion to offer him the leftover beef Stroganoff she'd made the other night. She was wary of his bossy nature, but drawn to the confidence he exuded all the same. Extending handouts wouldn't keep him out of her lane.

"I keep chef's hours," Cam said with that

brutal honesty of his. "And I've got a well-developed palate."

She absorbed his not-so-subtle swipe at the Bent Nickel's food and offered a not-so-subtle salvo in return. "Hey, I'm not the one with a string of kitchen fails today." Kid saboteurs notwithstanding. She let her words settle between them, then added, "Not that success in the kitchen translates to happiness." Because the seldom-smiling, never-laughing chef didn't seem happy.

"I assume we're talking about your ex-husband, the one who left Second Chance in pursuit of wealth and glory."

"You can assume whatever you please." And she'd try not to let his assumptions get under her skin, even though they all seemed to place her at the bottom of the kitchen hierarchy, somewhere at or below a part-time dishwasher. *I can handle Cam.* He didn't tear down her heart the way her ex-husband had. "Culinary success is difficult to come by and most often achieved at the expense of a personal life." Oh, she was on a roll, preaching from the pulpit without any of the gentleness Laurel had wanted her to use. "Hence the saying 'It's lonely at the top.'"

And good heavens above, Cam seemed

like the loneliest of souls with a demeanor that didn't foster easy friendships. A chef like Cam wouldn't relate to any of the choices she'd made. To him, culinary excellence was the prize worth any cost.

The area's night creatures came alive, filling the silence between them. Coyote yips. Cricket song. Even an owl had something to say. But not Ivy. Not anymore. She'd said too much.

"Thanks for the dessert." Cam got to his feet. "I hadn't realized frozen molten-lava cakes had gotten so good."

Frozen? Ivy's blood practically boiled. How she wanted to tell him she'd made those cakes from scratch. How she wanted to convince herself that his rude character should make him less attractive.

"You could probably put them on your menu," Chef High-and-Mighty continued in the same vein.

"Probably, but I won't." He was so tall and proud and sure of himself that it took effort not to shout her reply.

"Drawing a line, are you?" Cam made a sound of disbelief. "You could reconsider. In Vegas, I changed my menu all the time."

Ivy drew a deep breath to tell Cam exactly

where the line that bordered her lane was and what he could do with it.

"Mom?" Nick shuffled out onto the porch in his baseball-themed pajamas, eyes mere slits and voice hoarse. "My ear hurts."

Ivy laid a palm on her son's forehead. "You're burning up." She swung him into her arms. He was subject to ear infections that snuck up without warning. "We need to call the doctor in Ketchum." And Sarah Quill, who covered the Bent Nickel for Ivy and watched her kids if need be when emergencies like this came up.

She paused at the slider, tossing Cam a dismissive glance over her shoulder. "If there's one thing in Second Chance that needs changing, it's the availability of medical care, not my menu, not my cooking. Tell your brother."

CHAPTER FIVE

THE BENT NICKEL had more morning patrons than Cam expected, more than yesterday.

Perhaps they were drawn by Ivy's welcoming personality, the same way Cam was. She was as straightforward as her food, telling it like she saw it. Since he'd won a Michelin star, no one outside his family talked to Cam the way she did with that balance of hard truth and gentle support.

But this crowd… They couldn't all be here for her generous spirit or down-to-earth pearls of wisdom. So why was an empty seat hard to come by?

Sure, there was the community coffeepot to draw them. And, yeah, there was the gaggle of elementary and middle-school students chattering at the back tables presided over by their homeschool teacher. But there were people actually eating breakfast.

Pancakes. Waffles. Eggs. Omelets. Oatmeal. Although… Upon closer inspection, the food looked worse today than the day before. Ivy wasn't following the-first-pancake-is-always-spoiled-and-should-be-tossed axiom. Sad-looking pancake stacks sat on several tables. The oatmeal in bowls was lumpy and the scrambled eggs on plates were overcooked and crumbly.

Cam entered the kitchen with his blue-striped apron clutched in one hand and a bag of groceries in the other.

An older woman with a silver streak in her short black hair flattened a pancake with her spatula. "Customers aren't allowed in the kitchen. Take a seat and I'll get your order shortly." She waved him off with the spatula. The pattern on her purple polyester blouse was as busy as the diner. An old-school, frilly white half apron was tied around her waist.

R.J. stood on a stool at the stainless-steel prep table, tongue peeking from the corner of his mouth as he slowly sliced oranges. "He's the chef," he said without glancing up.

"Chef Camden Monroe." Cam put on his chef's apron and then stirred the hash browns on the grill. "Where's Ivy?" Because this woman was burning the potatoes and the Bent Nickel's reputation for quick, edible food.

"She had to take Nick to the doctor last night

and hasn't returned." The woman looked him up and down, as if he wasn't to be trusted.

"Is Nick okay? I know he had an earache last night." Cam glanced around the kitchen, unable to believe the rambunctious little boy he'd met yesterday had spent the night away from home.

"Nick gets ear infections a lot." The woman continued to study Cam with suspicion. "A chef who's a Monroe. Will wonders never cease? Are you as domineering as Shane?"

"No one is as overbearing as my brother." Cam edged her out of the space by the grill, flipped her sorry excuse for pancakes into the trash and poured out new ones. "And you are?"

"Sarah Quill." There was pride in her voice, although Cam couldn't imagine it came from her short-order-cooking abilities. "Ivy told me about you."

Was he supposed to know who Sarah was? He flipped the hash browns. "When do you expect Ivy back?"

"Soon." Sarah watched Cam poke the heating tray that was filled with limp bacon, then frowned when he slid it in the oven to crisp. "Ivy lets me use her kitchen to can my preserves and jellies, and in return I watch the kids and the diner sometimes."

Ivy let this woman—the maker of the apricot jelly he'd used yesterday—run her kitchen? And she'd tried to refuse Cam the same privilege? Did Shane know?

"I always watch out for Ivy." Sarah took two fingers and tapped the bridge of her nose in front of her eyes.

"Good to know the Bent Nickel has someone watching over it." Cam glanced at the orders that needed filling.

"I like your diced apples, Sarah." R.J.'s knife slipped and rattled the table, along with Cam's nerves. "Shoot."

"Here." Cam extended his hand toward the paring knife. "Let me do that."

"No, I've got to learn." R.J. scrunched his face in a determined grimace. "All this will be mine someday. It's just… I suck at cutting oranges for—for—"

"Garnish," Sarah said, otherwise not making herself useful, not even to caution the boy not to expect the Bent Nickel would be his someday.

"I suck at cutting *garnish*." R.J. sawed the knife through the orange.

"Spiraling is quicker." Cam took the knife and made a swift spiral of another orange.

"And then you cut it into pieces." He demonstrated. "See?"

"Wow," R.J. said. "You're almost as good as Mom."

Cam scoffed, returning his attention to the grill and the unfinished orders. "Sarah, why don't we divide and conquer? You can take orders and serve drinks. I'll handle the food." Thankfully, nothing on Ivy's menu required more than three ingredients.

"I'll have to call Ivy to make sure it's okay," Sarah said carefully.

"Or you could just do it and keep all the tips for yourself," Cam said slyly. "I bet canning jars don't come cheap."

Sarah shifted her stance in squeaky sneakers. "Someone should keep their eye on you."

"Likewise." Cam nodded.

Grumbling to herself, Sarah left to make the rounds through the dining room.

"I'm hungry," R.J. admitted. "Can you watch me make my breakfast before I go to school?"

"Watch me," not "make it for me." Cam was struck by a memory of himself at about R.J.'s age—he'd been desperate to get in the kitchen and cook his own meals, anxious to carve out a place in the Monroe family that even Holden couldn't attack. His first impulse was to say yes to the boy. But Cam had orders to fill and lacked eyes in the back of his head. "That depends. What did you want to make?"

"Crepes." R.J. came around the prep table and grabbed a worn, red-and-white checked cookbook from the counter. "Apple crepes. I'm not supposed to make it down here, but it's so much easier on the grill than in a frying pan." He stared up at Cam with big puppy-dog eyes. "Please."

Cam's resolve softened. "Do you have all the ingredients?"

"Oh, yeah. I can use Sarah's diced apples for filling." R.J. kept looking up at Cam and forcing a smile, as if were he to glance away, he'd lose his chance.

"For really great crepes, you'd want to make your own compote," Cam informed him.

"Chefs make their own filling." R.J. didn't so much as blink. "Down here, it's short-order cooks and shortcuts."

"That much is the truth." The boy sounded so much like Ivy.

In between completing orders, Cam helped R.J. with his crepe batter. The kid showed promise in the kitchen, as long as he could find where Ivy had squirreled her supplies. It took some digging around the pantry to locate Sarah's diced apples, which was maddening. A chef needed to know exactly where his ingredients were. In between organizing the refrigerator and pantry, Cam supervised the kid making crepes, which was surprisingly easy.

"You've got talent, kid. Good job."

"Thanks." R.J. removed his apron and then carried his meal to a table where his friends had congregated for their daily schoolwork.

Ivy entered the diner, carrying a red-cheeked, sleeping Nick in her arms. She took stock of Sarah chatting at someone's table and Cam flipping pancakes in the kitchen, then stomped across the checkerboard floor. "I don't recall leaving you in charge, Chef Interloper."

Her pink tote banged around her knees, along with a pharmacy bag. There were dark circles under her brown eyes. She heaved a sigh, as if the weight of the world—or of sturdy little Nick—was too much for her.

"Even at a diner, everyone chips in during an emergency." Cam took her purse and the bag of medicine, depositing them on her small desk at the back of the kitchen. When she didn't speak, not even to argue, he removed Nick's sneakers, because that's what his mom used to do when he was a little kid and had fallen asleep. "Sarah may be talented at canning, but her short-order-cooking skills leave something to be desired."

Ivy heaved another sigh. "If I wasn't exhausted and you weren't right about Sarah, I'd argue your right to be bossy." She opened a door at the back of the kitchen and climbed the stairs. Half an hour later, she returned, still looking worn out. She leaned against the refrigerator as if she needed it to stay upright. "Thank you, but back away from my grill. You're only supposed to practice making wedding food here."

Cam bit back a smile. She was nearly as stubborn as he was. "Have you been up all night?"

"Yes. All because your brother hasn't hired another town doctor." Ivy rubbed her face, as if in doing so she'd work up the energy to run the diner. "It's an hour's drive to the nearest medical clinic. But I can nap with Nick while Sarah takes care of the lunch crowd." She made a shooing motion with her hand. "It's Tuesday, second lightest lunch day of the week."

"I've got you covered." Her menu was as straightforward as she was. And as upsetting as it was to realize, it was a refreshing change to cook for speed rather than culinary excellence. He'd been here for hours and had had no complaints. No panic attacks, either, although that was something of a mixed blessing. He wouldn't want to get comfortable kitchen-slumming.

"I can do without your coverage, thank you." Ivy's eyelids drooped as much as her shoulders. "You're probably adding spices to omelets and apple compote on top of pancakes." She gestured to the open jar of diced apples R.J. had used in his crepes.

Cam gave a mock gasp. "You mean I'm putting my stamp on the food? Like any good chef would?"

"There are no chefs allowed in this kitchen." Her tone was steely and yet, there was that vulnerability in her eyes that he'd seen yesterday.

Again, he wanted to soothe her fears with a touch or some chocolate confection he whipped up.

Before he could act on anything, Sarah came to stand in the doorway, black hair with its white streak just as shocking as it'd been at first glance. "You and the chef have everything covered." She removed her frilly white apron and retrieved her purse from a cupboard.

"I'm leaving before the lunch rush gets here and my daily shows start. But don't forget…" She tapped the bridge of her nose with two fingers and gave Cam a squinty-eyed stare. "I'll be watching you."

Cam saluted her.

"But…" Ivy gaped at Sarah's retreating back.

"Well, now," Cam said like a judge preparing to point out the obvious. "Don't tell me you're going to put your pride before your need for rest and kick me out, anyway."

Their gazes met and locked. Something flashed in her eyes and it wasn't vulnerability. It was awareness. Of him.

Cam had to admit, he was aware of her, too. It was hard to overlook that spunk, harder still to resist walking over, giving her a hug and telling her that everything was going to be all right. There was just this feeling, a tug of intuition like the need to add pepper flakes to a sauce, that if he had her in his arms, he might not let go.

Ivy blinked first. She pushed clear of the fridge and tapped the menu hanging there. "Do you see this? You don't deviate from it." She made a double-hand motion, up and down, like a ground crewman directing an airplane to its gate. "This is the Bent Nickel's lane. Stay in it. Are we clear?"

"I know what you expect in this kitchen." It was outside the diner that she perplexed him. Cam moved to Ivy's side, took her elbow and escorted her to the staircase door, stopping only to hand her the pharmacy bag. "I've got this. Get some rest and take care of Nick."

"I don't trust take-charge men who try to take charge of me." She froze, perhaps realizing she'd said too much.

"Don't worry," he told her. "I'm the last person who wants to take charge here. And if it makes you feel better, I'm sure we'll have plenty to argue about later."

Like her freshly reorganized pantry.

IVY WOKE WITH a start, reflexively drawing Nick closer on the couch.

"You okay, Nicky?" She thought she'd heard him cry out.

Nick didn't wake, but he didn't feel as hot as he had before, and he wasn't whimpering about ear pain. She eased out from under him, and went to get a glass of water in the kitchen.

There was another distress cry. Not from Nick in the living room, but from R.J. one floor below her.

Ivy flew down the stairs. "R.J.? Honey, are you okay?" She burst through the door into the diner's kitchen.

R.J. sat on a metal stool at the prep table, gripping his wrist and whimpering.

"Chefs cut themselves all the time," Cam said. "Hold still." He had a small tube of glue from her first-aid kit and was running a bead along a bright red gash on R.J.'s knuckle.

Both males glanced up at her guiltily. Using his free hand, R.J. covered a fourteen-inch chef's knife with a dish towel.

"How deep is that?" Ivy fought a rising tide of panic and frustration. Her son was bleeding. She'd have to call Sarah back and drive R.J. to the urgent-care clinic in Ketchum. "You look like you need stitches."

"Nah." Cam pressed the edges of R.J.'s skin together. "It'll hold fine with liquid stitches. And if he has a scar, all the better. It's a sign of a good chef."

R.J. choked back a sob.

You want to be a good chef, don't you? Her mother's voice, sympathetic but firm as she bent over Ivy's cut finger.

Good chefs keep going. Her father's voice. *Even when it hurts.*

Even when the hurt wasn't inflicted in the kitchen. Ivy understood that now.

Her tide of mixed emotions climbed higher. Fighting to remain calm, she went in for a closer look, relieved to realize R.J.'s wound wasn't in need of stitches. Almost instantly, relief turned into anger. "He's my son, not a chef." She uncovered the blood-streaked fourteen-inch chef's knife. "And he's not allowed to use anything larger than a paring knife."

"But I want to be a chef," R.J. said bravely, choosing not to address the use of an off-limits kitchen utensil. "Like Mr. Cam. And Dad."

Not *like Mom*.

Ivy drew a deep, calming breath, the kind that was supposed to bring peace and perspective. "Are you having fun, R.J.?"

Her oldest glanced up at her, bottom lip trembling. He knew her first rule of the kitchen. He couldn't be cooking in here unless he was having a good time. "Ye-e-e-s-s."

Ivy gave him a quick, one-armed hug. "It's okay to say no." Little boys didn't need to carry on when they got hurt.

"No-o-o." R.J. sniffed, reversing his decision in the face of her understanding.

"I was dicing carrots at speed when I was

R.J.'s age." Cam took R.J.'s finger and wrapped it in a bandage. "A few more close calls and he'll always be careful. He's not done here. We've still got cucumbers to slice for this evening's garden salads."

"A few *more* close calls…" Ivy echoed, feeling faint. It was one thing for an adult to cut themselves while cooking, and another entirely to think about an eight-year-old having a similar accident.

Shane and Laurel stood in the dining room, its lone occupants. They seemed to be bickering. Shane's expression darkened, like a gathering thunderstorm. Ivy imagined her expression mirrored Shane's.

R.J.'s cut was frightening, and Cam was trying to make light of it for all the wrong reasons.

"I appreciate your help," Ivy told Cam, trying to be gracious, trying to retain control of her temper. He'd covered for her at the diner today, after all. But there was her son's blood on the prep table and he was reaching for the chef's knife again. She stayed R.J.'s hand. "But my son only cooks for fun. He's not a chef in training. In fact, he's done in the kitchen for today. R.J., go upstairs and sit with your brother."

"Can I watch TV?"

"Only on low volume. Nick needs his sleep."

"Okay." R.J. sniffed and went upstairs without protest. He was shaken, all right. No matter how brave a face he put on for Cam.

Ivy closed the stairwell door behind him and in doing so saw artichoke leaves in the trash. There was nothing artichoke-based on her menu. And she doubted Chef Overstep had had time to play with his wedding food. Conclusion: artichoke hearts had been added to something.

"Do you have a problem with my food?" she asked, her back to him.

"As long as I'm not eating it, no." Cam sounded perplexed by her question and perhaps a little annoyed, as if she'd questioned the essence of his chefness.

Don't touch my dish, Ivy. You'll just ruin it. Her ex-husband's voice echoed in the kitchen, in Ivy's head, in her very bones. He'd yell and whisper and hiss that she should stay away, and then he'd contradict himself. *You knew my sauce needed more basil. What kind of idiot lets it go out that way?*

Robert was a classically trained chef with the characteristic chef's ego. And yet, despite his training, he lacked a true feel for food, and he tried to make up for it by belittling everyone around him.

Kind of like Chef High-and-Mighty.

Ivy drew a deep, calming breath. The Bent Nickel was no longer a place where she was made to feel worthless and a fool. Harlan Monroe had made sure of that. And Cam wasn't Robert. He'd never said anything to her as nasty as Robert had, or at least he'd disparaged her food and her skill, but not her as a person.

In spite of acknowledging the difference between the two men, the past closed in around her, making Ivy feel small.

Stay in your lane, Ivy, and you'll be just fine.

That's what Harlan Monroe had told her the last time she'd seen him alive.

Her lane didn't have room for men in her kitchen who didn't obey her rules.

She faced Cam with the backbone Harlan had helped her develop, the one she needed every time her husband came back to town for a visit. "You need to leave." She'd said those words to Robert, too. She'd said them with Harlan at her back. She glanced over her shoulder, but no one was backing her up this time.

"Let me clean up first." Cam swept bloody

carrot slices into the trash. "Wouldn't want the Health Police to walk in and see this."

Ivy pressed her lips closed and her arms against her chest. "It's too soon for jokes."

Stay in...

R.J.'s blood, Cam's teasing, the reality of his reference to the health inspector. Fog settled over her brain, clouding her with indecision.

"And what if new customers saw this bloody mess?" Cam continued. "That would turn them off your chicken nuggets, for sure."

Ivy's breath was ragged. Her face hot.

My lane...

She couldn't remember what her lane was. There was just a man in her kitchen making fun of what had just happened. It triggered something inside—self-preservation. Immediately, her legs became unsteady and her hands shook as the instinct to flee warred with the sense that this was her home. Her safe home.

Cam chuckled. "Although seeing a kid cooking back here probably isn't good PR, either."

That laughter… He was enjoying this, the same way Robert used to enjoy putting Ivy in her place.

"You need to leave now!" Ivy shouted, completely laneless.

Cam stopped talking and stared at her, not moving.

Shane and Laurel both turned to see what had upset her.

What upset her was Cam! "You can't just give a boy a large, sharp knife without asking his mother's permission."

Chef Reckless held up his hands. "Ivy, kids need independence when pursuing interests."

"How would you know? Do you have any kids?"

"No. But I—"

"Then you can't really say, can you?" Ivy banged open a cabinet and reached for the disinfectant spray, ignoring a small voice in her head that cautioned her to slow down and steer back to her lane.

"But I—"

"I may be forced to let you borrow my kitchen and disparage my food, but I don't have to let you put my child at risk." A fourteen-inch knife could do more damage than slicing through a thin layer of skin. "R.J. doesn't work here."

"Ivy, I'm sorry."

"Duly noted." She wiped her baby's smeared blood away with cleanser. "Please go."

"Ivy."

"I said, go!" She slammed the disinfectant bottle on the prep table and glowered at him.

"Ivy." It was Shane this time. Gone was the thunderous expression. In its place was a look of concern. "We need to talk."

"No. I was wrong here." Cam headed for the door. "The kid got hurt and I tried to make light of it. Leave Ivy alone."

CHAPTER SIX

"STOP RIGHT THERE." Shane stepped in Cam's way, took him by the shoulders and turned him around, guiding him back to the kitchen.

Ivy scowled. There was nothing like the heat and embarrassment of a complete meltdown to make a woman want a little time alone to recover. "This is unnecessary. I need all Monroes to vacate the premises."

"That's not happening." Shane blocked the kitchen doorway, trapping Cam inside with Ivy. "You both know I'm a patient man. But I'm running out of time to plan the Old West festival and make sure ol' Wyatt actually shows up to the wedding, which means I need to go to South America tonight. Evidently, he's filming there. Meanwhile, I'll just jump right in and address the elephant in the room."

Ivy crossed her arms over her chest, as did Cam. They both scowled at Shane, united against him.

"Ivy, as much as you want things in Second Chance to remain the same, I can't allow it." Shane put his hands on his hips. "Second Chance is living up to its name and coming back to life, the way my grandfather wanted it to. The Bent Nickel Diner needs to keep pace with that change. And that means—"

"No." Ivy shook her head. He'd been making noise about menu changes for the past month or so.

"Don't do this, Shane." Cam stepped closer to Ivy. "The Bent Nickel is Ivy's."

His declaration gave Ivy pause.

Shane began again, this time in a gentler tone. "Change is coming, Ivy. And that means that your food needs to step it up a notch."

Ivy's arms tightened against her chest and she tried to ratchet her mouth closed because if she spoke, it was going to be in her outdoor voice. She'd been lucky her boys hadn't come down to see what all the fuss was about, but they would if she continued to yell.

"In her defense, Ivy can make things that are interesting." Cam's arms were just as firmly locked across his broad chest. "Like tater-tot nachos and frozen cakes."

Ivy choked back a groan.

"But just because she can change up the menu, doesn't mean she will without a push."

Shane looked pained. He was a lot of things, but he wasn't a bully. He just always wanted things done his way. "As part owner of this town, Cam, you have to face up to responsibility, make hard choices and broach the difficult discussions that lead to progress."

"Ivy's menu should be under her control," Cam said tightly, signaling to Ivy with a flick of his hand to let him handle Shane. "Whoever manages the kitchen, manages the menu."

"Is that so?" Shane ignored Ivy, facing off against his brother.

I should jump in.

She didn't, because the feeling of insignificance had returned, bringing with it the urge to remain quiet and still. But that urge was warring with the impulse to toss her arms in the air and toss out words right with them.

"We all rise and fall together," Shane said with a significant glance at Ivy.

His comment poked deep enough to awaken Ivy's backbone. "Together?" She stepped in front of Cam. "This is my place. I rise and fall alone." The way she had been for years. No husband. No in-laws. No Harlan Monroe. "You can't tell me what to do."

"Until December thirty-first," Shane said in an emotionless voice.

"That's right." Ivy's stomach rolled. "I'm in charge until the end of the year."

"Steady," Cam whispered at her back.

It was a bolstering comment. One she'd have expected from Laurel. But Laurel stood silent in the dining room, palms pressing on her lower back, worry in her eyes.

"The way I see this—" Shane had morphed into his business persona, the cold-blooded, corporate CEO "—you don't have to change your entire menu. A standout item or two will do. Don't make it too hard on yourself. But give travelers an appetite to return."

Ivy's chest burned with anger. *Don't make it too hard on myself?* The Monroes thought she was nothing more than a short-order cook. The irony. She'd carefully crafted the image. And now, her secret was burning to come forth.

I'm a chef!

Shane knew nothing about Ivy's past or about the choices she'd made to stay in Second Chance. He'd never asked and she wasn't going to tell him, especially not after this.

"Much as I hate to admit it," Cam said, "Shane has a point on offering a couple of standout items. After all, a better menu means a better profit."

Ivy scoffed. "You know nothing about running a profitable diner." Especially one located fifty miles from any competition. "You couldn't even make a snack schoolkids would eat." She was so angry, she didn't care that Cam's food had been unfairly torpedoed by R.J. and his friends.

"Ivy's got a point." Shane was quick to take a jab at his brother.

"Hey." Cam gently moved Ivy aside. "Whose side are you on?"

"Second Chance's." Shane smirked. "How can I make that any clearer? But I want to thank you both, because I think I've just solved one of my problems."

"Back away slowly," Cam told Ivy, jaw jutted forward. "I recognize that look on my brother's face. He's got a plan and I guarantee you neither one of us will like it."

Ivy tended to agree with Cam, not that she'd ever tell him that.

"We expect hundreds of people to show up for the Old West festival," Shane said. "There's no way Ivy can handle all that business by herself. If there was a way—"

"Oh, no," Ivy said, seeing where Shane seemed to be heading.

"Nope, not interested," Cam said, echoing her sentiment.

"—for you two to work together—"

"Never," Cam said.

"Not in a thousand years," Ivy agreed.

Shane paused, eyes narrowed on Cam. "It's like that, is it? You couldn't win Ivy over with your food?"

"She pointed out my glaze was lumpy." Cam shrugged. "I wanted to make her a molten-lava cake but then she defrosted one for herself."

"You wanted to…" Ivy's jaw dropped. "Why?"

"Everybody needs comfort food." Cam shrugged again. "Isn't that what cooks of any skill cook for?"

It was. But that was the last answer she expected from him.

Shane sighed. "You two leave me no choice."

"Wait a minute." Was Shane going to kick her out now? Today? Ivy stomped her foot a little, but with sneakers, it didn't amount to a lot. "I have a lease."

"And you want another." Shane let his words sink in.

"You can do that?" She barely had enough air in her lungs to ask.

"No." Cam crossed his arms over his chest

again. "You have five votes of twelve, Shane. That's not a majority. You can't offer her a lease."

"You're my sixth vote, Cam." Shane wore that calculating expression on his face again. "And everyone agreed to wait to vote until the end of the year as a way to honor Grandpa Harlan."

"I'm voting to sell," Cam insisted.

"Maybe…" A grin grew slowly on Shane's face. "Wouldn't you look like the star in the family, especially with Holden, if you swung my vote the other way?"

"What?" both Camden and Ivy exclaimed.

"You can't do that," Ivy said, as angry as she'd ever been at Cam. Shane held her future—her family's future—in the balance and he was being glib about it?

"You'd change your vote?" Camden eyed his brother suspiciously. "After months of harping about how we need to retain ownership of Second Chance?"

"Yes. Because I love you and I want you to be happy. You deserve to be happy, too, Ivy. I've tried reason. Tried compassion. Now I'm willing to make a deal. What I'm proposing is this. For a week, we offer two menus at the

Bent Nickel. One from Ivy and the other from Cam."

"What's the catch?" Cam demanded.

"Whoever earns the most money, earns what they want." Shane's voice was as sharp as Ivy's chef's knife, ready to dice up dreams. "If Ivy wins, she'll earn another year's lease at the low rate of one dollar. And if Cam wins, he'll get my vote on what to do with Second Chance."

Ivy swallowed. "If I do this, you'll offer low leases to everyone?" To Roy and Mack and Mitch and the others who'd sold to Harlan.

"No." Shane shook his head. "Only you. And no one else can know."

Ivy wanted to turn him down, if only because it wasn't fair to the rest of Second Chance. But at the same time her heart raced. Another year safely in her lane, protected from Robert. Another year in the black, not worrying if she'd have enough money to pay the winter heating bill or the quarterly taxes.

Working yourself to an early grave.

That was Robert's voice in her head. Cynical and unwanted. She could bear the long summer days knowing that she'd hardly have any business during the long winter months when snow closed the passes.

"I'll take that deal…" Ivy almost thrust out her hand to shake on it, almost forgot that a low lease wasn't the only thing she wanted in Second Chance. "With one stipulation. You hire a town doctor now or I'm not playing this game." They hadn't had one since January. It was almost June. What if one of the boys got sick during the diner competition? What if Nick's ear infection flared up again?

"You know I've been working on that," Shane said with a frown. "Dr. Carlisle will be here later in the week managing the updates to the clinic. I expect to hire someone shortly after Laurel's wedding."

"You're interviewing candidates?" This was news to Ivy.

"It's a moot point." Cam reentered the negotiations. "Ivy can't win if I don't play."

"Afraid I'll steal your secret recipes?" Ivy asked, tossing his words back at him.

Cam scowled. "Let's face it. You have no chance against me."

"You know nothing, Chef Big Ego." Nothing about what kind of patron entered a diner or about how loyal Second Chance residents were. "Put that Michelin star where your mouth is." She did thrust her hand forward then, but at Cam, not Shane.

The big, bad chef hesitated before accepting her challenge. His hand was large and warm and strong. His handshake said he wasn't going to go easy on her. But his eyes… His eyes said something different altogether. The challenges they spoke of weren't ones to be found in a kitchen.

Unless you liked being kissed in a kitchen.

Ivy jerked back her hand and tried to look as if he hadn't shaken her.

But now she knew what his skin felt like.

And she was shaken.

CAM LEFT THE diner in need of air and perspective. The wind rushed down the mountain, granting him his first wish. As for perspective…

Was he happy to be the one to show Ivy her food left something to be desired? *No.* But this bet would ensure Cam was never fired again. He'd find a way to lessen her embarrassment when Bent Nickel customers realized that instead of frozen food, they could be eating a fresh meal prepared by a world-renowned chef. Ivy was tough. If she could stand up to him—and Shane—she could ride out an ego-battering week. Just the memory of her facing off against his brother was enough to make Cam smile.

And the feel of her soft hand in his…

The wind tugged at his button-down. He'd done more than discover Ivy's spunk and softness. He'd found her trigger point. She was fiercely protective of her kids and the status quo. He didn't think any less of her for that outburst he'd witnessed. She'd been right on all counts. But Shane wasn't going to throttle back his drive to build Second Chance into a thriving town. The best way to help Ivy was to show her the power of a good menu.

The plot of land next to the Bent Nickel was bare, a field filled with nothing but wildflowers, as if someone had removed all evidence of a building. At the foot of the sloping property, the Salmon River rushed past, not eager to provide perspective.

Cam proceeded north toward a cluster of small businesses.

Was he troubled to realize he hadn't minded cooking the fast-paced, simplified items on Ivy's menu? *Yes.* He loved the intricacies of food. Plain meat? Frozen potatoes? Unseasoned eggs fried in butter? It was beneath him. And yet, the joy on little R.J.'s face when he cooked had somehow translated to joy inside his own hardened heart. But the feeling had quickly deflated when R.J. had cut open his finger. How scary was that? He'd put on a brave front for Ivy, but it had shaken him. What if the cut had been worse? With no doctor in Second Chance...

Shane was always talking about responsibility—to the family, to their grandfather, to this town. If Cam was going to take this challenge seriously, he had to be more responsible with Ivy's kids.

He reached a covered sidewalk fronting several small stores. The first store-window display was filled with stuffed animals and handmade dolls. The placard in the window read Mountain Lovelies. Open 10-5 for Summer.

A slender, older woman in blue jeans and a pink appliquéd sweatshirt opened the door. "You must be a Monroe. I'm Joley Sunday." Her shirt appliqué was a glittery pile of books and the words: I'm on a Regular Diet of Reading.

Cam introduced himself and then stood awkwardly, staring at a sock monkey with its embroidered smile pressed against the glass.

Like me, in a small-town fishbowl.

"You're the chef," Joley said kindly. "You know, I have some aprons in the back you might like. Thick material and clever sayings. They sell well."

Cam didn't budge. "I'm afraid I'm not a words-on-an-apron type."

Her smile never faltered, the sign of a seasoned retailer. "Well, if you're ever looking for a one-of-a-kind gift, just stop by. Most days, I close at five." Which was an hour from now. "But today has been unusually slow." She returned to her shop and flipped her Open sign to Closed.

Cam walked on, passing an empty space that said it was once an insurance business, but it had something suspiciously like a bakery display case in the back. Weird.

In the next retail space, a woman was locking up just as he reached her. She swung the door open instead. "Oh, hey. You must be the Monroe chef."

Cam glanced down at his jeans and rumpled button-down, which seemed cleaner than her paint-stained jeans and T-shirt. "How can you tell?"

"Besides the apron in your hand, no one else but a recent addition to town would be window-shopping the streets of Second Chance on a weekday afternoon," she confided. "I'm Claire Manley. And I don't get much foot traffic, anyway." She glanced toward her shop. "Vintage Furniture and Restoration. I get a lot of browsers from Egbert's fly-fishing place next door." She tilted her head toward the two-story house nearby. "I won't bore you with the usual complaints. Shane knows how I feel about not having a doctor in town. Diabetic." She tapped her chest and then flexed her fingers slightly. "Arthritic." Her expression turned rebellious. "And I won't make any excuses about being a snowbird or about closing early when business is nonexistent." She paused, as if waiting for him to argue. When he didn't, she shut the door, locked it and flipped her sign to Closed.

Cam was gaining a new level of respect for Shane, in having to deal with Second Chance residents. But attitudes like Claire's made him more determined to sell the town. Monroes had a strong work ethic and expected their business partners to have the same.

The sidewalk ended next to a gravel driveway for that fly-fishing business. On the other side of that was a really old-looking building with a sign that said, Historic Smithy. Smaller print underneath directed those interested in smithy tours to the fly-fishing shop. And that was the end of the main drag on the river side of the two-lane highway.

Cam turned around, glancing at the few buildings across the road. The medical clinic's windows were dark and had a deserted feel. In the woods on the slope above it, lights winked, indicating there was life and people beyond. His sister, Sophie, lived somewhere up there with Alexander and Andrew, and her husband, Zeke.

What if his nephews got injured accidentally? With no doctor in town… Cam shuddered at the thought, suddenly sympathizing with Ivy and her demand for a town doctor ASAP.

Shane needed to move his butt on this medical problem, even if they were putting the town up for sale come January first.

Cam headed back toward the Bent Nickel and the Lodgepole Inn.

Shane stood on the porch of the inn, wind ruffling his short, dark hair. "I need a ride to the Boise airport. Jonah should be here any minute."

"Is that your way of asking me to drive?" Cam stopped at the bottom step, staring up at his brother. "I'm not your biggest fan right now."

"Leaders don't set out to be popular." Shane handed Cam one of their grandfather's lines.

Cam passed one right back. "Leaders get

the job done. What's the holdup on staffing your medical clinic? Seems like a pretty serious issue to me."

"It is." Shane didn't make excuses. "Good doctors don't just fall out of trees to begin with. And good doctors who want to practice in Second Chance are rare indeed."

"But you're close?" An image of R.J.'s frightened face came to mind.

"I'm close." And by Shane's tone of voice that was all he was saying on the subject. "If you drive us to the airport you can shop for groceries in Boise." He glanced toward the general store. "Although Mack would consider me disloyal for suggesting it."

The thought of doing his grocery shopping at just one store—and at this store—was unsettling, and enough to make him agree to be Shane's chauffeur. "Sure, I'll make the drive."

"You're sounding very amenable." Shane eyed him suspiciously. "And responsible."

As if he hadn't been backed into a corner? "As opposed to…?"

"A Michelin-star chef who wouldn't be caught dead cooking in a diner."

"I can be a team player." Cam bared his teeth in a smile. "And responsible."

As long as he won the bet.

THE KIDS SHOULD'VE been in bed.

Who was Ivy kidding? She should've been in bed, too.

R.J. was asleep, his head on a pillow in her lap. Nick was tucked into the corner of the couch beneath a fuzzy blue blanket, his bare feet pressed against her leg. The remains of three-ingredient strawberry-icebox cake sat melting on the coffee table.

Ivy touched R.J.'s hand near his bandage, reliving his upset and her fear. It could have been worse, so much worse. Kids had no place in a restaurant. There were dozens of ways they could get hurt. Cuts. Falls. Scalds. Burns.

Her chest felt as if someone had tossed a fifty-pound bag of flour on it.

She'd been avoiding the realities of running the Bent Nickel as a single mom for too long.

The weight on her chest pressed her into memories of her childhood. Of strict rules and high expectations. Some of her earliest recollections were of moments in the kitchen of Pastasciutta, filling in for employees who didn't show up—dishwashers, busboys, cooks of all skill levels. Summers spent in the sweltering kitchen. Holidays. Weekends.

Ivy sucked in a strained breath. She didn't want to become like them, to expect her boys to work to an adult's standards. Not for love, not for respect, not even for wages. Her parents had put the time and effort into building a reputation for their fine-dining establishment. They'd wanted a nice house, repeat customers, good reviews and perhaps a mention on a travel site or blog. If they'd wanted more, they'd never said.

More. For a chef, more was a Michelin star.

Cam had one. Robert had dreamed of one. And Ivy? She'd thought about it once or twice in passing. But she was a realist. She might as well wish for a star in the sky. Her idea of more had been similar to her parents—own a fine restaurant, one chosen by the locals for special occasions, such as graduations, marriage proposals and wedding anniversaries. But when she'd been at her family's restaurant— and with Robert—she hadn't been allowed the freedom to make the food that excited her. And now, she couldn't make it downstairs. She'd have to watch Cam flex his culinary muscles while she slogged through another long day, sweating over a hot grill and fryer.

Cooking should be fun. It should fill bellies and bring joy. And to do so, you didn't have to come up with complex ways to make a dish.

You didn't have to meet a culinary high bar. But you shouldn't have to scale back, either.

Fine food, good food, the kind she cooked in her dream kitchen, was made for family. Not for profit. Not for respect. But for love.

CHAPTER SEVEN

CAM ARRIVED AT the Bent Nickel Diner at 5:00 a.m., ready to defend his honor in the kitchen.

Last night, he'd driven down to Boise to shop for food, dropping Shane and cousin Jonah at the airport for their trip to South America to find the infamous Wyatt Halford on location and convince him to attend Laurel's wedding. Not only had Cam bought enough food for several days, but he'd also arranged for food deliveries later in the week.

Cam tried to open the diner's door. Unfortunately, it was locked, and dark inside. He juggled bags of food and knocked on the glass. Two hours to open. Ivy had to be back there getting food ready for the day. When there was no answer, he knocked again.

A window above him opened. "What are you doing?" Ivy had bed head and her eyes were mere slits. She wore a frilly, flannel pajama top and a frown. And yet, she still looked beautiful to Cam. "Seriously, the diner doesn't open until seven."

"I know. I need to prep." Cam wasn't going to go through another booger-waffle fiasco. His future was at stake. His food was going to be pleasing and perfect, and he needed time to make it so. "Don't you need to prepare?"

"I need to sleep." She slammed the window shut.

Cam waited in the cold, half expecting she'd shuffle downstairs and open the door for him. He waited a full five minutes before realizing she'd gone back to bed. He returned to the Lodgepole Inn on edge. Out of necessity, he began his food prep in the small kitchenette available for the use of guests. It was more like a wet bar in an alcove than a kitchen, but it had a bit of counter space and a minuscule sink. Luckily, he was never without his own set of knives and he'd bought a set of cutting boards in Boise. He chopped out his frustrations—*chop, chop, chop.* He flattened a clove of garlic—*smash*.

"What are you doing?" Laurel shuffled out of the downstairs apartment looking much the way Ivy had earlier—bed headed, bleary-eyed, wearing an oversized Chicago Bears football jersey that stretched over her pregnant belly. "It's not even five thirty."

"I'm prepping food for my breakfast service." The residents of Second Chance were in for a treat this morning.

"Is this going to be an everyday thing?" Laurel rubbed her hands over her face.

"Yes. Ivy didn't give me a key to the diner."

"Can you blame her? You're up at oh-dark-thirty." Laurel turned slowly back around. "Mitch. Don't you have a key to the Bent Nickel?"

"Yes…" came a muffled reply. "I have a key to everything. But I'm not getting out of bed to find it."

"I'll try to chop quietly," Cam said, heartened by the possibility of access to a key to the diner for tomorrow.

"You do that." Laurel closed the apartment door.

He resumed chopping. Potatoes, sweet potatoes, green onions, tomatoes, olives, spinach. But once the vegetables were cut, he was antsy to get in the diner's kitchen. He wanted to make batter for blueberry muffins and oatmeal crisp. He wanted to put the chalkboard sign he'd purchased and carefully lettered with this morning's menu on the sidewalk in front of the diner. But mostly, he needed to put his best foot forward in the kitchen and ease the anxious knots in his stomach.

He loaded everything up and traipsed back to the Bent Nickel to rap on the door. It was six. Ivy should be in the kitchen by now.

At his knock, the window above him slid open once more. Ivy was still in her pajamas, still bleary-eyed. "Go away, Chef Early Bird."

"Let me in and I'll make coffee," he said quickly before she could slam the window closed. He'd witnessed her coffee addiction these past few days.

There was silence. The window didn't close.

And then he heard her muttering as footsteps thundered upstairs. She was still muttering when she appeared at the front door to unlatch it. "This is not how I saw my day going. My long, long day. Jeez, you have no idea what you've gotten yourself into, have you? It's a twelve-hour shift—cooking, serving, busing tables and running the register."

She wore fuzzy white socks, black plaid pajama bottoms and that frilly pink flannel top. She hadn't fixed her hair. It swayed across her shoulders as she hurried back the way she'd come.

Cam suppressed a chuckle. "You give new

meaning to the expression 'she looked like she'd just rolled out of bed.'"

Ivy paused, turned slowly and closed the distance between them. *"You."* She poked his chest. "You don't know how grueling running a diner alone can be. You'll have no sous chef. No pastry chef. No commis or saucier. No maître d'. No waiter or busboy."

"You made your point. I'll be fine." He tried not to grin. He tried not to move an inch lest she realize he found her adorable, from her floundering curls to her use of frozen food. His attraction made no sense. She was everything he wasn't. And yet, it made him—the master of the poker face—want to smile. "I know how to make coffee." He'd bought French-roast beans, a grinder and an espresso machine. They were in the trunk of his rented car just waiting to be unloaded and used.

"You better not be lying about that." She poked him in the chest one more time and then spun about, more pep in her step.

Cam set his food down in the kitchen and hurried back outside for the coffee apparatus.

There was more at risk than dollars earned and votes won. Cam was going to prove to Ivy that *average* wasn't the way to run a restaurant.

"Mom! Mom!" Nick shouted from the diner's kitchen a floor below. "Stranger danger!" He ran up the stairs and grabbed her arm, pointing downstairs with his other hand. "The booger man is in the kitchen."

R.J. pushed past them and ran down the stairs.

"Good morning," Cam said to R.J. in his deep, even voice.

That voice shouldn't send excited shock waves through Ivy's system. But it did.

"Mom." Oblivious to Ivy's distress, Nick dragged her toward the stairs, and the intoxicating smell of rich coffee and something that smelled suspiciously like blueberry muffins. *The booger man.*

"It's Chef Early Bird," Ivy reassured him. *Chef Shock-to-My-System.* "He's a Monroe, remember?"

She'd best remember that, too. And remember that she'd encountered two kinds of Monroes—the ones who wanted to honor their grandfather by improving the standard of living in Second Chance, and the ones who wanted only the dollars that two thousand acres of mountain land would bring. She might find Cam handsome. She might envy him his achievements. But he was just a man using

Second Chance and the Bent Nickel as a stop on his way to somewhere else.

They emerged from the stairwell into a kitchen redolent with welcoming aromas. Ivy paused and closed the door to their upstairs apartment behind them. No one had cooked for her here since she and Robert were married.

No one is cooking for me today, either.

But there was a handsome chef in her kitchen.

Cam wore blue jeans and a black button-down shirt beneath his blue-striped chef's apron. He looked ready for his magazine close-up, preparing breakfast for what he assumed would be paying customers streaming through those doors when they officially opened at 7:00 a.m.

Good luck with that. There was seldom a stream at seven, or even a trickle. Locals trundled in between seven thirty and nine as they dropped off their kids or stopped by for a cup of coffee or to check on the local news. They'd be in for a news flash today: a Monroe was cooking in the Bent Nickel.

"As promised." Cam handed Ivy a cup of steaming coffee as black as his eyes. "Apologies again for the knife incident. I'm making breakfast."

That was nice of him, if unexpected. And the coffee smelled heavenly. His gaze beckoned her closer, bringing to mind small gestures of appreciation between a man and a woman, private smiles laden with meaning, a lingering kiss as an accent on a goodbye. A kiss…

Her gaze drifted to his mouth.

"Feel free to drink the coffee." Cam cradled one of Ivy's hands in his and raised the mug a few inches higher. "That's what you do with coffee, after all. Or have you forgotten because your mind was elsewhere?"

Oh, my word. He knows I was thinking about kissing him.

Ivy shrank back. "We're not paying for breakfast," she said quickly, before she followed through on her impulse and his invitation to—to… "Thank you, anyway."

Enough of that, girl.

"I wasn't going to charge you." Cam frowned.

Yeah, he was going to kiss me.

And I was going to enjoy it.

Ivy sucked in a breath, cautioning herself to leash her overactive imagination. And if that didn't work, to remember the trouble impulsive kisses caused and that she didn't do impulsive anything.

Stay in your lane.

"What is that?" R.J. pointed at the sausage. It was fresh sausage, not the frozen kind Ivy bought that came in sticks and patties.

"That's sausage for my sweet-potato-and-sausage hash." He slid Ivy a sideways glance and an almost smile. "That's one of my breakfast specials today. Would you like some?"

"Hash sounds yucky," Nick said, having inspected Cam's ingredients. The medicine was working. His fever had broken overnight. He was back to his larger-than-life little self.

R.J. measured a stare at his younger brother and then measured another one at Cam. "I'll try it if you show me how to make my own."

At Cam's nod, R.J. ran across the kitchen to get his apron and a stepping stool. He was just as enamored of Cam as Ivy was, except he did nothing to hide it.

"Not too close." Cam adjusted the stool so R.J. wouldn't be standing too near the grill. "Do you know how to scramble eggs?"

R.J. nodded. "It's the first thing Mom taught me. I don't hardly burn them anymore."

"Burning eggs is a rite of passage," Cam said solemnly. "Master the art of a soft scrambled egg and you can cook just about anything."

That wasn't true. But R.J. seemed to like hearing it nonetheless.

Nick did, too. He'd wandered closer, sniffing the air. "I smell something good." He pointed at the oven. "Are you makin' muffins?" At Cam's nod, he jumped up and down a few times. "Yay! We only get muffins on holidays and snow days."

Days when Ivy was guaranteed slow traffic, or no one at all. She sipped her coffee. It tasted as good as it smelled. She spotted the shiny espresso machine on the counter. "Hey, you didn't brew this for the dining room." She set down the mug and hurried to get the community coffeepot going.

"Why would I make coffee you're going to sell?" Cam teased. "This is a contest I intend to win."

"I thought we were just cooking." R.J. sounded awestruck. "Will there be judges and timers and stuff like on cooking shows?"

"Cool," Nick said.

"It's not like that, is it, Chef Blabbermouth?" The competition was supposed to be a secret. Ivy turned on the dining-room lights, and then the neon Open sign, even though it was a few minutes early. Her gaze caught on a sandwich board on the sidewalk. "Hey, is that your sign outside?" Without waiting for her competition to answer, Ivy went through the door to the sidewalk and breathed in the brisk morning air as she read the sign:

Breakfast Specials!
* Sweet Potato & Sausage Hash
* Blueberry Muffins
* Stone Fruit Oatmeal Crisp

The good news was their menus wouldn't overlap and his were priced at least ten dollars more than hers. The bad news was his specials sounded better than her two-egg breakfast. Thankfully, he'd priced his hash at twenty dollars.

She hurried back inside and set about making coffee and hot water for tea. Cam was showing R.J. how to chop hash on the grill. Her stomach growled nearly as loudly as the brewing coffeepot.

"I heard that," Cam said without looking up.

She ignored him.

A timer went off. Cam opened the oven door and frowned. "What the…?"

Ivy knew right away what the problem was.

"Don't forget that baked goods require less sugar and baking powder at high altitudes." She wouldn't give him a superior smile. That would be petty. She was the better person, after all, someone who didn't rub a person's mistakes in their face.

Okay, maybe just this one time.

She gave Cam a lofty smile.

"Muffins need more liquid, too," R.J. said, making Ivy proud.

"This batch is ruined." Cam removed the muffins from the oven and set the hot tin tray on the stainless-steel island.

"No-o-o-o," Nick howled. "You promised muffins."

"I'll make another batch." Cam's gaze lingered on the oven. "I think my oatmeal crisp should still be good."

Ivy couldn't get so lucky as to have two of his breakfast items fail. She handed Nick a banana. "You can eat it with cereal, or you can wait and see if Chef Sea Level's blueberry muffins turn out this time."

Cam scowled. Nick pouted.

A large white van pulled up outside and about a dozen teenagers tumbled out wearing hoodies emblazoned with a high-school logo. Some headed for the general store, which would open any minute, and some entered the Bent Nickel. A second van joined the first. Unexpected, but a good start to the morning.

Ivy entertained a wicked thought: *Teenagers probably didn't have twenty bucks to spend on a hash breakfast special.*

"Welcome to the Bent Nickel." Ivy came out of the kitchen to greet the crowd. "Menus are on the table. Bathrooms in the corner. Coffee is on the honor system and is almost done brewing."

Cam appeared at her side. "Today's specials…" He parroted what he'd written on the sandwich board. "The muffins are a bit behind schedule but anything else will be up in no time."

Ivy caught a whiff of something burning.

"Cam?" Back in the kitchen, R.J. must have smelled it, too. He sounded worried.

Cam wasn't worried. Or his nose wasn't as sensitive as Ivy's. "Can I get anyone started on a special?"

Jeez. If he burned his special, the smell would linger for hours. Ivy drew Chef No Nose back a few steps. "Let them settle in. You need to check your oatmeal crisp. Now."

Cam sniffed and hurried to the kitchen.

Ivy took orders for eight two-egg breakfasts,

four short stacks of pancakes and one order of French toast. Cam sold one hash plate and one oatmeal crisp.

An hour later and the two vans had left, making way for the first wave of locals. Ivy cleared tables and wiped them clean.

"Where's Shane?" Roy demanded as he entered. "He put in a work order for me to prep six cabins for use." The old man was paid to maintain the Monroe buildings. He took a seat at the counter. "Aren't there enough rooms at the inn for all these wedding guests he's expecting?"

"They're Monroes," Ivy said, as if that explained everything.

"You won't find Shane around for a few days," Cam called from the kitchen. "He's gone on family business to South America."

Ivy and Roy exchanged like-minded headshakes. Normal people did not have family business in South America.

Nick took a seat next to Roy and announced, "I got a banana for breakfast."

"Nick..." Ivy didn't have to see her son's face to know he wasn't happy about that banana. But she looked, anyway.

Roy took a fruit cup from his jacket pocket and handed it to Nick.

"Hey." Ivy pointed at Roy. "You need to ask before giving my kid food."

"What? This? It's wholesome goodness." Roy produced a second fruit cup and lifted the plastic seal. "Each one of these peach cups has a full serving of fruit." The old man tapped his cup against Nick's. "Bottoms up."

The pair slurped their diced peaches as if they were a pureed smoothie.

As if they'd shared fruit cups before.

Ivy shook her finger at Nick, all but forgetting the booth still needed to be cleaned. "You're only getting away with that because you're five, young man."

Slapping his empty fruit cup on the counter, Roy advised, "I'm proof you can get away with it longer than that, Nicky, my boy!"

Nick wiped his mouth with his sleeve, giggling. "Peaches and banana for breakfast." He peeled his banana, offering half to the town handyman.

"I don't eat bananas." Roy leaned away as if Nick had offered him fried rattlesnake. He made a horrified face. "Yucky texture. Creepy brown spots. Clingy strings. Banana-phobia. It's a thing."

Nick stared at his banana. He rewrapped it and set it aside. "I've got banana-phobia."

Oh, no, he didn't. "Eat that banana, Nick, or you'll be confined indoors the rest of the day."

"Mo-om." Nick kicked the counter with his sneakers.

Ivy tossed her rag onto the busing tray. "Nicholas Parker. You love bananas." She waited until Nick began to eat it, then returned to the kitchen, lugging the heavy tray.

R.J. was copying check amounts on the whiteboard near her office.

"What are you doing?" She hefted the tray onto the counter. "Math homework?"

"I asked R.J. to log every order—yours and mine separately." Cam stirred a new batch of blueberry-muffin batter. "R.J. is a fair and impartial judge."

R.J. giggled, not sounding impartial at all. Not that it mattered. Ivy had outsold Cam five to one. And the day was just beginning.

Cam added more water to his batter. "Just so you don't get cocky, I should point out one hash special is the same price as about three of your two-egg breakfasts."

"And yet, I'm more than double your total." There was no way she couldn't say those words without gloating.

"I'm not concerned," Cam replied glibly.

"You should be." Because she hadn't been

running this diner for years to lose to a man who struggled with muffin batter and tried to price-gouge her customers.

Advantage: Ivy.

CHAPTER EIGHT

"WHY DOES IT take you so long to fill an order, chef?" R.J. stared up at Cam from his kitchen stool with what had earlier been worshipful eyes.

The knots in Cam's gut were back.

"There are no chefs allowed in here." Ivy breezed through the kitchen and into the pantry.

R.J. huffed. "Well, *this cook* has been working on his panini order forever."

Oh, from the mouths of babes.

"Not forever. Twenty minutes. Tops." A lifetime to a customer, though. Cam threw his latest attempt at aioli sauce in the trash. "I'm searching for perfection in my plates, including condiments that complement smoked turkey. If at first you don't succeed..."

"I would've eaten that," Nick said from his perch on a beanbag chair in Ivy's office. "You toasted it on bread and it smelled yummy-yums."

"You have an order to fill," R.J. reminded Cam. "Mom says customers shouldn't wait."

Cam made a noise of acknowledgement. He knew he was stuck in a loop. It just seemed wrong to let something he wasn't pleased with go to a table. Everybody was a critic nowadays and he couldn't afford bad press. Of course, he couldn't afford to turn away sales, either. Was there something he'd recommend instead? Ivy's grilled cheese perhaps?

Heck, no. She made it on thin white bread.

"Who moved my paper straws?" Ivy demanded from the pantry. "*Who...?* Chef Overstep, why did you rearrange my pantry?" She stood in the doorway, hands tossing like salad.

"It's got a more efficient layout now." Cam frowned at the small amount of fresh garlic remaining on the prep table. Was it enough to make another batch of aioli *and* his dinner sauce? "You should thank me. Your packaged rice was hidden behind the microwaveable popcorn."

Ivy lowered her hands and blew out a breath. "Just tell me... Where can I find my paper straws?"

He told her, without so much as a thank-you in return.

"But Mr. Cam, what about your panini?" R.J.'s impatient tone sounded a lot like Ivy's.

Ivy emerged from the pantry, straws in hand, frowning. "What's wrong with your panini?"

"My panini is fine. It's my aioli that isn't cooperating." Food critics had raved about his aioli sauce. No one was going to rave about it today, especially the couple at the table in the middle of the dining room, the ones with their heads bent over their cell phones. "It didn't strike the right note with the bread I chose, or my cheese and smoked turkey."

Ivy inspected Cam's handful of ingredients. And then she gave him a funny look. "Aioli isn't that hard. I have a jar in the fridge. Doctor it up if you don't like the basics. Just get your food out there. Now."

Cam's gut knots twisted. "Everything I make is fresh."

"Everything?" Ivy asked archly. "You *never* use premade anything?"

"Well, besides bread, never," Cam said firmly, with a mirrored expression of affront to her two boys just so they'd know the standards this chef had.

"That's not true." Ivy tsked, making light of Cam's entire being with one small noise. "If you've ever plated French fries, you've served premade ketchup. R.J., get him the jar of aioli."

Oh, the look Ivy gave Cam. It was the look he'd given many a kitchen worker when he was being disobeyed.

Cam's nervousness grew, making him stammer like an entry-level apprentice. "I can't… I'm not…"

"You can and you will." Ivy's gaze softened. She touched Cam's arm, as if understanding she was asking him to bend his very being, not just his condiment standards. "I'll tell your table their order will be out in five minutes."

A family of four entered the diner, talking about bathrooms and the need to hurry.

"Back here." Ivy sped out of the kitchen to show them the way. She always went the extra mile for her customers, just not where her food was concerned.

"Do you want me to make your panini?" R.J. asked hopefully. "I know how."

"Sure." Cam admitted defeat.

Grandpa Harlan would say that was the coward's way out. Holden would say his cousin had sold out. Ivy would say he'd made a customer happy before they made their way out the door. And Shane? He'd agree with Ivy because it fit his scheme of establishing the Bent

Nickel and Second Chance as a reputable rest stop for travelers, one with decent food, clean bathrooms and a row of quirky shops that allowed for the stretching of legs.

I'm stretching something, all right.

For the first time, Cam faced the idea of losing. He could forfeit in the name of his chef's honor. But all it would save was his honor, not his dream of restaurant ownership and culinary domination.

Back on his stool, R.J. was assembling panini ingredients on the counter next to the grill. "My mom says the secret to a good panini is for everything to be hot." He brushed both sides of two slices of bread and put them on the grill, followed quickly by Swiss cheese on each. He opened the jar of aioli and spread a layer of it on both slices of cheese, followed by turkey slices and a sprinkling of pepper.

"Now comes the magic."

Nick watched raptly, hunger in his eyes. "Can you make one for me?"

"In a sec." R.J. squirted water on the grill and then covered the sandwich with a melting dome. "Mom says the lid makes it get hot faster. And the steam keeps the bread and turkey from drying out."

Cam knew this, but he was surprised R.J.

did, and not because he was young. "I thought paninis weren't on the menu."

Clutching two green plastic army men, Nick turned onto his stomach on the beanbag, swishing the contents nearly as loudly as the panini sizzle. "That don't mean we don't eat them."

"But that doesn't explain how you know how to make paninis." Cam had learned how to cook by watching his family's chef, recording cooking shows, poring over cookbooks and watching videos online. These kids only seemed to hang out in the kitchen with their short-order-cook mom.

"Order up," Ivy said via the pass-through. She stuck a tag on the rotating ticket wheel. "One cheeseburger, no garnish. One quiche special with extra cheese. Two chicken nugget meals." Ivy veered toward the soda machine.

"I've got the cheeseburger and nuggets," R.J. said, which meant he knew how to get them started.

The quiche was Cam's other lunch special and not to be modified.

"I can't put extra cheese on my quiche," Cam said to Ivy. That would destroy the balanced layers of flavor he'd worked so hard to achieve. "Tell them the special comes *as is*."

Ivy seemed not to hear him over the ice machine filling cups.

"Mom says if folks are paying, they have a say on what they eat." R.J. took out a plate and decorated it with a pickle and an orange slice, then tumbled an order of fries on the side, possibly too early given when he'd put the panini on the grill. Next he went to the freezer for chicken nuggets and a burger patty.

"Mom says even if you don't like pickles, they have to go on the plate." Nick yawned.

"Mom says—"

"I get the idea." And the message—diners at the Bent Nickel ordered food any way they pleased. Culinary rules didn't matter. Chef recommendations didn't matter. Edible art didn't matter. Cam took out a slice of quiche from the oven, where he'd been keeping it warm, and then sprinkled fresh Parmesan on top—*just this one time*. He slid it back into the oven to melt the cheese. "Shouldn't you guys be upstairs watching TV or something?" Not down here witnessing him sinking to new lows.

"Mom says we're not old enough to be upstairs alone." R.J. dumped the nuggets in the fryer and dropped the thin patty on the grill.

Nick slid to the floor in a swooshing of

beanbag. "Mom says too much TV turns brains to mush."

"Your mom says a lot," Cam mumbled. And she did a lot, too. She rarely sat still other than to drink a bit of coffee.

His agent called. Cam sent him to voice mail again.

Hours later, Cam had survived the breakfast rush, the lunch rush and the dinner lull. Ivy had been a veritable Energizer Bunny. She didn't rest and she didn't stop smiling. If Cam had been the smiley type, he would've stopped around lunchtime. His back ached. His feet hurt. But, more importantly, his confidence was dragging.

"It's been a long day," Cam said to Ivy out of a need to make polite conversation while she continued to putter around the diner, seemingly as fresh as she'd been at 7:00 a.m.

"If you want to call it a day, by all means head back to the inn." Ivy studied the contents of the refrigerator. "There's less than thirty minutes before we close and I need to make the boys dinner." She glanced at Cam over her shoulder. "Whatever you're making looks fancy. Are you practicing wedding dishes?"

"No... I..." Cam had filled three large bowls with quinoa and jerk chicken with fresh pineapple and peppers. "I made you and the boys dinner. It's a long day for ones so young." And it wasn't like he had customers to sell his dish to.

"A long day for…" Ivy's gaze sharpened. "Are you implying something about my parenting skills?"

"No. I think you're doing a great job. Your boys are awesome and amaze me with their food knowledge. You've been generous with your kitchen and the reorganization of your pantry." That was as close to an apology as she was going to get. The pantry had a more efficient layout now, after all. "I just thought it would be nice if someone made you a meal for a change."

Honestly, he'd been bored and had decided to make the meal on the off chance that a customer would walk through that door and be unable to resist the smell of his food.

But based on his lie, Ivy's expression changed. Softened. She looked highly kissable. And totally out of his league. How this woman ran a diner alone, cared for her kids and kept a smile on her face was beyond him. It was hard work. Historically, Cam spent most of his day scowling at less-than-perfect dishes and barking orders.

"Dinner, fellas." Ivy took two bowls and set them in the booth nearest the kitchen.

The boys had been engrossed in a video game in the pantry, timer set for a precious hour of playing time. They scrambled to the table regardless, as if they were starving. Cam held his breath, waiting to see if they'd reject his food the way old Roy had rejected Nick's banana this morning, or his booger waffles the day before. But they continued to surprise him, digging right in. If only all Bent Nickel patrons had such an appreciation for fine food.

Ivy brought them glasses of milk. And then she rejoined Cam in the kitchen, picking up her bowl. "You didn't make enough for four?"

"Honestly?" Cam patted his stomach, relaxed for once. "I tasted so many kitchen fails today that I probably won't eat until breakfast tomorrow."

"I see you finally mastered high-altitude muffins." She nodded toward a container filled with muffins on a shelf, then took a bite of his chicken. "This is lovely. The sauce... Wow. Is this one of your staples?"

"Yes." Cam hadn't realized he'd been waiting for her reaction, too, and was pleased that she liked it. "I created that sauce recipe when I was twelve."

"It's truly inspired. So many layers of flavor and yet they all blend together." She took another bite, pleasure spreading across her face like the colors of the sunset he'd watched with her the other night. "Seriously. If you stayed in Second Chance, you and Sarah could can the most wonderful assortment of things."

"I'm not staying in Second Chance." Cam stopped watching her eat and scrubbed his workspace clean. "I need to be where people appreciate my food."

Ivy smiled at him. It was a tender smile, one of the few she'd given him since they'd met. "I appreciate your food."

"Me, too." R.J. said.

"Me, three," Nick added.

"Really?" Their praise lifted his spirits.

"Have we surprised you, Chef Saucier?" Ivy asked between bites, her nickname more of a compliment for once, a reference to his skill with the sauce. "Did you think that because we make a living selling burgers, nuggets and French fries that we'd never had jerk chicken? Or quinoa? That we wouldn't like sauces that are as hot as liquid fire?"

He nodded. But then he remembered that she'd known what apricot-glazed waffles were. Where Ivy was concerned, he couldn't make assumptions.

Especially when one assumption he had was that she'd be like liquid fire in his arms.

"GOT YOUR GROCERIES." Mack shouldered her way in the back door, carrying a large box.

Ivy came forward to help with the load. "Everybody chip in." So they could unpack groceries and finish this very long day.

"I'm still on garbage duty." Nick pushed the big plastic garbage can toward the back door. "Why is it so heavy today?"

"Because of Mr. Cam." R.J. hefted a large container of ketchup from the grocery box and carried it to the pantry. "He throws a lot of food away."

"That's the honest truth." Ivy shook her head. The man had one speed—slow—and a very high standard. He tossed more food than he plated. If there was ever a rush on his specials, he'd be in trouble.

The group made short work of the groceries, and then Ivy helped Nick with the trash, since he'd given up at the back door.

"What's this?" Mack stood in front of the whiteboard with the columns of the day's check amounts.

Ivy felt a swell of pride looking at how many orders she had relative to Cam's.

"Mr. Cam and Mom are playing a game." Nick sat on the bottom stair to their apartment.

"Mom's going to sell the most food." R.J. swung the stairway door open and closed, open and closed, nearly catching Nick's toes each time. "She's going to win."

Mack turned to Ivy, the beginnings of a smile on her face. "And what do you get if you win?"

Shoot. Too late, Ivy remembered this challenge was supposed to be a secret. But it had been Cam who started the tally, right there where anyone in the kitchen could see. She explained about the stakes—Shane's vote to keep the town versus her low lease.

Mack whooped and hugged her. "If you get a low lease, then I get a low lease." She high-fived each of the boys. "Low leases for everybody!"

"That's not what Shane promised." Ivy tried to squelch her friend's enthusiasm and obtain an agreement to secrecy.

Which she did, but not without a qualifier from Mack. "If word gets out, I am totally recruiting residents in town to order from your menu." She practically skipped out the back door as he shouted, "Low leases for everybody!"

CHAPTER NINE

CAM'S FEET DRAGGED as he left the diner.

Laurel stood on the front porch of the inn, staring across the highway at the mercantile and trading post. The buildings had been turned into retail space for Laurel and Sophie. She smiled at Cam as he approached, rubbing a spot on her belly. "How'd it go today?"

"Some might call it a failure." Most, actually. Cam crumpled his apron in his fist as he climbed the inn's porch stairs.

Laurel hugged him. "You need to win the locals. Gabby told me you were charging twenty dollars a plate. That's steep."

"It's a fair price for a dish made by a celebrity chef."

"A celebrity chef they've never heard of?" Laurel gathered her long red hair so it didn't blow in the breeze. "Up here, people don't care about fancy food or name-brand footwear, much less a celebrity. Well, maybe everyone but Gabby."

"You don't think I can win." Heck, Laurel might even want him to lose given she was voting to keep the town.

"I don't want to argue. Let's walk over to the church where the wedding will be held." His cousin looped her arm through Cam's and led him back down the stairs. "I believe you can win, if you can adjust to the tastes of Second Chance. Maybe you'll learn something from what Ivy's done."

Cam rolled his eyes, then tossed his apron toward the front door of the inn. "I could learn how to stay upright and log ten thousand steps a day." That was uncharitable, but he was cranky.

"Oh, Cam." Laurel veered south toward a white-steepled church on a grassy slope dotted with occasional wildflowers. "You've always been so serious, which is good given your choice of occupation, I suppose. But sometimes people who are serious are also seriously inflexible. Look at Ivy objectively. She's good at modifying her menu to people's expectations."

But she didn't exceed expectations. "I'm not going to win this competition by cooking a better burger."

"Maybe not. But you might win if you

bridge the gap between Ivy's basic burgers and filet mignon." She pointed to level ground above the highway. "I thought we could set the reception tables there. It has a grand view of the valley, don't you think?" She turned him to face the Sawtooth Range, much as Ivy had done the night they'd hung out together. "Staring at those mountains makes me feel like all my problems are relatively small."

For her sake, Cam hoped so. But when he looked at the mountains, his problems still felt insurmountable. "Let me help those problems shrink. How hearty do you want your reception menu to be?"

"How much do you want to show off?" Laurel asked him in return. "Guests won't have too many places to eat before or after the wedding besides what they can buy in the general store or at the Bent Nickel. They'll be hungry."

"Hollywood royalty in the Bent Nickel." Cam tsked. "There's a thought that probably gives your mother hives." Aunt Genevieve was a multifaceted snob—food, fashion, social status. "We've talked about some options on the phone. I'll put together a sample menu tonight." He needed to go online and check that all his ingredients could be delivered here without compromising quality. "Did you reserve linens and silverware?"

"Not exactly. Ow." Grimacing, Laurel pressed her palm against her belly. "Practice contraction. I, uh, thought you'd be arranging all that." She contorted her body as if that would ease whatever practice contractions were.

"Can I do anything for you? Rub your shoulders? Run for help?" Cam added Laurel to the list of residents who'd sleep better at night if there was a doctor in town. At this rate, a doctor would help him sleep better at night, too. "Seriously, what can I do?"

"Be my wedding planner?" Laurel's smile didn't look much different from a grimace. "Ashley and Mom are busy, meeting with studios and producers. I don't want to take Mitch away from his crusade to save Second Chance. Sophie's superbusy and—"

"You always come at the bottom of someone's priority list," Cam remarked.

She blew out a beleaguered *"Yes."*

"You know, I'm pretty good at putting on events with food." Which was a good thing since it was less than two weeks until her wedding day. "Have you rented tables and chairs?"

"No." Laurel's mottled face pinched and tears gathered in her eyes.

Cam wrapped an arm around her and guided her toward the Lodgepole Inn. "That's okay. No worries. Your wedding planner is on it." He'd start with his sister, Sophie, who'd gotten married two months ago in that same meadow with nothing more than a wedding cake, a few tables and folding chairs. Of course, she'd had less than fifty guests and Laurel was expecting at least three times that.

"I'm not totally unprepared." Laurel sniffed, torso beginning to relax. "I have a wedding dress. It's almost finished."

Cam contained the urge to laugh. His cousin enjoyed designing and making her own clothes, so he should have guessed her dress would have been her first thought. "Should I ask if you've selected colors?"

"Periwinkle blue and silver. Pink was always Ashley's color."

He remembered. "A nice soft blue it is."

They reached the inn's porch steps. She was a bit shaky in the climb.

Cam helped her to the door. "You'll be all right?"

Laurel nodded. "I'll be all right. Should I

call Sophie and tell her you're on your way over?"

"What makes you think I'm going to pay Sophie a visit?"

"Because Monroe men are so predictable." She took hold of his shoulders. "You are not allowed to chastise her for the state of my wedding preparations. I should have stayed on top of things and been more adamant that my mother didn't hijack the guest list."

"How did superwoman fall so far behind?" Cam teased, even though this was crunch time. "I promise not to berate Sophie for failing in her sidekick duties."

Laurel kissed his cheek. "I can't imagine why people think you're such an ogre to work with."

"Hardy har," he grumbled.

"Well, maybe not everyone, only Ivy." Laurel sighed. "You need to make it up to her. She was frightened about that kitchen business with R.J."

"I'll add it to my list, right beneath my wedding-planner duties." But, for now, he needed to find his sister and some help with wedding preparations.

Which involved traipsing up a hill on the other side of the two-lane highway toward a cabin near the medical clinic. It was just one of many cabins in Second Chance and he hoped it was the right one. He paused halfway up the path to look across the road at the Bent Nickel. The lights were off downstairs. There was no sign of Ivy or the boys. But it was the closest cabin. He'd take a chance it was Sophie's.

"Hey." Roy swung open the door just as Cam reached the cabin's front porch. "Are you coming to make me dinner? I already had soup. Chicken noodle." Standing in the doorway with the light behind him, Roy looked rail-thin and in need of a heartier dinner than soup.

"I'm looking for Sophie's cabin." But there was something about Roy's lack of weight and dinner choice that nagged at Cam. "Can I come in a minute?"

"Sure." Roy stepped back to let him in. "But the directions to Sophie's cabin don't need to be written down. She's just up the hill a little ways more."

Cam crossed the one-room cabin—past a pair of red velvety recliners, past a black pot-belly stove, past an unmade single bed and into a kitchen that wasn't large enough to deserve the title. There was one cabinet, a small sink, a microwave and a minifridge. Not surprisingly, the cupboards mostly contained canned soup and fruit cups. And the refrigerator was empty.

"Is this what Monroes do now?" Roy asked, without losing his upbeat tone. "Inspect the premises? What's next, bed checks?"

Cam rubbed his forehead.

No matter where Grandpa Harlan traveled, he'd had a nose for folks in trouble. He'd spot cars on the side of the road and stop to see if they needed help. He'd order extra plates at restaurants to give to whoever couldn't afford a meal. He was always buying new sleeping bags for his monstrous motorhome because he was always giving them away to people who were down on their luck. He fed them, found them jobs, helped them get home.

Cam faced Roy, who stood before him in threadbare blue coveralls and thick gray socks with red yarn on the toes. This man needed help. Cam knew it like he knew Laurel could use a hand with her wedding.

Cam rubbed his forehead again. He had a lot on his plate. Did he really want to add a side of food-phobic Roy? "When was the last time Shane was in here?"

"I don't know." Roy sat on the edge of his bed. "Maybe March when I had that heart attack? He and Mitch brought me some clothes when I was in the hospital." Roy placed his elbows on his knees and leaned forward, brow furrowed. "Did I do something wrong?"

"No." But Cam was feeling like he had. He'd been living in a tunnel, focused on his own goals. And in the meantime, a world with real issues and real problems had been revolving around him. A world Grandpa Harlan had always wanted to make a little bit better. "You like pork chops, don't you, Roy? Cooked carrots? Salad?"

"I'll eat anything."

Cam covered his laugh with a cough and turned toward the door.

"Are you gonna inspect Sophie's kitchen?" Roy followed him out to the porch. "Is this gonna be a new term of my lease?"

"Don't worry, Roy." It seemed like worrying was Cam's stock-in-trade now. Or at least until Shane returned. "These aren't new lease terms." They were old ones his grandfather would have wanted upheld.

Cam bid Roy good-night and walked on. The trail grew steeper and the trees gave way to a small, cheery cabin. Despite it being hours until sunset, the lights were on inside and a plume of smoke rose from the chimney.

At his knock, Sophie opened the door and

immediately pressed a hand to Cam's chest. She gave him a stern look from behind her thick glasses. "Before I invite you inside, I just want to say we're building a house next year. This is only temporary, so don't judge." She backed up, letting him in.

"How can I judge when I haven't even said hello?" Cam stepped inside.

Sophie and her family lived in a nicer cabin than Roy's, but it was still a cabin—log walls, a stone fireplace, a bigger kitchen, what looked like two bedrooms and one bath. It wasn't the lap of luxury Sophie had lived in while working in Philadelphia, but she seemed happy and relaxed.

"Uncle Cam, did you bring booger waffles?" Andrew squirmed in his seat at the kitchen table, grin wide enough to split his little face.

Alexander rested his chin on the edge of the table and grinned at Cam, like he was the keeper of a big secret that Cam wasn't in on.

"Careful now." Zeke was sitting at the table with the boys and a stack of children's storybooks. The lean cowboy looked like he'd showered after a day of wrangling rodeo stock at the Bucking Bull Ranch north of town. "I hear your uncle Cam makes a mean apple pie. Hint, hint."

"He does." Alexander sat up. "And pumpkin, too."

"Message received." *And thanks for that much-needed vote of confidence in my food.*

"What brings you by?" Sophie straightened her glasses and studied Cam's face. "I was about to get dinner started. Unless you're here to cook for us?"

Cam shook his head. "Can we talk?" He gestured toward the fireplace and two chairs. He waited until they were settled before explaining about Laurel's lack of wedding plans and his offer to help.

"The practical arrangements are the least of Laurel's worries. The other *situation*… It's a mess." Sophie leaned forward, lowering her voice. "At this point I think Laurel should call it off but she's determined to clean up the chaos she's made with Ashley and Wyatt before the baby comes. Everyone wants to be the one to tell Wyatt—Ashley, Aunt Gen, Mitch, Shane—but Laurel's adamant that she does it her way before she walks down the aisle. With all this pressure, is it any wonder she's fallen behind with wedding plans?"

Cam nodded. "I have permission to take

over, but what do I know about putting on a wedding?"

"I'll be your chief assistant." Sophie turned her chair so she faced him, not the fireplace. "Zeke and I borrowed dining tables from friends in town. All kinds of stuff. Our wedding was simple, but it was farmhouse-chic, wasn't it?"

That was a stretch, but Cam dutifully nodded. "We should just make some calls to rental companies in Boise."

"No, no, no, no. We're on strict orders from Aunt Gen not to use the Monroe name on anything."

"I hate to burst your bubble, sis, but with over one hundred people on the guest list, you can't just borrow stuff from neighbors. Dining tables and chairs, serving tables, linens, china, glassware." The list was daunting and his sister was dreaming if she thought the Monroe name didn't need to be thrown about with less than fourteen days to prepare.

"What about that Parker lady?" Zeke closed the book he'd been reading with the twins.

"Ivy?" Did Ivy have enough basic dinnerware for the wedding?

"Naw," Zeke replied. "Um, Diane Parker? She lives out past the Silver Spur. I recall someone saying she used to host weddings or fancy teas or something."

"I've heard that, too." Sophie nodded. "She was Ivy's mother-in-law. I bet Ivy can take you out there. You know, people here tend to hang on to things."

"That's the very definition of your grandfather, honey. *Hoarder*." Zeke stared at Cam's sister with so much love in his heart, it made Cam uncomfortable. He stood and prepared to make his exit.

"Uncle Cam." Alexander ran to his side, brown cowlick at attention. "Can you make me booger waffles tomorrow?"

"I can. But will the kids laugh if you eat them?"

"Who cares?" Andrew rubbed his tummy. "Booger waffles are so good."

Cam gave each of his nephews a stern look. "Where was that love when I needed it the other day?"

They giggled and hugged him, and promised to eat all his booger waffles forevermore.

CRÈME BRÛLÉE.

It was a must after the day Ivy had had working side by side with Cam. Her feet hurt but that was a given. It was her heart that ached more. Watching a master chef at work, fingers itching to jump in, to add seasoning or a bit more powdered sugar or crushed garlic. To motivate him to move quicker than his meticulous snail's pace. To tell Cam his aioli was superb...because she'd snuck a taste when he wasn't looking.

But they weren't colleagues in the kitchen. And there was the specter of Robert in the diner, a presence that made her defensive any time someone cast shade on her food.

"Is that...?" Footsteps tread steadily on her porch stairs. *"Crème brûlée?"* Cam appeared at the landing. "I hope you made enough for everyone."

"And by everyone, you mean you, Chef Trespasser?" She was getting used to seeing his handsome face, ever serious. But his presence still made her heart stutter.

I'll faint if he ever smiles at me.

He sat on the lounger next to Ivy's. She uncovered a plate and handed it to him, then retreated to her apartment to get another serving and a glass of water for him, shutting the drapes behind her.

"This is becoming a habit." She sat in her lounger and propped her feet on a pillow. The sun was setting. Second Chance was hunkering down for the night. Ivy was ready to count the days until the next big snowfall, skipping the summer completely. She longed for the kind of snowstorm that closed passes and allowed her to spend her days baking with the boys and making unhurried dinners.

Cam tested the texture of her dessert with his spoon before taking a bite. "Don't expect me as your dessert companion forever. Laurel's wedding is a week from Sunday."

"Not to mention there are six days left in our competition and I'm beating you." She took a bite of her crème brûlée. *So good.* "You'll be moping around the inn when you lose." That statement shouldn't give her a twinge of regret.

"Not so fast." He pointed at her with his spoon. "You haven't won yet. At my prices, I can catch up easily. All it'll take is a tour bus."

"We don't get many of those up here." The two vans carrying the high-school sports team that had passed through this morning were a rarity.

"Doesn't mean we couldn't get a big bus." Cam set his empty ramekin on the table. "Your crème brûlée is ordinary."

"Of course, it is." Ivy smirked. "That's why you ate the whole thing." Pride tried to work its way out of her chest and into her words.

"Another frozen concoction, I assume. You must get one of those specialty food trucks to deliver this ready-made." Cam waited for Ivy to answer, and when she didn't, he added, "Or perhaps one of those home-delivery meal services. They drop off boxes with everything you need to make the meal."

The desire to confess she'd made this from scratch was strong. But what would it serve? If the Monroes knew she was a chef, they'd expect her to cook like one.

"You know, you can concede now and make me the winner," Cam said smugly. "We don't have to draw this out."

Every time Ivy started to like Cam, he found a way to remind her he was the most infuriating man. "Did you miss the part where I'm winning?"

Cam yawned. "I heard from Shane. He and Jonah landed safely in South America."

"And this should concern me because...?"

"Laurel's baby daddy doesn't travel incognito. Wyatt loves the spotlight. And if Shane convinces him to come to Laurel's wedding—which we both know he will, because my big brother is a force to be reckoned with—then every booth in your little diner will be full of Hollywood types who are used to top-notch cuisine, and they will gravitate toward my specials."

A tremor of apprehension shuddered through Ivy. She willed it away, bolstered by years of experience staying in her lane—a single mom in Second Chance making simple food.

Find what you do well and stick with it. Another of Harlan's platitudes. He'd also told her Robert couldn't touch her in Second Chance, not anymore. If only he'd made plans to keep Cam away…

"Obviously, you're clueless about timelines," Ivy said in a tone designed to discourage. "That actor guy is supposed to show up a week before the wedding, which is just a few days from now." She'd been briefed by Shane. "That doesn't leave you enough days to win." Especially at the pace he made food. The urge to feel sorry for him resurfaced. She squashed it. "Now be quiet. The sun's going down."

As usual, he didn't listen to her. "You know, most cooks who put in a twelve-hour day would be soaking in a bathtub right now."

"Do you know how much energy it takes to heat a bathtub?" It was cheaper to fill her spoon with crème brûlée. "Or how loud the diner is all day?"

"Silence is your bubble bath?"

"Yes." She shushed him and tried to relax.

"I like your boys," he said.

She smiled, shushing him again, despite being pleased that he was charmed by her kids.

The Sawtooth Mountains became painted in their subdued grays, purples and blues as the sun dropped behind them. For several minutes, neither she nor Cam spoke. It would have been nice if she wasn't aware of him sitting next to her, this chef who liked her kids.

"Quite the show." Cam sat up and picked up their empty ramekins. "I'll do the dishes."

"No need." Ivy stayed his hand, which required her touching him, which made her skin tingle, which made her think about kisses. Which had no place in the kitchen—hers or the diner's. But out in the twilight? She sighed.

"What's wrong? You don't want me to see your dirty kitchen?" Cam set the dishes back on the side table. "My grandfather used to say it's best to clean as you go, whether you're working on an engine or working on a soufflé."

She nodded. "I liked your grandfather. A lot."

Cam slanted her a quick, questioning glance. "You don't blame him for coming into town and contributing to your marriage crumbling?

When he bought you out, he changed everything."

"No, I don't blame him." If not for Harlan, she might still be unhappily married. "Robert and I looked at the world—culinary and otherwise—in different ways." It would have been nice to know that before they got married. But that's what men like Robert did—smoke and mirrors as they courted women.

Cam was quiet. Thinking about Ivy's failed marriage? She thought not.

"You blame your grandfather for all this," she realized. "Shane did, too, when he first arrived."

Cam stared at the Sawtooth Mountains, denying nothing.

"Harlan only wanted the best for you." The old man had often talked about his legacy and his grandchildren. But Ivy couldn't share those conversations with Cam. She'd signed a nondisclosure agreement that wouldn't run out until her lease expired at the end of the year.

"He wanted the best for me?" Cam huffed. "I was in a really good place when he died. And then I found out his last wish was to sever my ties to my family and create ties to this place."

"He didn't want you to sever ties with your

family," she pointed out gently, confident she could share that much. "He wanted to remove your fallback plan. After all, no one with a first-class seat reaches for the stars." One of Harlan's best quips. "Although sometimes the things that drive us are the most painful moments in our past." Another one of his sayings she'd taken to heart.

Cam's features were as stony as the mountains holding his gaze.

Ivy wondered how she could make him understand. She couldn't quite grasp why it was so important to her that he did. "Robert wasn't happy here. He labeled everything as an obstacle to his dreams—the town, the diner, me." She hurried on before the bad memories intruded. "When he left, I had a three-year-old and a newborn, and a contract with Harlan Monroe. But what I didn't realize was the freedom I'd gained. Without Robert's pessimistic attitude—" without his emotional abuse "—I took charge of my life. I could make the menu any way I wanted and set hours that fit motherhood."

"You mean you…" His dark gaze turned on her, eyebrows raised. "If you weren't a single mom, you'd change up the menu?"

She tsked. "Don't go telling Shane that. He'll try and fix me up."

Cam cocked an eyebrow, visible in the light of the rising full moon.

Don't let him judge you.

Ivy lifted her chin. "How many fine-dining establishments are a one-man—or a one-woman—show? Few. If you'd been in my shoes—a single parent in need of an income—you would have made the same trade-off, the only responsible choice." She reached across the space between them and squeezed Cam's hand, foolishly wishing there were no secrets between them, no divergent ideas in the kitchen. He was a good man but pride seemed to be holding him back. He didn't recognize that food didn't have to be five-star to be satisfying. "Instead of blaming your grandfather for lost opportunities, take back your destiny and be grateful for the chance to do something new. Maybe this journey will help you find a lane that makes you happy."

From the disdainful look Cam gave her, she knew her definition of happiness and his were worlds apart. A chill wind rushed past.

Ivy got to her feet, stacked dishes and gathered them so she could bring everything inside in one trip.

"Can you take me to your mother-in-law's house?"

Ivy nearly dropped the dishes.

"Hey, careful there." Cam steadied her arms. "I need to talk to Diane Parker. She's your mother-in-law, isn't she? The one who used to host events up here? Sophie mentioned her name. Laurel hasn't made arrangements for anything for the wedding and…" He peered at her. "Are you okay?"

"I'm fine." Far from it, Ivy set the plates and glasses back on the table and sat down. She didn't like going out to the Parker place and neither did the boys.

"She's the person I need to talk to, though? About tables and china and such?" Cam sat across from her. "Diane Parker?"

"Yes. The Parkers used to run the Bent Nickel and host events on their property. Summer weddings were their bread and butter, I think." It was why they'd sent Robert to culinary school. They'd hoped he'd continue the business and expand it. "I don't know what they still have." And she didn't want to know.

The moon was illuminating the broad valley, normally a calming sight for Ivy.

"Can you take me there? Or…" Cam studied her. "If you give me directions, I can drive out there myself."

"It's kind of hard to find." Two country roads and an unmarked driveway. She'd never understood why they couldn't more clearly mark the way to their property when they did business on it. "And the Parkers are…" She wasn't sure how to describe them. "Collectors?"

Cam shook his head. "Like hoarders?"

"You'll have to see for yourself. I suppose I can drive you out there during the afternoon lull, as long as Sarah's available." Ivy stood, needing to find her sea legs. It had been years since she'd been to the Parker home. For visitation, Robert usually picked up the boys from the Bent Nickel.

Cam got to his feet. "Sounds great. Thank you." He kissed her forehead.

"Uh." Now it really felt as if Ivy was at sea. Her knees were rubber.

Chef Surprise was already heading for the steps, perhaps without realizing he'd just caused a cosmic shift in her world. "Oh, I almost forgot to ask." He turned at the top of the steps.

"Hmm?" Apparently, her ability to form words had fallen overboard.

"How many meals does Roy usually eat at the diner?"

"Roy?" Roy who? "Oh, *Roy.* It varies. Why?"

Cam shrugged, almost looking embarrassed. "I'd like to feed him sometimes. He's too thin." He hurried down the stairs.

So nice. So out of character from Chef High-and-Mighty.

Or not.

Ivy stood for several minutes before picking up the dishes, letting the cool breeze bring her back to reality.

She'd been worried about the impact of Cam's smile? She should have been worried about the power of the honorable character he hid behind the mantle of chef.

CHAPTER TEN

GABBY KINCAID HATED being twelve.

Everything about twelve was a major embarrassment—blemishes, bras, braces.

Zits dotted her chin in constant rebellion against the pimple cream Dad bought her. Her braces had come off only to be replaced by retainers, which gave her a slight lisp. The bras had come on, and woe-be-it to her if she forgot to wear one. No one had told her that would be a problem, not even her soon-to-be stepmom, Laurel Monroe.

Laurel was the most awesome person she knew, cooler than Laurel's cousin Shane. Forget for a moment that Laurel was pregnant and that she was marrying Gabby's dad. She was seriously cool. Laurel used to make clothes for movies and TV shows and famous people, like her identical twin sister, Ashley. And the cherry on the cool-factor cake? Laurel was inviting famous people to her and Dad's wedding, which was happening in less than two weeks.

Which meant Gabby had to get rid of her zits, practice retainer enunciation, remember to wear a bra and find something supercool to wear. Which for a twelve-year-old living in Second Chance was practically impossible. Dad had taken her shopping a week ago in Boise and had refused to let her venture into the junior section of the store. He'd taken her to the girls section and demanded she choose a dress with lace and bows and a poofy skirt.

Totally for ten-year-olds.

They'd had words and since Dad used to be a lawyer, he'd argued his case with annoying points that Gabby refused to acknowledge were right on all aspects but one: twelve-year-olds who wore a bra needed dresses in the junior section.

I rest my case.

Dad had taken one look at the short dresses on the ultrathin mannequins in the junior department and hauled her out the door.

But today…

Today, the coolest ever soon-to-be stepmom was taking Gabby shopping for a dress, just as soon as Laurel had her phone appointment with her doctor. That's right. Gabby was going with the hippest person on the planet to buy the hippest dress in the department store. She had Dad's credit card in her purse, which was a hand-me-down from Laurel and designer— *squee!*

Laurel's cell phone rang.

"Hey, Dr. Carlisle," Laurel said from out in the inn's common room.

Gabby took her laptop and went to sit at the inn's check-in desk, because she was allowed and because it allowed her to witness everything that went on, like conversations and telephone calls. And since the Monroes had begun coming to town, there were a lot of conversations and telephone calls to listen to.

It was fun to pretend to know what the person on the other end of the phone was saying.

"Like I'm carrying two baby horses in my belly, both of whom pack a wallop of a kick," Laurel said.

Gabby choked on a laugh. She bet Dr. Carlisle had just asked Laurel how she was feeling.

Laurel looked at Gabby, raising her perfectly plucked red eyebrows, which in cool stepmom speak meant "I hope you're not eavesdropping."

Gabby adjusted her laptop screen as if she'd

been watching something funny and wanted to see it better.

But really… Eyebrows. Gabby's were bushy and a soft red. They stood out almost as much as her pimples on her pale skin. That was the next thing on her list after a dress. She wanted to learn how to pluck eyebrows. Or better yet, have Laurel pluck her eyebrows. If Gabby plucked her own, she might not end up with any.

"Twenty-five weeks," Laurel said, most likely in response to "how far along are you?"

Gabby pulled up a profile of Laurel on the public-encyclopedia site online, the one anyone could add information to. It said Laurel had been the stand-in for her famous sister from age five, and that she'd gone to fashion school. There were photos of some of her designs, including an evening gown that Ashley was supposed to have worn to an awards show. It was long and pink and sparkly, and considered Laurel's crowning achievement.

Not to mention it was also worn by moi.

Only in the Lodgepole Inn, but still.

"The same. I eat. I sleep. The babies wake me." Laurel sighed, sinking deeper into the couch cushions.

That was for sure a response to the doctor

asking if anything about the way Laurel was feeling had changed.

Gabby returned her attention to the screen. Laurel's childhood. Her education. A couple slam dunks on the red carpet. And then…nothing. Not even the fact that she was pregnant with twins.

"No. I don't know when Holden is coming to town." Laurel stared at the ceiling. "Oh, yeah. He'll be here for the wedding."

Ugh. Gabby couldn't think why anyone would want to know if Laurel's cousin Holden was attending the wedding. Maybe she'd ask Mack. She had all the town gossip, Monroe or otherwise. She'd know why Dr. Carlisle would ask that particular question.

While Laurel finished her conversation with Dr. Carlisle, Gabby opened the update-information box on the encyclopedia site and typed in: pregnant, twins, father Wyatt Halford.

Her pulse began to pound.

Gabby knew just typing that information in a box was wrong. She fully intended to erase it all in a moment. But it was thrilling to be in on this secret. Her stepmother-to-be was having the babies of the sexiest man alive! At least, that's how the magazine had described him. It stank that she didn't have anyone to tell. Dad had made her promise not to share the news with Mom, who lived in Chicago. But this. This Gabby could do. She could type in Wyatt Halford's name and believe she was important enough to know something before the rest of the world.

"Gabby."

Gabby jumped, slamming the laptop shut and practically squishing her thumb in the process.

"Come feel the babies kicking."

Gabby hurried over, because it was totally awesome to have baby feet press against her palm, or baby knees bump her fingers. She was starting to think she might want to be a doctor.

Laurel smiled at Gabby, reaching for her hand. "It's okay for me to take Gabby dress-shopping to Boise, isn't it? I've got Odette covering the store today but I know that Mitch would want me to ask. You know how he worries." Laurel caught Gabby's eye and then rolled hers.

Dad was a worrier, all right. If he had his way, Gabby would show up to the wedding in a parka and Laurel in a wheelchair.

Laurel rolled Gabby's palm across her belly as if it was a computer mouse. One of the baby girls was stretching her legs—*poke, poke, poke.* A little foot tested itself against Gabby's palm.

Gabby giggled.

Laurel moved her hand around to the other side of her stomach, where something about the length of Gabby's hand was hiccupping.

"I can't wait to meet my little sisters." It may suck to be twelve but it rocked to be a big sister.

"Yes, Dr. Carlisle, that's Gabby." Laurel burped. But it was Laurel, so it was a dainty burp. "Excuse me. Yes, Gabby's nose is fine."

Gabby placed her fingertips along the bridge of her nose. She'd broken it in February, right after her birthday. It was an omen about becoming twelve.

"Yes. I'll see you in the office next time. Goodbye." Laurel pushed herself to her feet. "Put your laptop away and let's get going."

Gabby carried her computer back to her room. She opened it, just to close out all the programs running. A big box sat in the middle of her screen.

Submitted.

Submitted?

"NOT THIS PLACE." Nick fell back into his car seat as Ivy turned down the Parkers' long driveway.

"The plastic palace." R.J. sounded sad.

"Yes, this place," Ivy murmured, just as displeased to be at her former in-laws' home as her boys. She was only doing this for Laurel.

The gray ranch house sat next to a large red barn on a rise near the Salmon River. The gardens were overgrown. The knee-high lawn didn't appear to have been mowed in months. The first feelings of trepidation pressed down on Ivy's shoulders.

"They used to host weddings here?" Cam peered out the front window. "I'm guessing that was a long, long time ago."

"It used to be pretty." Ivy slowed to play tour guide—anything to delay the inevitable. "There was a gazebo over there at the bend in the river." It was a pile of lumber now. "And a beautiful arched trellis with blooming roses over here." It tilted at a precarious angle. "And Diane had the loveliest dishes. She used to tell each bride which set best fit her personality."

"You got married here," Cam mused.

Ivy nodded. "Don't go romanticizing it." She'd been a starry-eyed bride after a whirlwind romance. "That's the last time I saw my parents."

Cam's curiosity was like a palpable thing, but she'd already said too much.

Ivy parked in front of the house.

"It's shady under that carport," Cam helpfully pointed out.

Robert's parking spot.

Nope. Not happening.

"Will you look at that?" Ivy drew her keys from the ignition. "The car is already off." She helped the boys out of the car, but the threesome clustered together without moving toward the front door.

Cam came to stand next to them. "Why didn't you tell me?"

That my former in-laws are intimidating? That the Parkers are outside of my lane? That this would be awkward?

Cam nodded, seemingly reading her mind. "We could leave."

Ivy shook her head. "Laurel needs plates and tables to put them on."

The Parkers came out to the front stoop, staring at their visitors without smiling.

Diane had bright blond hair that was swept into a neat chignon at the base of her thin neck. She wore a quilted burgundy vest over a white blouse and capris. Jarvis wore a crisply pressed white button-down over his blue jeans. His gray hair was short and receding. They looked forbidding but normal.

"You should have told me," Cam murmured again.

"Hindsight," Ivy murmured back, glancing into the rearview mirror of her past and flinching.

"Why do you always make my parents feel stupid?" Robert was driving too fast on the country road, as if he couldn't escape his parents soon enough.

"I don't know what you mean." Ivy was thinking they had gotten along so well.

"Can't you just...?" Robert growled. "Can't you just say less?"

"O-kay?"

Ivy had tried saying less. She'd tried being invisible. She'd tried baking gifts. She'd tried lending a hand when they had an event out here. But whatever she tried hadn't been good enough. Not for Robert and not for his parents.

"Hey, Grandma. Grandpa." Like a trooper, R.J. made the slow walk of the dutiful grandchild across the front walk to the stoop.

Diane nodded to acknowledge him. Always

the more expressive, Jarvis smiled and patted R.J.'s head.

Nick tried to scamper up the steps and into the house, but Jarvis caught him, swinging him upside down and over his shoulder.

"Gently, please." Ivy hurried forward.

"I'm gonna hurl," Nick cried.

"No one passes without saying hello properly to your grandmother." Jarvis bounced Nick for good measure, eliciting a groan.

Cam strode past Ivy and swung Nick upright and onto his shoulder. "Hi. I'm Camden Monroe." He stood like a superhero without a cape.

"I didn't know you'd be bringing a Monroe." Diane fixed Ivy with a stare cold enough to freeze the Salmon River.

Ivy had purposefully withheld that information.

"I didn't want any fanfare." Cam winked at the Parkers and then got right down to business. "You may not have heard that my cousin Laurel is getting married in a few weeks. We're in the planning stages, gathering things like tables and chairs, place settings and the like. I heard you used to be in the event business."

"We closed that." Diane clasped her hands

and let her gaze flow over all their heads. "After the divorce."

Ivy kept quiet. In their eyes, she was to blame for their son leaving town. And without him, they seemed to have lost the heart for the business.

"But you still have everything." Cam made it a statement. "Word around town is that you have a fine collection of china."

"We do not cater anymore." Diane's frosty gaze landed on Ivy.

We should go.

Ivy couldn't work up enough saliva to say the words.

"But…" Cam set down Nick and glanced around, his expression that of Chef High-and-Mighty. "I really don't need to see any more." He turned toward the car.

Ivy's mouth dropped open. She drew the boys to her side.

Diane stopped him with a delicate hand on his arm, delaying his escape. "My china collection is fit for royalty."

"Second to none," Jarvis said obediently, the way Ivy would have done during the later years of her marriage to Robert if she'd stayed married to him.

"Huh." A Michelin-quality chef stared down

at where Diane's fingers rested on his arm. "Somebody's going to have to take your word for it."

Diane lowered her hand, and hissed softly like a leaky balloon.

Ivy drew the boys closer trying to catch Cam's attention. Whatever he was up to would only make things harder on Nick and R.J. later.

"Because I just can't see china fit for a king being kept here." Chef High-and-Mighty turned up his nose. "And I don't want to embarrass anyone."

Such a lie. Cam wanted to rattle Diane.

"Are you talking about Grandma's dishes?" Nick frowned.

R.J. shushed him.

Nick broke free of Ivy's hold and scurried to Cam's side. "They're everywhere. Gazillions of them. But you know what? Maybe they're not so good. We only eat on paper plates here and only in the kitchen. By ourselves."

Indignation built in Ivy's chest and flared up her neck. Her boys were well-behaved—there was no need to isolate them like that. Kids made messes. That was a fact of life. She glared at Diane, who only had eyes for Cam, so she glared at Jarvis, who stared back unemotionally.

"Excellent support for the point I was making." Cam bared his teeth. His words carried a bite. "There's nothing here of any consequence."

Suddenly, Ivy was glad Cam was kitchen royalty and grateful he knew how to handle the likes of the Parkers.

"Diane's collection is exquisite." Jarvis's comment earned him a frown from Diane. Regardless, he pressed on quietly, to Diane, "I told you people in town would forget who you are. This is our chance. *A Monroe*."

"We need to be going." Cam checked his watch, poking the bear.

"Diane." Jarvis reached for the doorknob, waiting for his wife's permission to let them in.

Diane gave Jarvis a stiff nod and went inside as soon as he opened the door for her.

"Shoes off, please," Jarvis told Cam before scurrying inside.

"Ugh," Nick whispered. "Do we have to go in the plastic palace?"

"We can't let Mr. Cam go in there alone," R.J. whispered back. "Come on." And he marched up the stairs without looking back.

Crossing the threshold, Ivy touched Cam's arm. "What are you up to?"

"Something that's long overdue." Cam slid out of his loafers.

Before she could tell him that whatever he had in mind was a waste of time, Jarvis urged Cam to hurry.

Cam didn't hurry, but he did disappear down the long hallway.

Ivy had never liked the plastic palace. It was dark, even in daylight. There were no can lights. The bulbs in the few ceiling fixtures were dim. And then there were the plastic runners covering the white carpet. She, and the boys, and Cam were all going to be charged with static electricity before this pointless visit was over.

Ivy led the boys to the back of the house, where everything was covered in plastic— the couch, a wingback chair, the dining-room chairs and barstools. Only the two prim gray recliners in the living room were plastic-free. Neither boy ran around or rushed to take a seat. And who could blame them? Ivy had been forced to sit on the plastic-covered couch long before the boys were born.

I should have taken that as a sign.

They'd raised Robert in this house with strict rules, although they countered that by indulging his every whim as a reward for good behavior. Ivy could never live up to their unrealistic standards. Her boys could never live up to them, either. And now, she was determined they'd never have to.

Eat by themselves.

Anger strengthened her steps.

They joined Cam and the Parkers in the large dining room, which had six hutches filled with china.

Diane tugged on a pair of white gloves, a slight smile on her face. Jarvis stood nearby, ready to do her bidding.

Ivy pulled a dining-room chair across the plastic runner and sat down on the plastic seat, beckoning the boys into her lap. If Diane was getting her gloves on, the show was about to go on.

"The lavender Wedgewood is the gold standard." Cam practically pressed his nose to the glass for a better look. "And the Spode Blue Italian is classic."

Diane smoothed the gloves over each finger ritualistically. "I can bring out a plate, but you can't touch. Which would you like to see? The Wedgewood or the Spode?"

"Neither." Cam backed up, sliding his stocking feet backward across the runner, making a zipper noise and giving the boys the giggles. "I've seen enough."

Diane's smile plummeted into a frown. She'd been interrupted midpresentation. Nobody interrupted Diane, not in the dining room of the plastic palace.

"You've got quantity here. But quality…" Chef High-and-Mighty tsked. "Lenox? That's everyday. And Desert Rose? That's so twenty years ago. And look at that. You must have at least two hundred place settings."

"One eighty," Jarvis said. "We lost some when a bunch of cowboy groomsmen used them for skeet practice."

Diane trembled, a volcano ready to blow. Ivy recognized the signs from her years with Robert.

"You're lucky you weren't serving those cowboys on the Spode." Cam chuckled.

Diane jerked as if she'd had a muscle spasm.

"Well, this has been interesting." Cam wiped a finger over the cherry dining table, and then rubbed dust from his finger. "But this collection is too…small. Did I mention we're hosting Hollywood royalty? Not just my cousin Ashley Monroe. Wyatt Halford will be there, too."

"Wyatt Halford, the movie star?" If Jarvis

had a vote in renting china, it would be yes. He trembled like a young Labrador with a tennis ball in his sights.

Diane, on the other hand, had stiffened. "Nothing is for rent. Or sale."

"As I mentioned, I'm not interested in…" Cam waved a dismissive hand. "This. We're bringing in the family Raynaud Duchesse."

Ivy swallowed a gasp. The French porcelain made by Limoges had gold inlay and cost over one thousand dollars a plate. It did indeed put anything in Diane's collection to shame.

"Thank you for the informative peek." Cam retraced his steps toward the door, regal despite being in his stocking feet.

Red-faced, Diane made a strangled noise. Jarvis looked like a stiff wax statue.

Ivy herded the boys ahead of her, apologizing when her touch gave them each an electric shock.

Darn plastic runners.

Diane and Jarvis remained in the dining room, not bothering to see them out.

They all stuffed their feet into their shoes and hurried back to her car. No one spoke.

As Ivy backed out, she imagined Diane's howl of rage. She imagined Jarvis cringing in a chair while Diane circled him on the plastic runner, shouting about his stupidity.

She might have felt some sympathy for the man. If he'd ever done anything to help her in any way. Ever. If he'd ever allowed her boys a modicum of dignity.

They ate dinner alone!

Ivy hadn't gotten her wheels under asphalt before the regrets began, as bumpy as the road.

She was going to have to get a lawyer, a good family-law attorney, because there was no way she was letting Nick and R.J. stay in that house again.

Cam took her right hand from the steering wheel and held on to it without saying a word.

Only then did Ivy realize she was shaking and that the boys weren't saying anything.

"Milkshakes for everyone when we get back," Cam said. "My treat."

CHAPTER ELEVEN

"ARE YOU FEELING OKAY?" Laurel asked Gabby.

"Umm…" Gabby was still in shock from the "submitted" notification.

They'd circled the junior section of the department store twice. Gabby hadn't been able to enter. She'd had the cell phone her mother gave her for her birthday taken away from her, so she hadn't had time to resubmit information to the website saying, *My bad. Total rumor.*

News traveled fast in cyberspace. Gabby had to tell Laurel what had happened, except if she did, Laurel would be upset, which was bad for the babies, and she'd probably cancel the shopping trip, which was bad for Gabby. And if she didn't tell, Dad would be furious, which was doubly bad for Gabby. He might never give her cell phone back.

There was no winning in this situation.

"Gabby?" Laurel stopped near a display of dresses. No lace. No bows. No puffed skirt. "How about one of these?"

"These are awesome." Gabby took one and held it up to her shoulders, website dilemma forgotten. "What do you think? Does it bring out the color in my eyes?" She'd heard that on a TV show.

"Your eyes are beautiful." Laurel was craning her neck, looking around, while pressing her palms into the small of her back.

"I think the dressing rooms are over there." Gabby had spotted them during one of their laps around the section. "Should I grab this really cool black dress, too?" On second thought... They might use it for her funeral when she finally came clean. She forced out an awkward laugh. "Oh, hey, no. Black is not a wedding color."

And back to the rack it went.

"Right." Laurel grabbed two different dresses in two different colors and then headed for the dressing room. She passed a display of black moto jackets and grabbed one. She passed a display of pastel sweaters and grabbed two.

Total score.

"Way to give Dad a heart attack." Gabby snagged a jean jacket with frayed cuffs and rhinestones on the collar. If only the shoe department was closer.

Laurel barreled into the dressing-room corridor and hung the clothes on a hook. "I'll be in that chair waiting for your runway show." She lumbered to the end of the corridor and sat.

Gabby hesitated, sensing something wasn't right. There was a fluttering in her stomach that she'd only experienced one other time—when Roy had his heart attack. "Are you okay?"

"Yes." Laurel waved a hand. "Darn practice contractions."

Worry kept Gabby's feet glued to the floor. "How do you know they're only practice?"

"Go. I can call Dr. Carlisle while you change." Laurel dug a bottle of water from her bag. "And I'll hydrate. The babies love hydration."

"Okay. I'll be quick." Gabby arranged her items into outfits, hanging them on different hooks and over the door. None of the dresses were bra-friendly. She removed hers, placing it on a hook with the moto jacket. She chose a pale blue dress and a matching sweater, and then stepped into the hallway to show Laurel.

"Love," Laurel panted, already off the phone. "I think you should wear makeup for the wedding."

"Really?" Gabby squealed.

Laurel held up a thumb and forefinger that were practically touching. "Just a little."

"And my eyebrows? Can you show me how to pluck my eyebrows?"

"Yes." She panted some more, her cheeks super red. "Do you want to try on anything else?"

Gabby spun around, looking at herself in the mirror. "No. This is awesome. You're awesome." The world was awesome, except…

Submitted. Gah!

"I guess I'm through." Literally, if she couldn't unsubmit.

"Good. Because Dr. Carlisle wants me to stop by the hospital before we go home."

Gabby yelped and dove back into the dressing room. She threw on her clothes, grabbed the dress and sweater and left everything else where it was. They paid. Laurel panted. On the way to the parking lot, Shane called Laurel, asking about some bet with Ivy that Laurel said was okay, but then she told Shane she had to hang up because of the false contractions.

Which seemed pretty real to Gabby.

They hurried out to the SUV. Laurel paused at the door.

"What's wrong?" Gabby hurried to her side. "Did your water break? Do I need to call 911?

I should have my phone back for just this reason."

"No, I…" Laurel laughed. "False contractions. They just stopped." She wiped her face. "Silly girls. These silly girls." She rubbed both hands over her belly.

"I'm going to have a heart attack. I'm twelve. I shouldn't have to worry about things like this, or…" Gabby swallowed, thinking about Roy's pale face when he'd collapsed in March.

"Things like what?" Laurel squeezed Gabby's shoulders.

"Life…" Gabby gestured toward Laurel's tummy. And then she stared at the sky. "Or death. Like—like…" She whispered, "Like when Roy almost died." And she and Zeke had saved him. Gabby sagged against the SUV's door.

"Honey." Laurel drew Gabby into her arms, which was great and awkward considering there were two volleyballs between them. "Have you been worried about that?"

"I'm twelve," Gabby grumbled, still holding on to Laurel. "I worry about everything." Her blouse scratched her chest. Gabby leaped back and pressed her palms where her bra cups should be. "OMG! OMG! I left my bra in the changing room."

They stared at each other for a moment.

And then Laurel laughed. "Come on." She slung her arm over Gabby's shoulders. "Let's go back. If we hurry, we'll make it home in time for your dad's dinner."

"No." Gabby dug in her heels, freeing herself. "I'm not reclaiming my bra. It's mortifying."

"Okay. But you'll have to pay for a replacement with your own money. And bras aren't cheap, even training bras." Laurel took a step toward the mall, holding out her hand.

Gabby's cheeks felt as red as Laurel's had been before, but she took her hand. "Twelve is the worst age ever."

"THERE'S A STORM blowing in." Ivy stared up at the sky from the front windows of the Bent Nickel.

She looked lonely to Cam. Or perhaps it was Cam who was feeling alone. He wanted to talk about what had happened at the Parkers earlier that afternoon. With the boys in the back seat on the return drive, he and Ivy hadn't said much of anything, a trend that continued through the afternoon when a school bus full of seniors on a day trip stopped in town, keeping them busy.

Well, Cam hadn't been busy. He'd taken down his sandwich-board specials before they'd gone to the Parkers and hadn't put it back up when they returned. He'd supervised R.J. in the making of French fries.

Nick snored softly on his beanbag. R.J. played checkers in the dining room with Roy.

"That smells good." Ivy entered the kitchen and took a peek at his pork chops. Her T-shirt proclaimed Cooking Is a Professional Sport. The funny thing was that she worked as if it was true. "You don't need to make us dinner every night."

"I certainly need to tonight." Not to mention Cam was in need of comfort food, too. He wasn't sure what to make of the Parkers or whether they were just plain cruel. Kids shouldn't be ignored. He wanted to hug those two brave boys until he was reassured they'd never go through that again.

Ivy did more than peek at his dish. She took a fork and moved a chop to rest on its fat, making it spit and hiss. "There are five pork chops here."

"You've been paying attention to Eli's math lessons." Cam grinned. He liked teasing her. Her smile reassured him that the Parkers hadn't broken her or the boys. "Actually, I made one for Roy." He'd prepared Roy's vegetables in the steamer with a light, buttery seasoning even a picky eater wouldn't complain about. "Can you get me a box? I see his checker game is almost over." And the old man would want to head home before the storm hit.

Ivy went into the pantry. "I'd like to go on record as saying what you did was risky at the Parkers' today."

"Don't defend them. I saw how small you made yourself when we turned down their driveway." He spared her a smile as she returned and set the open food box on a nearby counter. He'd never seen anyone physically withdraw into themselves the way she had. He'd wanted to tell her to turn the car around. And then, when Jarvis flipped over Nick, he'd almost run up and knocked him down. "The vibe the Parkers give off is… Well, I shouldn't talk out of turn about your in-laws."

"*Former* in-laws." Ivy knotted her knuckles together. "And you have better intuition than I had. Intuition like that would have saved me an ugly marriage. All that plastic. The white-glove ritual." She shuddered.

"But it would have cost you two great kids."

"True."

Thunder rumbled on the mountain.

"Roy, I've got something for you. Don't leave yet." Cam reached over and brushed Ivy's cheek with his knuckles. "What's bothering you?"

She tried to smile. "My dear friend Laurel's wedding is dishless."

He knew that was a ruse. "And?"

Ivy glanced at Nick before checking that R.J. was still occupied in the checkers match. "The Parkers are worse than before. Part of my custody agreement was that Robert only have the kids in a supervised environment, which at the time was deemed to be his parents' home."

"Ew. Yeah. You need a good attorney." He placed Roy's food in the box, closed it up and handed it to Ivy before realizing she wasn't waitressing. "Who did you use last time?"

"Harlan's legal counsel. Daniel something. He was here at Christmas." Her gaze shuttered, as if she wasn't supposed to have mentioned that, given her nondisclosure agreement with his grandfather. "I'm sure there's someone locally who can get the process started. It's just… Robert's summer week is coming up and I can't let them go there."

"Then don't." Cam began plating their dinners, the pork chops and steamed vegetables with a mustard-cherry glaze. "I know Daniel Cross. I'll give him a call tomorrow."

"Thank you. Now, about the Raynaud Duchesse." Ivy deftly changed the subject. "I called my restaurant supplier about dish rental. I can't get you those rare plates. But he does have some very nice Wedgewood." Ivy picked up Roy's to-go box. "I can order them, and tables and chairs, if you'll pay."

Cam reassured her he would. "Like a Monroe would stiff you with the bill." He wanted to keep teasing her and keep that soft gaze upon him. It made him forget about Nick and R.J. spending a week in the plastic palace. "You're only being kind to me because I'm so far behind in this cooking challenge."

"There is that."

They were grinning at each other for no reason. But Cam couldn't seem to stop.

Thunder rumbled again, breaking the connection between them.

"I guess I won't be out on the porch tonight." Ivy spun away, taking Roy's boxed dinner with her.

"No dessert. That's a shame." Cam stopped putting vegetables on plates to watch her sashay to Roy's table.

"I didn't say I wasn't having dessert," she

said over her shoulder. "Only that you won't be having it with me."

Now that really was a shame.

"ARE YOU KIDDING ME?" Gabby fell back on her bed. "Gah!" She pounded her fists into the mattress. "Grrr-gah!"

Her change to Laurel's online-encyclopedia entry had been accepted. And now it wouldn't accept her attempts to point out the information was incorrect.

Error.

Maybe there was a silver lining here. Laurel wasn't the best-known Monroe. A change to her profile might go unnoticed, perhaps for a week or more, perhaps until after the wedding.

The dress she and Laurel had picked out hung from the tall mirror on her dresser. In hindsight, it looked too cute and innocent. Gabby should be wearing villainous black.

All the careful preparations that had been made, all the ways Laurel and Dad had practiced how to tell Wyatt he was going to be a father—it could all be ruined.

Maybe her stupid computer needed a reboot. Gabby turned it off and on. And then she tried the website again.

Error.

"Seriously? Who programs this stuff?" She searched FAQs for how to report false information. She searched for a technical support line. She searched for complaints about the site. *"Full of inaccuracies."* That complaint wouldn't hold up in a court of law as her defense. "Gah!"

"Gabby, what are you doing?" Dad knocked on her bedroom door once before opening it.

"Dad! Boundaries." Gabby slammed her laptop shut. "What if I was getting dressed?" That would be more mortifying than having to walk back to the department store and admit you'd left your bra hanging on a hook in the changing room.

"You've been in here yelling at your computer for the last thirty minutes. I know you're not naked. And if you had been, it's not like I haven't wiped your bottom."

"Ew, Dad! Boundaries!"

"I have to agree with her, Mitch." A few feet away in the kitchen, Laurel was eating ice cream from the carton. "You can't say things like that. In a few years, she'll be dating and the last thing she wants you to reference in front of her man is you changing her diapers."

Dad looked like he might be having false contractions. He was red-faced and panting.

"In a few months, I'm going to be the only man in a household of four women. Maybe you two need to learn how to talk to me." He stomped off.

Laurel dug in the ice-cream carton, then shrugged. "Nerves."

"Wedding jitters?" Gabby had read about those, and guys getting cold feet.

"New-baby jitters." Laurel put a big spoonful of ice cream in her mouth.

"Yeah, about that." Gabby was going to come clean. With Dad in a mood, Laurel would handle this error herself. She'd know what to do.

"Do you think I've gained too much weight?" Laurel turned sideways, showing Gabby her profile. "I feel huge."

Gabby may have been twelve, but she wasn't stupid. "The correct response is no?" She backed into her room.

"Smart girl." Laurel dug in the carton. "We'll get through this. Just a couple more weeks to go, right?"

"Right." Gabby closed her bedroom door and leaned against it, feeling a zit form on her chin.

Two weeks? She was going to be grounded

for the rest of her life once Dad found out about this.

Was it too much to hope that Wyatt Halford had no internet in South America?

It was. Who would deny the Sexiest Man Alive access to social media?

Two weeks. What could possibly go wrong?

CHAPTER TWELVE

Meanwhile, somewhere in South America...

WYATT HALFORD, AKA the Sexiest Man Alive and the highest-paid action star of last year, didn't know what was worse—the back he'd thrown out during a stunt on his latest film, or the physical therapy that was supposed to speed his recovery, which currently involved being strapped into an immersion table, hung upside down and having to breathe through the "good" pain.

"You can't come in here." His assistant, Jeremy, sounded upset.

"Too late," an unrepentant male voice said.

"Dang, it's hot." Another male voice.

"Jeremy?" Upside down, in his skivvies, and back to the door, Wyatt was at a disadvantage.

"Gentlemen, please leave before I call Security." Jeremy was trying, but he was a stick figure of a man, and better at logistics and technology than throwing a punch.

"I think we'll stay to hear that call," the first male said in a cocky voice. "I'd love to see Security try and kick out your distribution representative. Might delay your movie's release a few weeks. It'd be too bad if your opening weekend coincided with the latest Marvel release, wouldn't it?"

Wyatt was an actor, not a prima donna. If a studio exec wanted to talk, he'd talk. He assembled a smile on his face and contorted himself into an upright position, blinking through the head rush. Jeremy helped him lock into the start position and freed his feet.

The world stopped spinning.

Two men stood just inside the door of his luxury trailer. One wore a suit and a smile that was too knowing for Wyatt's taste. The other was as skinny as Jeremy with red hair, a red goatee and a nervous slant to his blue eyes.

"Those are some nasty bruises," the suit said, not at all sympathetically.

"I'll live." But Wyatt wouldn't be doing any of his own stunts anytime soon. Good thing most of the exterior shots were finished. Another few days and he could fly home to the States, to his own doctor, his own trainer and the best physical therapist on the west coast. "What can I do for you?"

Jeremy helped him into a robe.

"We want to offer you a role." The redhead pulled a script from a messenger bag.

The suit held an arm in front of his overly eager companion. "We have a project that might interest you."

"Run it through my agent," Wyatt grumbled, reaching for his water bottle.

"We'd rather run it by you." There was something in the suit's dark eyes that said this wasn't a normal project to be presented through the usual channels.

Whatever it was they were proposing, Wyatt vowed to reject it.

"It's a Western." The redhead fanned the pages. "A gritty story with a grim ending. Ashley Monroe has committed to the project."

Wyatt's back spasmed. Ashley Monroe would never want him attached to a project with her.

"There are a few dimensions to the role beyond the film though." The suit assessed Wyatt with a cold glance that seemed to indicate he wasn't measuring up.

Could have been the bruises, the robe or the pain Wyatt was trying to disguise. He closed his eyes, centered himself and then opened them again. "Get to the point."

"There are public-relations opportunities with Ashley at the location where the film will be shot."

"I've done PR with her." A date that had been both surprising and unwise.

Ashley Monroe had been a much-beloved child star. She had a squeaky clean image that was the polar opposite of Wyatt's. What good would dating her again do for his career? Nothing.

Wyatt signaled Jeremy to show his visitors the door.

The suit laughed. "Here's the thing, *lover boy*." All traces of humor vanished from his facade. "You will play the role of Ashley's wedding date. The details are here." He dropped a fancy envelope on Wyatt's coffee table. "I need you to RSVP. Plan on staying a week or her people—*our people*—will release certain details about your last date to the tabloids." The suit walked out.

The redhead gazed down at his script, sighed and then shoved it back into his bag and followed him.

Jeremy apologized for the intrusion and made some excuse to leave.

Wyatt drank more water, but the bad taste from his unexpected visitors lingered.

He reached for his phone. If the Monroes were going to lean on him, he was going to do a little web crawl and see if there was any leverage to lean back.

Funny thing about web search results. They turned up the latest and the most frequently read information. In this case, he didn't find new news about Ashley. He found new news about himself!

Swearing, Wyatt opened the wedding invitation.

"THAT WENT WELL." Shane stripped off his suit jacket before claiming his seat in their rented SUV. He squashed a bug on the back of his hand, hoping his shots were up-to-date.

"Are you kidding? Wyatt didn't bite." Jonah collapsed into the air-conditioned seat next to Shane. "We never told him who we were. And he didn't ask me to leave the script."

Jonah was often overly eager when it came to his work.

Shane aimed the air-conditioning vents at his face and instructed the driver to return them to the airport. "You have a lot to learn about negotiation, cousin. Wyatt thinks we hold his future in our hands. He may have built box office gold as an action hero, but when he played a villain in that spy movie last holiday? His standing in Hollywood slid. That was why he wanted a date with Ashley in the first place. To help clean up his image."

And Laurel had gone in her place. Once the press got wind of Laurel's situation, it wouldn't only be Wyatt's career that took a hit. Ashley's would, too.

"Wyatt will never come to Second Chance. Not in time for the wedding." Jonah slumped in his seat. "And not for the Old West festival." Where they planned to put on a few scenes from Jonah's script.

"Oh, he'll show up. He wants to hold on to that brass ring."

"But then what? As soon as Laurel tells him the truth—that she was only pretending to be Ashley—he'll regain the upper hand." Jonah hugged his messenger bag to his chest. "Her wedding is going to be a disaster. And my movie will lose a bankable star."

His cousin might have a point. Shane made a mental note to make sure Wyatt's understudy in the festival was good. "You worry too much."

"I'm a writer. Until production on a film begins, it's my job to worry."

Shane's phone vibrated. He checked the display. "It's Ashley. Good news. Wyatt agreed to be her wedding date." Actually, it was kind of suspicious how fast Wyatt had given in. Shane frowned.

"This wedding is going to be a disaster," Jonah repeated.

"Not completely." Shane loosened his tie, trying not to absorb Jonah's pessimism. "The food is going to be excellent."

CHAPTER THIRTEEN

"WHAT SPECIALS ARE you attempting today, Chef Wedding Planner?" Ivy skipped down the stairs just minutes before opening.

She showed no sign of the exhaustion Cam was feeling. In fact, she brought an energy into the room. She was pert and perky, ready for another twelve-hour day.

Ivy brushed a hand over his shoulder as she passed. What had she eaten for dessert last night to recharge her batteries? Perhaps a defrosted chocolate mousse?

"Your customers are in for a treat today," Cam said optimistically, as if they'd be open to his specials. He'd been prepping for two hours and had already turned on all the lights and unlocked the door for customers, early or otherwise. "I'm making bacon-wrapped eggs and polenta, berry breakfast crepes and…" He carefully removed his pride and joy from the oven. "A personal serving of Parmesan-and-chive soufflé for early birds." He set the small ramekin on top of a plate as carefully as if it was a baby. "By Chef Early Bird."

"Wow." R.J. moved closer, donning his chef's apron. "I haven't had soufflé in forever."

"Soufflés don't come frozen, do they?" Cam ruffled the boy's hair.

Ivy gave Cam a funny look.

Cam thought he understood Ivy's no-chefs-in-the-kitchen rule. Her ex being a chef had soured her on the breed. Which was good since it meant despite the sparks between them, she'd never act upon their attraction. And since he didn't plan on staying, neither would he.

Easier said than done.

Cam laid his hand over hers as she counted the cutlery in a plastic tub. "I called Daniel Cross this morning. He'll be in touch about your revised custody agreement." He'd told Daniel he'd foot the bill.

"Thank you." Ivy stared at their hands then slowly withdrew hers. "Boys, can you roll silverware in napkins? We're running low."

The boys moved between himself and Ivy.

"So efficient," Cam said.

"Yes, well. Speaking of efficiency. How long will customers have to wait for soufflés?" Ivy didn't wait for him to answer. She moved to the dining room to start the large carafe of community coffee.

"Not long." Cam dressed the soufflé plate with raspberries and a sprig of fennel. "I've already got a customer for this one."

Laurel paced the dining room, her palms pressed into the small of her back. "Morning," she said to Ivy. "Don't mind me. It's just another round of false contractions."

"Speaking of false positives." Ivy's gaze found Cam's. "Even personal-size soufflés take thirty to thirty-five minutes. My customers expect to be in and out in forty-five minutes. Are you sure you want to attempt to offer soufflés?"

"They'll wait for this." Cam would. "I've got more batter in case anyone is interested first thing." He'd erase it from the chalkboard of specials after 8:00 a.m., since the batter spoiled quickly. "By the way, I fried your bacon and sausage for the morning." He offered Ivy's boys each a plate with two slices of bacon and two of sausage.

"You're hired," Nick said, proceeding to his beanbag, where he had a clear view of the kitchen. "Mom, can you make cinnamon rolls?"

"No, honey." Ivy stood near Laurel in the

dining room, staring out at Mack from the general store, who was gesticulating wildly as she talked to a few town residents in the parking lot. Ivy turned, caught Cam's eye and blushed. But only for a moment, before she moved on to make coffee.

Roy and another elderly gentleman who wielded a cane entered the diner. They asked Ivy for their "usual" breakfasts and claimed a booth near the kitchen.

"How was your dinner last night?" Cam asked Roy.

The old man gave him a thumbs-up. "Ate all the pork chop, but the vegetables were too mushy."

Mushy? His vegetables had been al dente.

"No cinnamon rolls?" Nick crunched his bacon as if he was famished. "Not even for midmorning snack?"

Perhaps the way to Second Chance's wallet was through dessert. What did Cam have to lose?

"I can make cinnamon rolls," Cam volunteered.

Ivy studied him speculatively. "What are you up to? Looking for extra credit by selling muffins and pastry?" She gestured to his display of blueberry muffins on the counter.

He'd marked them down.

"I'm just watching the bottom line." And formulating a campaign to win over the daily crowd, per Laurel's advice. And to do so, he had to think outside the box. "I was also thinking about my appetizers for Nick's kindergarten graduation."

"Summer is a day away," Nick said dreamily, mouth full of sausage. "Hiking. Tubing. Horseback rides. Adam said I could sleep over at his ranch."

"What are you making for Eli and the kids?" Ivy asked Cam as he delivered Laurel's breakfast and a mug of hot tea to a booth.

"I'm treating the crowd to smoked trout crostini." It had been one of the bestselling appetizers on his menu at Monroe hotels.

"Ew." Roy shivered dramatically.

"You should listen to Roy. He speaks for picky eaters everywhere." Ivy filled in two paper order tickets for Roy and his companion, and then stuck them on the rotating ticket holder. "Around here, people like the basics, which is my menu."

Cam rolled his eyes at the thought of her rudimentary menu, which lacked quality and interest. She'd do better running a dessert shop with those premade frozen concoctions.

"We'll see what people like today." It was time to institute guerilla warfare. Cam returned to the kitchen. If he'd learned anything about pushing new and exotic dishes in his years as a restaurant chef, it was that you had to establish trust between the customer and the chef to sell the dish. Entering the dining room, he carried a plate of bacon-wrapped eggs and polenta in one hand and a plate of berry crepes in the other hand.

Cam walked up to Roy and his elderly friend, trailed by Ivy's boys. "Can I interest you gentlemen in one of today's specials?" He explained each of the dishes, playing up to Roy since he'd fed him dinner last night. "Or perhaps a Parmesan-and-chive soufflé?"

"Hey!" Ivy called from the kitchen. "They ordered already."

"Give me a chance here." Cam slid the plates on the table, banking on Ivy's big heart to buy more time. "What do you think?"

Roy edged back in the booth. "I don't eat things like that."

"Things like what?" Cam kept his expression as neutral as Ivy's two-egg breakfast.

"Grits," Roy said in obvious distaste. "Those are grits."

"Polenta," Cam gently amended. "And you

did say to me once that you like to eat the scary stuff." Not that polenta was scary.

Nick giggled, gripping the edge of the table. "Roy is funny." His comment earned him a fruit cup from the town handyman.

"Roy is *picky*," R.J. corrected solemnly. "What do you think, Egbert?"

"Oh, I don't know." Egbert had a striking resemblance to Santa, although he wore a sky blue T-shirt with a fly fisherman on it. He stroked his full white beard. "Pancakes with berries look tasty. If only I wasn't on a diet." He patted his belly.

Cam could sense a sale. And one sale would lead to another. "The crepes are twenty dollars a plate. I can make you a fresh order."

"Twenty…" Egbert's bushy white eyebrows rose.

Roy put a fruit cup on the table and chuckled. "That makes Ivy's four-dollar oatmeal look like a bargain, eh?"

"Sorry, young man." And Egbert did look sorry. "I'm on a semiretired income. I'll be having coffee and Ivy's oatmeal this morning."

"Coming right up," Ivy called from the kitchen.

A tan, aging cowboy came in and sat down at the kitchen counter.

"Next customer, Mr. Cam." R.J. made a come-hither gesture, encouraging Cam to pick up his plates. "Hi, Mr. Bouchard. This chef is trying to sell his meals."

"For twenty bucks!" Nick danced around Cam's feet, almost tripping him. The boy stopped and glanced up at Cam. "Is there anything on our menu that costs twenty bucks?"

Cam shook his head.

Nick blew a raspberry. Translation: *good luck with that.*

R.J. gave his younger brother a gentle slug in the shoulder. "There could be twenty-dollar plates if people like it."

Shane would appreciate R.J.'s attitude, not that the boy could motivate Ivy to adjust the Bent Nickel's menu.

Cam took control of his selling efforts and began his sales pitch.

The cowboy was frowning before Cam had a chance to explain what polenta was. "The last time I paid upward twenty bucks for a meal was when I was in a steakhouse in Boise. And I had *steak* on my plate." Mr. Bouchard gave Cam a stern look, as if the chef had no right to be disturbing his coffee and the wheat toast he'd asked Ivy to make him.

Sarah entered, carrying a basket of jellies

and preserves—and an air of disapproval—
when she saw Cam. She strolled past on her
way to the coffeepot, eyeing Cam's plates and
shaking her head. "I knew you needed watching."

Cam and R.J. exchanged glances and shrugs.
Cam couldn't think of why she'd think he was
the town villain.

The schoolteacher and some kids entered the
diner. They headed toward the corner tables,
drawing Nick and R.J. in their wake.

"You're going about this all wrong." Ivy
pulled Cam away from her customers.

"This is the way it's done." Cam couldn't
keep annoyance from his tone. Experience was
on his side.

"The way it's done?" Ivy asked. "Like when
you wheel live lobsters around a restaurant on
a tray with the fresh beefsteak tomatoes and
cuts of meat?" Ivy rolled her eyes. "This is not
the right customer base for that."

"So you're saying I shouldn't show people
what I've made?" He was never going to win
this bet, never going to leave Second Chance
with seed money for his own restaurant.

Cam's phone rang in his pocket. It was probably his agent, calling to sever their business

relationship. And who could blame him? Cam couldn't even succeed cooking in a diner!

"I agree you need to show them." Ivy's glance bounced around the diner. "But I also think you need to give it to them for free."

Frustration filled Cam's chest, forcing out a single word. *"Free?"*

"Yes, free." She plucked the crepes from his hand and walked to an older woman with short white hair who'd just come in. "Odette, Chef Monroe made too many crepes this morning. Would you like some?"

"Careful," Roy called from across the room. "He's charging twenty bucks."

Odette put on a pair of reading glasses that were dangling around her neck. She peered at the crepes, at Cam, across the diner at Roy and then out the window toward Mack, who was on the phone. "What's the catch?"

"There's no catch," Ivy reassured her. "It's free."

Cam made a sound deep in his throat that earned him a dark look from Ivy.

"For real?" Roy scooted out of the booth and teetered across the room to Ivy's side. "If it's free, I'm trying it. Me. The man who likes dangerous food, as long as it's not grits or bananas or booger cheese." Roy took possession of the plate of crepes, pausing to stare at Ivy and Cam as if they might refute his claim. When they didn't, he retreated to his booth and a laughing Egbert.

"I'll take the gritty stuff if it's free," Egbert said, chuckling. "Are we going to need to do dishes to pay for all this?"

"Not this morning." Ivy delivered the polenta dish to Egbert. "Cam is interested in what people think of his food."

"I guess if you snooze you lose." Odette shrugged and joined Laurel at her table. "A cup of tea, please."

Cam followed Ivy back into the kitchen. "Listen, I love to cook and I love it when people enjoy my food. But the point of this exercise is for me to make sales. Not give food away." Not suffer humiliation at her hands. Not lose.

"Let me guess. You've never worked anywhere that food on the menu cost less than twenty dollars a plate." Ivy gave him a look that dared him to deny it.

He couldn't. "So?"

"So?" She sighed the way she did when Nick did something outrageous. "If you want to win, maybe you should think about the things you made when you were twelve, not the ones you built your reputation on twenty years later. I promise to get no pleasure from beating you. But if you continue like this, you won't just lose. You'll lose badly."

Cam knew what Ivy said made sense. But that didn't change the fact that he wasn't wired to cook that way.

"Now tell me." Ivy took hold of Cam's arm. "What's the deal with your super slo-mo food-prep style? I've seen grass grow quicker than you move in the kitchen."

"What?" His gut clenched. "I'm not slow." It wasn't a lie. Cam wasn't slow. He was slower than slow.

"Cam." Ivy pulled him deeper into the kitchen. "You have no confidence in your food. There are soufflés in the trash."

She knew.

She knew. She knew. She knew.

Ivy's gaze trapped his. "I watched you place individual blue-cheese crumbles on waffles the other day. One at a time, Cam."

He couldn't move, not even to frown at her.

It's true.

It's true. It's true. It's true.

She sighed. He noticed she sighed a lot when he was near. "Yesterday, you choked on mixing aioli."

Cam consciously took in much-needed air. He could wait out her interrogation, deny by his silence. Except there was the simple fact that she was right, still had hold of his arm and was huggably near.

"I was fired." Those three words burst out of Cam to land in between them with a thud. He glanced to his feet before lifting his gaze back to her face.

Her beautiful, intent face. "You mean, fired by your dad?"

It shouldn't have surprised him that she knew that. According to Shane, everyone with a lease in Second Chance knew a lot more about the Monroes than they let on. Heck, Grandpa Harlan had probably told her his plans regarding the will long before he died.

"Cam?" She touched his cheek briefly with her palm.

Here was where Cam should say yes. *Yes, my timing is off and my confidence is in shreds because my father gave me the boot.* Here was where Cam should insert a little damage control. Defend his reputation. Protect his ego.

Cam drew in a deep breath, prepared to deflect, and said, "I was fired by someone else. Last week. During the Saturday dinner rush." He clamped his lips together.

That's it. I'm done.

Ivy didn't laugh. She didn't say something snarky, like "Obviously, you were fired. Heck, I'd fire you, too." She gave him a half smile, rubbed his shoulder and said matter-of-factly, "Get over it."

Cam's jaw dropped. "Get…"

Get a grip, chef.

"Get over it?" Cam tugged her into the pantry and closed the door behind him. "Get over it? You don't just get over something like that. I… I can't just get over something like that. Do you realize that I've got a—"

"Michelin star?" She tried to get around him to the door. "Seriously, is that your excuse? Do you plan to put that on your tombstone?"

He shifted so she couldn't get out.

Ivy made a grumbly noise in her throat. "I can't believe this. Don't you realize—"

"No one with a Michelin star gets fired. No one." Cam grabbed on to her upper arms to hold her still. "Can you at least look me in the eye while we're arguing?"

Ivy stopped struggling. Her cheeks bloomed with color. Her gaze only made it about as far as his collarbone. "Hanging on to one event in your past isn't going to help you in the kitchen. Now—"

"Whoa, whoa, whoa. Aren't you the one who said it's the bad things that drive us?"

She nodded.

"Well, my bad thing has me driving the speed required in a school zone—nice and slow so nothing gets hurt." He huffed. He'd hurt quite a bit of food this week. And since she continued to stare at his collarbone, he puffed. "What does it matter?" He put a hand beneath her chin and lifted her face until she met his gaze. "Don't you get it? I'm not going to be allowed in kitchens of any consequence."

"You're allowed in mine." But she said it with that hint of vulnerability in her eyes, as if she knew her kitchen was of no consequence at all. And then her gaze slid away from him toward the door his back was against. "Unfortunately, you aren't going to get a chance to prove whether speed matters. You've locked us in the pantry."

Reflexively, he pulled her closer, as if there was something dangerous in the pantry besides him and his sudden need to kiss her.

"What are you doing?" She tilted her head back to look up at him with those eyes that saw too much.

"I'm trying to reassure myself you don't see me as a complete buffoon," he said gruffly, meaning it. If he gave in to the impulse to kiss her...

"You're not a buffoon." Ivy gave him a gentle shove, strong enough to give her some breathing room. "People get fired all the time for good reason, for no reason and everything in between." Her cheeks reddened. "My dad fired me."

"He was a chef?" Cam asked.

"Oh, yeah." Ivy nodded. "Fine Italian cuisine. Everything I learned about running a restaurant, I learned from him. He never ran out of gas. And if something bad happened, he'd pick himself up and drive himself forward, usually dragging the rest of the family behind him."

"Your dad sounds a lot like you." And Grandpa Harlan.

Ivy threw her arms around Cam's waist and squeezed. "I think that's the nicest thing you ever said to me."

"Mom?" R.J. opened the pantry door. "You know the pantry lock doesn't work. Why would you close it?"

Ivy elbowed Cam out of the way. "It was Cam. He was trying to show me where he put everything."

R.J. stood staring at Cam with his hand on the doorknob. "What was Mom looking for?"

"A pineapple slicer." Cam said the first thing that popped into his head. He walked out of the pantry.

Sarah stood in the doorway to the dining room, frowning.

"But…" R.J. dogged his heels. "We don't have any pineapple."

"I know." Cam wasn't giving up on this ruse. "I told her she shouldn't buy any until she had one."

R.J. stopped in the middle of the kitchen. "But… I'm confused."

So was Cam. But it wasn't pineapple and pineapple slicers that confounded him.

It was Ivy.

CHAPTER FOURTEEN

A FLASH OF sunlight on a passing car caught Ivy's attention midmorning.

The diner had been packed with locals since it opened, Mack's work for sure. Second Chance residents were ignoring Cam's specials and ordering off the regular menu. Who had spilled the beans that a competition was on? Mack had promised not to meddle until word got out.

But there was a lull in the restaurant now, and Dr. Carlisle had just driven by, heading toward the medical clinic.

Ivy hurried into the kitchen and washed her hands. "Cam, can you cover for me for a few minutes?" She didn't look at him when she asked. They'd been avoiding each other since R.J. had released them from the pantry.

Cam had been unusually quiet, perhaps regretting his confession about getting sacked. He needed time to process that those terminations didn't matter. And she needed time to hide the fact that she'd almost kissed him. It was enough to keep her from starting up any more conversations.

R.J. scurried into the kitchen behind her. He'd been with the schoolkids. "I'll help Mr. Cam."

Nick skipped in behind his brother. Both boys were spending more time in the kitchen since Cam had arrived. "I'll make sure nobody gets locked in the pantry."

"Sure," Cam said dejectedly. "I've got nothing better to do." He'd gotten no orders, not even when Roy and Egbert sang his praises.

"We'll make pizza for school snack." R.J. headed for the freezer, back turned so he didn't see Cam's helpless expression.

He'd been fired and now he was serving frozen pizza. Ivy wanted to toss a chef nickname his way to lighten the moment, but she couldn't think of any clever ones, and then the moment passed as the boys began chattering at him. Ivy hurried out the door and crossed the highway to the medical clinic.

"Dr. Carlisle." Ivy waved to the woman as she opened the door.

Dr. Carlisle turned slowly, her hand on her lower back. "Hey, Ivy. The clinic is coming together, isn't it?" She entered the cabin Shane had hired her to update. It was now filled with new medical equipment, a sharp contrast to the old furniture still in the waiting room.

"Yes," Ivy said absently, trying to wrap her head around a fleeting impression of something…and failing to put her finger on it.

Dr. Carlisle adjusted her black glasses and tugged down her pink scrub shirt. "I'm expecting delivery of two patient beds today. I couldn't sleep last night because I didn't think they'd both fit and I couldn't remember if we'd rewired the wall with enough electricity for them." She walked into the exam-room space, which was now divided by a curtain hanging from the ceiling. "Good. It is."

The clinic was housed in a small cabin built in the last century. The last few town doctors had also lived there, sleeping in the loft above the kitchen. Ivy could understand Dr. Carlisle's concern about space. It was tight. But she'd come over for a reason, not a social call, or to check on Dr. Carlisle's progress on modernizing the clinic. Updates meant nothing without a doctor on staff.

"Nick had another ear infection a few nights ago." Ivy kneaded her knuckles. "It came on without warning." That wasn't quite true. He'd played in the rain the day before, but it wasn't like he'd had a fever or been sick.

"I'm sorry to hear that." Dr. Carlisle had great bedside manner. She gave Ivy a soft smile. "He's better? Did you ask his doctor about putting in tubes?"

"No. We went to the medical clinic in Ketchum, rather than his regular doctor." Ivy promised to report the event to Nick's pediatrician. "I was just wondering if you'd heard of any doctors interested in working here. Shane said he had someone in mind, but you know Shane." That Monroe played his cards close to his chest. Ivy kept hoping he'd persuade Dr. Carlisle to take the job. She was single, bright and caring, and had visited Second Chance many times.

Dr. Carlisle surveyed the space with a wan smile. "These Monroes..." She pressed a hand to the small of her back once more.

The movement made something in Ivy's mind click into place, filling in the blanks from her earlier incomplete thought. The gesture was the same thing Laurel had been doing this morning in the diner, as if her back ached from stretching ligaments.

Ivy's hopes sank. "Are you pregnant?"

"You've never heard about Merc'less Mike Moody?" Nick sat on his beanbag, a line of plastic green army men on the floor at his feet.

It was after four. The lull was in full swing. Just not where Ivy was concerned. Her orders had increased. Not that pulling away from him had made her happy. She'd been in a prickly mood since asking Cam to cover for her earlier. Her smile was strained around the edges and she'd burned two grilled-cheese sandwiches at lunch. In a row.

Whom had she spoken to outside that had upset her?

Cam had been stuffing red bell peppers and wondering if Ivy would tell him what was wrong if he asked, or if she'd take a conversational detour back to his methodical performance in the kitchen. And then the boys had brought up the topic of this Mike Moody character. "Was Merciless a lovestruck cowboy or a miner or something?" He wiped his hands and then adjusted the green army man in his back pocket, the one Nick said he needed poking his head out as lookout.

"Merciless Mike Moody was a bandit." R.J. poured cheese sauce over elbow macaroni. He'd made it with hardly any supervision or advice from Cam. "But he wasn't even the baddest bandit around."

"That was a girl!" Nick nearly slid off his beanbag. His feet wiped out his army battalion. "A girl robbed the stagecoach."

R.J. nodded. "And she killed people."

"Don't talk like girls can't do the same things as boys." Ivy carried dirty milkshake glasses into the kitchen from the diner's last group of customers.

Cam sprinkled shredded cheese on top of the sausage-stuffed peppers, and then he slid them into the oven. He was making Ivy and the boys dinner. Not because he was bored, but because they all deserved to be cared for the way Ivy cared for everyone else. She reminded him of his grandfather and how he had always watched out for others. "Is this really a good time to talk about equal-opportunity murder and mayhem?"

"Is there ever?" Ivy loaded the dirty glasses into the dishwasher. "Your cousin Jonah has been writing her as the hero of his movie script. Mike was her brother."

"Oh, that Mike." The character Laurel's baby daddy was supposed to play in Jonah's film. "And the celebration of this brother-sister duo is the theme of Shane's Old West festival?"

"Yes," they all said in unison.

"Cam…" Ivy came to stand next to him. "Can we talk for a minute? Outside?"

"Of course." Cam followed her out the back door to a porch beneath the one where she ate dessert every night. "Listen, before you start, let me apologize for this morning. I got upset in the pantry."

"Oh… No… That's not what… Thank you, but…" Her fingers knotted, unknotted, knotted again. "I was wondering…"

Cam laid his hand on top of hers. "Tell me what's bothering you."

She stared at their joined hands. "I'm thinking of… I think it's best…"

He waited.

Ivy lifted her pained gaze to his. "I'm forfeiting the challenge."

"No," he said reflexively, momentarily forgetting his goals in the face of her distress.

"What's the point?" She shifted her hands to grip his. "We're never going to get a doctor. It's irresponsible to raise kids here without local medical care. I'll finish out the summer and close the Bent Nickel for the winter. That'll give me enough money to start elsewhere. And I won't have to lie awake at night worrying about my lease."

"No." Second Chance without Ivy? She was the heart and soul of the small town. "I'll talk to Shane. I'll make medical care in town a priority."

The pain in her expression eased. "That's sweet, but... If I forfeit, you'll get your vote. I just wish..." She gave a little laugh. "I wish a lot of things."

The way she stared at Cam made him wish, too.

"I'm just sorry I let the rest of the town down by quitting. Maybe Shane will figure things out, but..." She had the most expressive eyes. They flashed tenderness, regret and longing. Her emotions were laid out like an engraved invitation, inviting Cam to return in kind, perhaps with a kiss. "It's for the best. We'll both move on from Second Chance."

Cam couldn't move. Not to speak. Not to let her go from him and certainly not from Second Chance.

He drew her closer, until their clasped hands were over his heart. "Don't go." His words sounded like a growled command. Not that she'd ever heed a word he said. He had to show her why it was important that she stay. He had to make her see. He had to...*kiss her.*

His lips came down upon hers, not to stop

her from ending the contest and leaving, but to show her what she'd be missing. His touch. His tenderness. His gratitude for standing up to him and telling him to stand up for himself.

Cam was good with food. He wasn't good with people, except when it came to this person—Ivy Parker, short-order cook and all-around superwoman. He was good with her even when he didn't realize he wanted to be good. She put up with his guff. She called him out on his ego. She seemed to understand what he was going through, which meant more to him than he could put into words.

And her kiss… Cam was lost in it and he didn't care. He wouldn't care if he never saw a kitchen again as long as Ivy inched a little closer, kissed a little longer, squeezed his hands a little tighter.

The Salmon River rushed past, mere feet away. Wind rustled the pines. Somewhere a bird sang. The gentle sounds of nature. A backdrop he'd always associate with her.

He didn't know who shifted first, who sighed, whose fingers loosened. But he'd remember staring into her eyes for what seemed like forever. They were a deep brown. And her expression… It was relaxed and open. Those lips that had returned his impulsive kiss were curling into a smile.

"Don't go," he said again, in case she'd forgotten what he'd said earlier.

"But…" There was wonder in her eyes, wonder in her voice. "Why?"

He kept her close, bodies touching so there was no need to whisper. He whispered anyway. "Because I made you dinner."

In the history of reasons men had given women for staying with them, that had to rank up there among the worst.

There were shouts from inside the Bent Nickel. Probably from eavesdropping boys who thought Cam was being ridiculous. Their repetitive shouts took a moment longer to penetrate his brain.

"Dad! Dad!"

"DAD! DAD!"

Ivy's kiss-muddled brain took a moment to process Nick and R.J.'s shouts.

It took another moment to release Cam and enter the Bent Nickel's back door, dreading what she'd find.

She stumbled through the kitchen, only to stop in the doorway leading to the din-

ing room, needing to lean against its frame.
"Robert?"

She and the boys hadn't seen her ex-husband
since last summer. In December, he'd claimed
the snow in Second Chance was too great to
visit, and he didn't want to be stranded in town
and miss work. Ivy had been relieved.

"Honey, I'm home," Robert said in a sing-
song voice. He thought it was endearing. Ivy
was only mortified.

Cam came to stand behind Ivy, positive energy radiating from him like the summer sun,
warm and too bright to look at directly.

They'd kissed. It had been marvelous, like
a spoonful of the most decadent dessert when
you'd been on a diet. They needed to talk about
that.

And Shane's silly competition. They needed
to talk about that, too. Ivy was serious about
quitting and moving on to somewhere safer
and more practical for the boys, although it
was a crushing decision. She loved Second
Chance.

"Mom, look who's here," R.J. said, glowing
with a tentative happiness.

"What a surprise." Ivy hoped her tone con-
veyed it was a pleasant one. She tried so hard

to be neutral when it came to outward emotions toward their father.

"What did you bring me?" Nick demanded, used to being spoiled by his father.

There were no locals in the dining room, no passing customers, no Monroes, either—if she didn't count Cam.

How can I not count Cam?

She could practically feel the heat of his body behind her. If she'd been younger or weaker, she might have taken a step back and leaned into him, drawing strength from someone who cared what she did with her future.

Don't go, he'd said. As if he planned to stay and couldn't bear the thought of living in Second Chance without her.

Don't dream, a small voice in her head cautioned. *You know where dreams lead.*

Oh, she did. *Dead ends.*

Robert pulled up a boy in each arm and swung them around. Their feet flew out and upward, hitting chairs.

"Robert, stop. Stop before you hurt someone." Ivy rushed forward, straightening chairs as she did so. "Why are you here?" Okay, there was more than a little suspicion in that question. "You're early."

Robert stopped spinning and hitched the

boys into the crooks of his arms. "I heard my little man was graduating."

"Tomorrow is my last day in kindergarten," Nick confirmed, grinning from ear to ear.

"And my last day in third grade," R.J. said, heartbreakingly aware that he wasn't Robert's favorite.

"We didn't expect you." Ivy cast a nervous glance around the Bent Nickel. It looked fine. All tables clean. All napkin holders, salt and pepper shakers filled. No one, not even Robert, could find fault with anything today.

Don't let him judge you.

She swallowed. What didn't show was the abundance of cash in the register and the tally of accounts that said she was having her best year ever. Had Robert's parents told him she was doing well? Since the divorce, they rarely came to the Bent Nickel. She'd let them know about Nick's graduation a month ago via email and Jarvis had told her they'd attend. But they'd said nothing about Robert, not even when Ivy was there. She'd had no warning.

Her gaze collided with Robert's. There was a calculating look in his eye that unsettled her insides. He wasn't just here for his child's kindergarten graduation.

Suspicion tried to become panic, tried to

make her hands shake. She couldn't show any outward sign of weakness or Robert would pounce. Not physically. He was too smart for that. His was a mental game of cat and mouse.

"Boys, don't you have something to do in the kitchen?" Cam asked, perhaps sensing Ivy's trepidation.

Nick shook his head. R.J. shrugged, fiddling with the bandage on his finger.

My boys...

She'd do anything to keep them from falling under Robert's spell the way she had.

"Hey, I just got here. There should be no chores. There should be milkshakes." Robert carried the boys to a booth near the kitchen. "Come sit with us, Ivy. Have the new guy make us some."

"New guy?" Ivy's gaze collided with Cam's. His expression was as cold and hard as it had been the morning she'd told him to get out. Her mouth went dry. She gave a very small headshake, trying to tell him this was her battle to fight.

"Yeah, the new guy. Your cook." Robert pointed to Cam before settling into the booth, flanked by the boys. "You must be doing well. I see you're doing specials again." He gestured toward the sandwich board outside.

"Oh, him." Ivy found her voice, somewhere down by her toes. "He's not my cook. He's Laurel Monroe's wedding caterer. He's renting space for a few weeks. Those are his specials on the board outside, test runs for the big day." She was babbling. Why didn't she identify Cam as a Monroe? And what would she rattle off next? Her monthly profits? "I'll get those milkshakes started." She walked to the freezer on unsteady legs.

"You didn't bring me anything?" Nick asked Robert, flabbergasted.

"It looks like your mother can spoil you with that rent she's getting from those *Monroes*."

Too late, Ivy realized her mistake. Robert had hated Harlan. And now he was going to use the Monroe card to paint her as a bad mother who didn't spoil her kids when she could. Next he'd chip away at her cooking ability and denigrate her management of the Bent Nickel.

Ivy got out the ice cream, pressing the large, cold container to her chest, hoping the chill would get her brain moving the way it was supposed to. She had to figure out what Robert wanted. She had to make sure she was his focus, not R.J. and Nick. And she had to stuff all her feelings about Cam and that kiss deep down inside, where Robert wouldn't see.

She carried the ice cream to the milkshake machine, which was halfway between the kitchen and Robert's booth.

"I'm always amazed this place is still open." Robert shifted gears. "You still taking Monroe charity, Ivy?"

Cam joined her. He set down a metal cup filled with hot water and handed her the ice-cream scoop. His gaze was colder than the ice cream, but it was a chill directed at Robert. He touched her hand briefly, so lightly she would have thought she'd imagined it if not for the flash of compassion in his eyes.

For the second time that afternoon, she wanted to touch Cam, to draw on his strength. She hated that she didn't want to face Robert alone. That's all she'd done for years. She could be good at it if she had time to mentally prepare herself.

Ivy nodded to Cam, hoping to convey she was fine even though she wasn't. Her emotions were a whirling vortex of uncertainty.

And really, was there a reason to be fearful? Other than that brief flash of calculation on Robert's face, he was just being…

Well… Robert. She could handle shade and put-downs.

"Something smells good in the kitchen." Robert drummed his hands on the table. "The new guy must have made it."

Something did smell good. And for the life of her, Ivy couldn't think what she was cooking. The diner was empty and it wasn't time for her to make dinner yet.

She added chocolate syrup and started the machine.

"I made Ivy and the boys dinner," Cam said over the whir of the milkshake machine. "Practice for the wedding. Sorry, but I didn't make enough for four." He smiled at R.J. and Nick. "And I've already shut down the kitchen for the night."

Ivy wanted to hug Cam. He'd just blown off Robert without telling him to get lost.

Don't go, he'd said. *I made you dinner.*

Cam wanted to go somewhere he was appreciated? That was here, in Second Chance. She appreciated him.

Cam disappeared into the kitchen. Or he would have disappeared if not for the pass-through. He stood where Robert couldn't see him. But Ivy could see Cam. She couldn't tear her eyes away.

Because Cam was smiling. At her.

Her heart swelled enough to knock her out of her lane.

Small-town, short-order cook, single mom. Three inconsequential things that defined Ivy and made her less threatening to Robert. She could be so much more if she smiled back at Cam.

Lane? What lane? She could feel the corners of her lips rising.

"Ivy, where are those milkshakes?"

"Coming right up."

CHAPTER FIFTEEN

"FRIED PEACHES AND cream-cheese tarts?" Robert stood in the diner's kitchen after hours, leaning against a counter like he owned the place. He had rebuffed all Ivy's hints to leave. "Seriously, Ivy. That'll go right to your hips. And hippy waitresses don't make good tips."

Ivy bit back a retort about fat shaming. It would only fall on deaf ears. Instead, she said in a reasonable voice, "You know how hard it is to run this place. I'll walk it off, but thanks for your concern."

The boys were upstairs watching a little bit of television before bedtime. Cam had left before she started making her tarts, but not before asking if she needed him. She'd lied and told him no.

Cam had shown her genuine concern these past few days. His stuffed peppers had been delicious. His macaroni and cheese comforting. All that was missing tonight—besides Cam's kiss—was the warm culinary hug of fruit and rich cream cheese, batter-fried. She removed them from the fryer and placed them on paper towels to soak up the excess oil, her skin crawling when Robert leaned in for a closer look.

"If I was running the Bent Nickel, it would have been filled for dinner," Robert said with an air of authority Ivy immediately resented. "I knew it was a mistake letting you handle things."

Letting me? It had been a term of her divorce.

"Robert." Ice. It was in her veins. She tried to chunk it out in her words to discourage him. "You gave up the right to influence what goes on at the Bent Nickel a long time ago. Fridays are always slow."

"As are all days ending in a *Y*. You need me to run things around here." He took a half step closer and wielded the smile that had won her over. He was handsome when he smiled. But run the diner better than her? No way. His face was tan. There were no worry lines radiating from his eyes like the ones she had. And there were the beginnings of a gut at his beltline. Robert wasn't running a kitchen. He wasn't running anything but at the mouth.

Not that he'd ever accept he lacked the acumen to run a restaurant.

Just thinking about telling him made her pulse pound and increased her instinct to flee. She reminded herself Robert was just spewing words. She'd been taking in Cam's words for days. But that wasn't the same, not by a long shot. Cam hadn't brainwashed Ivy or tried to control her.

Robert's chuckle echoed ominously in the empty kitchen. "I'll never know what Harlan Monroe saw in you. But I guess that well is dry now that he's dead, huh?"

No matter how much Harlan's passing hurt, Ivy had to remain impassive.

He just wants a rise out of me.

Ivy dusted the tarts with powdered sugar, hiding her trembling hand with quick movements. She flipped the tarts with tongs to cover both sides.

"I bet you're barely hanging on. I bet you're looking to cash out of your lease." He took out his wallet and placed a one-dollar bill on the counter. "What do you say?"

"Thanks, but no thanks." Ivy transferred the tarts to a small Dutch oven to keep warm. She began closing down the kitchen, making sure things were off. She'd come down later to drain and clean the fryer once it cooled. "We manage just fine."

"Managing isn't success." Robert's smile grew. "Face it, Ivy. You need me back here to manage the business, to make it grow." He inched closer. "To build it into something our boys would be proud to run, unlike this dump you've let it become."

He's right. Her voice, small and meek. The Ivy she'd been after years under Robert's influence. He'd verbally beat her down until she didn't believe she could cook a scrambled egg.

He's wrong. About everything.

Heart pounding, Ivy placed her hands flat on the counter on either side of the covered dish and looked him squarely in the eye. "I keep telling you, we're doing fine without you. The Bent Nickel is—"

"Ours." Robert tried to capture her hands.

Ivy snatched her hands away. "The Bent Nickel doesn't belong to either one of us. We sold it to Harlan. And you—"

"Should have thought about it a while longer." He studied her through half-lidded, calculating eyes. "I was coerced into the deal. Now that the old man is dead and I find myself between jobs, I want what was mine."

The restaurant. The boys. Her.

Ivy struggled to think, to remain calm. He'd been fired again. An assumption, but he was always between jobs when he visited Second Chance.

Robert's gaze slid away, taking inventory of the kitchen, of the white board tally, but his chilling smile remained. "You need me."

A fearful, wounded noise tried to work its way up her throat. She swallowed. "It doesn't matter. The deal is done."

"Agreements are ripped up all the time." Robert's brow creased, but his eyebrows didn't lower. "Especially deals with dead guys."

"Don't you dare talk about…" Ivy suddenly remembered the door to the apartment stairs was open and the boys could hear them argue if they weren't fully immersed in their television show.

If Robert knew they'd heard this argument, he'd make them choose sides. He'd berate them relentlessly and box them into a corner until they'd choose him. That's how abusers worked. They targeted the innocent and the weak.

"Robert." *Breathe. Try to smile.* She did both but couldn't quite meet his gaze.

She had to put him off without challenging his ego. *Pretend to be no threat, no challenge.* She told herself a backbone was only good if it wasn't broken. He hadn't shattered her defenses today. He'd pushed familiar buttons, but to no avail.

"It's been a long day, Robert. I'm tired. And I've got to get the boys to bed. We can talk about this some other time." Or never. Ivy grabbed the diner keys from a hook on the wall and headed toward the front door. "I'll let you out."

Ivy barely kept herself from running across the dining room. She unlocked the door and held it open, holding on tight. Only then did she notice Robert lingering in the kitchen, staring at her, at this woman he used to be married to, the one he'd berated daily, the woman who'd never stood up to him without a millionaire at her back.

Harlan would want her to lift her chin, to look as if she couldn't be pushed around.

Oh, but inside she was a feather. One good hard argument from Robert and Meek Ivy would return, blown in whatever direction Robert wished.

The boys. She had to be strong for the boys.

She lifted her chin higher, sealed her lips together, but not forcefully enough that she couldn't attempt to smile.

And still, Robert hung back, measuring her resolve like a predator assessing his quarry.

She could have asked him if there was something wrong. She could have asked him if he wanted to take a tart with him. But things had changed in Second Chance. *She* had changed. All she needed now was for the change to stick. He'd never tested her like this before. Something had happened to him and she didn't think it was Harlan's passing. He felt angry with the world, not happy at the opportunity to return to Second Chance.

"Good night, Robert." She rattled her keys, leaving her ex-husband no graceful way to stay and try to make her believe she needed him.

Ivy locked the door behind him and tested the latch twice before returning to the kitchen, shoving aside his dollar bill.

She waited until he'd driven away.

Instead of grabbing the tarts and carrying them upstairs, she lurched into the pantry and slid to the floor, letting the fear and mortification out in deep, wracking sobs she tried to silence in a dish towel.

She didn't want the boys to know their father wasn't a good man. She didn't want her boys to know their mother had once been too timid to stand up to him. A coward. She'd been a coward. Her father had berated her for it. He'd seen it on her wedding day and she...

Ivy's shoulders curled inward. She knew most people didn't want to acknowledge words could be debilitating or dangerous. Most people, including her parents and some of her friends in Second Chance, didn't understand Ivy's fear, couldn't understand she'd lost nearly five years of her life to that man.

Sticks and stones may break my bones, but names will never hurt me.

Harlan had made her see what Robert had done to her. Her husband had made her second-guess every action. He'd limited her friendships and taken control of her life by making her feel she couldn't survive without him.

He wants to do it again. What good are lanes when Robert didn't stay in his?

Ivy felt lightheaded. It was exhausting to stand up to Robert. Look how shocked he'd been when he'd encountered her backbone, how he'd pivoted with determination and come at her with a different line of logic. She hadn't felt this vulnerable since Chef Camden Monroe had walked through the Bent Nickel days ago. And even then...

He's not like Robert.

Not bossy. Not a prima donna. Not a dreamer when it came to culinary success.

Okay, he's like Robert, except...

Cam could back up his culinary ego. He was good with the boys. Patient. Caring toward all of them. Loving.

Don't go, he'd said, as desperately as if he wanted to make a life together.

What if Cam just wanted someone to run the Bent Nickel, his family's business investment?

No. That was Meek Ivy talking, a woman who'd been under Robert's thumb.

Cam would never have kissed her if his being here was only a business maneuver. Cam was many things, but he wasn't dishonorable. He didn't use people the way Robert did, manipulating them to do what he wanted because he'd either convinced them they were worthless, or worn them down with his verbal wars. Cam was different.

Don't go, he'd said.

They needed to talk about those two words. And that kiss with all its promise of something more.

Love.

She didn't dare even think about the word.

It involved a level of trust she wasn't sure she could give.

And besides, Ivy couldn't think about flowery emotion. She needed to manage Robert, the way Harlan had shown her.

She gathered herself together, wiped away her tears and carried the tarts upstairs.

"Where did the peaches come from?" R.J. climbed onto a barstool after she put his tart on a plate. "They smell so good."

"I had some of Sarah's peach preserves downstairs." She'd had to rummage around Cam's reorganized pantry to find them.

"I liked Mr. Cam's macaroni and cheese." Nick joined his brother at the counter. It was late for them. They both had sleepy eyes. "Can we add it to the menu? It's better than boxed mac."

High praise indeed. Boxed macaroni and cheese was a favorite of her boys, not that it was on the menu.

Ugh. Don't think about menus.

"I made it," R.J. said with pride.

"Good." Nick smacked his lips. "You can make it when he leaves."

When Cam leaves…

Ivy's heart clenched in protest. But what

could she do? No Michelin-star chef would be happy in Second Chance.

While the boys ate their tarts, Ivy paid some bills. She answered an email from Harlan's lawyer—yes, she was interested in revising her custody agreement. This time, she'd have to present it without Harlan standing at her back. When Cam leaves…

She couldn't wrap her head around his absence, which was surprising given the short amount of time he'd been in her downstairs kitchen. But thinking about him was like imagining veering out of her lane. And she couldn't consider that. She couldn't create dreams about love or the future. She couldn't think beyond tomorrow, not when Robert was in town. Normally, her lane was safe. Normally, Robert didn't present ideas that included her. Nothing seemed normal anymore.

Ivy put the boys to bed and reheated the remaining tarts in the microwave—two, because she expected Cam.

A few minutes later, tarts and water on the outside table, Ivy settled into her lounger beneath Nick's blue fuzzy blanket. The sky tonight was an orangey pink. The wind was picking up. A storm was on the horizon, due to roll through tonight.

She'd survived the eye of Hurricane Robert, but her head was pounding and she was bone-weary.

Exhausted, she closed her eyes, letting herself relax, embraced by the silence, if not by Cam.

FOR ONCE, CAM climbed the stairs to Ivy's porch without feeling like he was intruding.

That's Chef Trespasser to you.

Or Chef Interloper. Or Chef Overstep. Or any of the dozen or so nicknames Ivy had come up with for him. He smiled.

He was later than usual, having reviewed menu choices for the wedding with Laurel. The sun had already gone down. The stars were already coming out. He reached the top stair and stopped.

Ivy was asleep on the lounger, burrowed beneath what looked like a cozy blanket.

"So she really does sleep." He crossed the porch quietly and stared at her under the light of the stars. She was beautiful. How could he not have seen that the moment he'd laid eyes on her? "Ivy, honey, wake up."

They needed to talk about what had happened before her ex-husband had barged into the diner. They needed to talk about her ex-husband. The guy was a jerk. That wary look had returned to her eyes when he showed up.

Ivy didn't stir.

A sweet smell, like peach pie, tickled his senses. He could sit in his usual spot and serve himself whatever dessert awaited him in the covered dish on the table. The clank of cast iron and silverware would undoubtedly wake her.

"Ivy," he said softly.

She didn't so much as sigh in her sleep. Poor thing. She needed to be in bed.

Cam scooped her into his arms and carried her to the apartment. He'd never been inside before, but he knew which window was hers. He gently drew the curtains aside and stepped through the slider. There was only one light on over the stove.

The apartment was open-concept. Small living room. Small dining room. Big kitchen. He did a double take. A big, beautiful kitchen with plenty of work surfaces. A six-burner gas stove. A huge stainless-steel refrigerator.

Ivy snuggled deeper into his arms.

Ivy, who he'd accused countless times as being a culinary hack.

Ivy, who had offered him delectable desserts he'd assumed weren't made from scratch.

Ivy, who kept the diner's kitchen neat and tidy, fully stocked with everything a chef could need to cook fresh ingredients if they had fresh ingredients.

The kitchen was well-equipped because Ivy was a chef.

"Ivy, honey. Wake up." He pressed a kiss to her crown.

Ivy simply sighed.

Much as Cam wanted to have this conversation, it was clear they weren't having it now. He carried her down the hall and into the front bedroom, a space that was pink and frilly, everything Ivy hid from the outside world beneath her jeans and T-shirts.

He laid her in bed, removed her sneakers and tucked her under the covers. He kissed her forehead, half wishing she'd wake up, stretch, wrap her arms around him and draw him down next to her so she could explain this double life of hers. Plain short-order cook by day. Sophisticated, feminine chef by night.

But she didn't so much as heave a sigh this time. So Cam turned and walked back down the hall. He brought in the dishes from the porch. Only then did he lift the lid and discover a pair of beautiful peach tarts, still warm. He couldn't resist. He found a fork and took a bite of one.

"It's good, isn't it?" R.J. stood at the end of the island in race-car pajamas. "I hope I can cook like she does someday."

"Me, too," Cam whispered, meaning it.

"I'm sorry about your waffles." R.J. clung to the counter's edge, looking like he might cry.

Over waffles? "It's okay. They weren't perfect." Ivy would have made them divine, though.

"I told the kids not to eat them," R.J. confessed in a small voice. "Because you scared my mom."

"You told…" Cam frowned. He'd been sabotaged because… "Your mom was mad, not afraid."

R.J. opened his mouth, perhaps to argue.

"Wait." The wheels in Cam's brain were turning. "You liked my waffles?"

R.J. nodded miserably. R.J., the kid who'd eat anything Cam offered him. The kid who wanted to learn how to cook everything. The kid who'd been raised by Ivy, the chef, who probably made soufflé on the regular. It all made sense now, except the scaring part.

R.J. inched closer, moving along the island as if the counter was a swimming-pool ledge and he was a nonswimmer in the deep end. "My dad came back today."

Cam nodded, unable to resist taking another bite of peach tart. It was nearly as irresistible as Ivy.

"Mom and Dad argued." R.J.'s brow furrowed.

Cam nodded. He'd seen that coming. It had been one of the reasons he'd left Ivy alone with the guy. "Sometimes ex-husbands and wives disagree." And sometimes they needed to work it out alone.

"He makes her scared, too." R.J.'s words barely carried to Cam. And the little guy's eyes were luminous, shining with a familiar vulnerability.

Cam had trouble swallowing.

The fear in Ivy's eyes. He'd noticed it the day he'd told her the kitchen downstairs didn't inspire him. And he'd seen it again tonight when she was dealing with Robert. Oh, there were other times, but he chalked that up to her concerns regarding her lease and the doctor. Still, he felt the need to deny it. "I don't scare your mom. Or at least, I don't mean to." Her ex… That might be another story. Robert, plus his parents… Cam didn't want to think about Nick and R.J. in that plastic palace with those three.

"But…you and Mom argue," R.J. pointed out, still in a voice Cam could barely hear.

Cam raised his fork and shook it from side to side. "With us, it's more like banter. There's a difference." At least, there had been since Shane had forced them to work together. And look at that. Shane was finally good for something. "You see, I was angry—not at her, but the world—but I think I'm over it now."

And he was. The bitterness and blame he'd clung to were receding and had been since Ivy had told him to get over it. Being fired shouldn't define him, just the way being divorced shouldn't define Ivy. There was more to each of them than that. He could finally forgive his grandfather his last wishes, and his father for carrying them out, and perhaps find the happiness that Shane and Ivy thought he deserved.

"You're a good cook." R.J.'s frown hadn't changed. His grip hadn't lessened. "But don't scare my mom anymore." He paused and then added, "Please."

"I won't." But R.J.'s hang-up on Ivy's state of mind had him worried.

Was her ex-husband a serious threat to her

safety? To the boys' safety? Supervised visits weren't imposed for no reason. Cam tensed, gripping the fork so hard it pressed into his palm. Robert's acerbic tone and his air of superiority were classic traits of a bully. And Ivy… He realized now he never should have left her alone with the man.

"I should go to bed." But R.J. didn't let go of the counter.

"Do you want some tart first?" Cam gestured toward the dish because he needed something warm and soothing, and the kid probably did, too.

R.J. shook his head. "We can't have seconds of desserts."

"Just like you can't have seconds of French fries." He'd figured that much out the first day he'd been dragged to the Bent Nickel.

R.J. nodded.

"Then this one is for your mom." Cam covered it up and opened the refrigerator, intending to put it inside. "Holy moly."

This was what he'd hoped to find when he'd opened her refrigerator downstairs days ago. Blocks of Parmesan and gouda cheese. Fresh cuts of meat. A vegetable drawer filled with uncut produce. A leftover container of Stroganoff made with strips of beef, not hamburger.

Yep, Ivy was a chef, all right.

Cam found a spot for Ivy's peach tart and closed the refrigerator. "R.J., I'm going to leave. Can you lock up after me?"

The kid gave a big nod, fingers still white-knuckling the granite. "I'll tell Mom you were here."

Cam bent down to the chef-in-training's level. "Maybe you shouldn't. I mean, she'd worry that she fell asleep outside with the door open. Anything could have come in."

"Bears." R.J. nodded solemnly. "Coyotes. Mosquitoes."

Loud, obnoxious fathers that should have restraining orders.

"We don't want to worry her." But now Cam was worried about her. And R.J. The kid was frightened. Impulsively, Cam drew the boy into his arms and hugged him.

The brave little man hugged him right back. "Can we make something tomorrow?" R.J. asked in his regular voice. "Something a chef would make in a fancy restaurant?"

"We should." Or not. Cam needed to think more about why Ivy wanted to quit the challenge and how best to let her know he knew her secret: she could win over anyone with food, especially dessert.

CHAPTER SIXTEEN

Ivy woke up to the alarm beeping on her nightstand.

She couldn't remember coming to bed last night. She must have been exhausted, drained by her discovery about Dr. Carlisle's pregnancy and the encounter with Robert. She'd slept in her clothes. Ugh. She tripped over her shoes on the way to the bathroom. Yep, she'd been out of it, all right. Usually she left her shoes near the stairs to the diner. And given the rain on her window, she'd slept through a storm, too.

"Mom, can I go downstairs with Mr. Cam?" R.J. had burst into her bedroom wearing clean clothes, his hair brushed and his shoes on. "He's making avocado toast."

"Me, too." Nick shuffled into the hallway behind his brother. He was still in his pajamas. His brown hair was wild, and his feet bare.

Ivy reminded them of the rules of going downstairs. "Clean clothes, clean teeth, hair brushed, shoes on." She left them on the honor system and got into the shower.

Her boys were both with Cam when she joined them downstairs.

"Avocado toast?" Ivy didn't want to admit that it looked good. "Please tell me you don't want to pressure me to add that to the menu. We never get good avocados up here." Her gaze snagged on more of Cam's work. "Chocolate cake?" Several rounds were cooling on a corner counter. "I thought you were making appetizers for the school's ceremony this morning."

"Change of plan." Cam handed her an espresso cup. "Thought you needed a jolt this morning."

"I can't imagine why," she said testily. She remembered waiting for him outside last night. And then…morning.

"We need to talk, for one thing." Cam ignored her irritation, smiling with a tender look in his eyes as if she'd kissed him hello.

Not a bad idea.

If she was the type to drift out of her lane, which she wasn't, especially with Robert in Second Chance.

Ivy wanted to go back to bed and start this surreal day all over again. Instead, she went about setting up for the day. It was only after the community pot was brewing coffee that she noticed Cam hadn't put out his chalkboard specials. And then she remembered she'd told him the bet was off. Her steps slowed.

In the kitchen, bacon and sausage were sizzling on the grill. Something wasn't right. Chef Early Bird was too chipper. Because she'd forfeited?

"Boys, why don't you sit down in a booth with your mother and have breakfast?" Cam didn't look at Ivy when he spoke, but there was warmth in his words nonetheless.

"I don't usually eat breakfast." Ivy didn't usually have time.

"I know." Cam lifted his gaze to hers, the look he gave her so direct, and yet that gaze lacked the huff and puff of his big ego. "You should eat. You should take better care of your-self."

"Come on, Mom." R.J. carried two plates of avocado toast to the booth nearest the kitchen, followed closely by Nick.

Ivy didn't move. "I don't understand."

Cam closed the distance between them. "Does a man need a reason to cook for a woman?"

"Yes." And yet he'd been doing it for days.

She found it hard to look in his eyes. "Have you told Shane you've won?"

"Nobody won." Cam brushed Ivy's hair behind her ear, his touch warm and welcoming.

"I made peach tarts last night," she blurted. For the life of her, she couldn't remember how they tasted.

"Your desserts have no bearing on…things." The way he stared at her… It surprised and comforted her at the same time.

"I don't understand. Your specials… Chocolate cake…" Yesterday's kiss…

Robert. Think of Robert.

She never wanted to think of her ex-husband again.

"We'll talk about everything. I promise." There it was again. The tender look in his eyes. "By the way, your ex-husband just parked out front."

Ivy practically gave herself whiplash in her rush to look. Sure enough, Robert had pulled up.

"I thought you might want to gird yourself for his presence. Hey." Cam caught her eye. "If I ever made you nervous or…*scared*, I never meant to."

She very nearly fell over in shock. "You've never intimidated me the way…"

"Robert does," Cam said, finishing for her as he squeezed her hand. "You know I'm here if you need me."

"Thank you, Chef I-Got-Your-Back." She was surprised to find she could still smile. Yes, the future was uncertain. But for the first time in a long time, Ivy felt like she could venture out of her lane.

If Cam was by her side.

Robert entered, sucking all the life from the diner, all the hope from her heart. He sat down with the boys and began eating her avocado toast. "Coffee over here, Ivy." He grinned at the boys. "I'll let you in on a secret. The service in this place sucks."

Ivy started forward as if on command.

"Take a breath." Cam drew her close to his chest, out of Robert's line of sight. "The service here is excellent."

"It is, but…" It was tempting to lean into that strong chest, to lean on another Monroe. But there was danger in that. Like Harlan, Cam wouldn't always be around to lean on. And there were the boys to consider. She didn't want Robert turning his temper on them.

"He's only trying to draw you out," Cam said softly.

"I know." What good did knowing his tactics do her? If he needed something, it was easier to give it to him.

Just not the Bent Nickel. Not her home.

"Tell Robert his coffee is brewing and give him a bill for the avocado toast." From behind her, Cam's words wafted warmly over her ear.

"I can't." She turned to face him. "He'll be livid."

"Then I'll do it." Cam would, too.

She could see it in his eyes, which were taking on that cold, determined look she knew so well. The one that didn't scare her. What did scare her was Robert's reaction when he learned Cam was a Monroe.

Cam rubbed her arms, and repeated, "I'll do it."

He wanted to be her shield? He was more like his grandfather than he knew.

"Waitress?" Robert called, setting Ivy's teeth on edge. "It's like this all day, isn't it, boys? Your mother is probably back there checking her phone instead of taking care of business."

"It's not like that at all," Cam whispered with a nod toward the dining room. He kissed her nose.

Chef Sweet. Ivy wanted to throw her arms

around him and get a real kiss—forget about ex-husbands and demoralizing pasts.

"It's like this all day," Robert repeated, louder this time.

Both men were waiting for Ivy to react. A long buried habit—her scurrying at Robert's beck and call—fought against the courage and strength of will she'd developed over the last five years. But it was Cam's strength that tipped the scales.

"It's not," Ivy said in a loud voice, earning Cam's smile. And then she was moving away from her Monroe rock. "It's not like this every day, Robert. Your coffee is coming right up." She paused at his table and placed a dollar bill in front of him. "You left this last night."

Robert's eyes narrowed.

While Ivy poured his coffee and tried to pretend Robert's reaction didn't make her nervous, Cam put an order ticket on the table.

"What's this?" Robert scowled. "I don't pay for food here. I own this place."

Without missing a beat, Cam said, "I thought the Monroes owned this place and this town." He towered over Robert, but casually, as if he considered her ex to be no threat. "And besides, my meals aren't on the menu and are billed separately."

Robert pushed his plate away. "Twelve dollars for toast. And it wasn't even good. The avocado was brown." He stood and tossed bills on the table. Twelve dollars. No tip.

R.J.'s eyes were huge. He gripped the table's edge.

"Dad, are you coming to graduation today?" Nick had avocado on his chin and hope in his eyes.

"I might not make it, sport. Your dad's a busy man." Robert headed for the door, but stopped by Ivy and said, "It would be better if you weren't around Second Chance to spoil things for me. Or my parents. Don't think I haven't heard what you did to my mother." He walked backward toward the door and whispered, *"Gone."*

A chill ran down Ivy's spine. That was a threat.

That was new.

She couldn't move until Robert had driven away. Only then did she breathe. She turned to her boys and reassured herself they were all right, telling herself threats were different than actions.

R.J. was staring at her. Nick was oblivious, asking Cam for seconds.

Cam was in the kitchen. "Ownership of the

Bent Nickel? We'll have to talk about that, too."

A couple with a baby entered the diner.

"Tonight," Ivy promised. If Robert was going to be a problem, her landlord needed to know.

"I'll be making test dishes this afternoon for Laurel to try." Cam handed Ivy another plate of avocado toast before turning bacon and sausage on the grill. "Get that couple settled, but then, please, have your breakfast. It's going to be a busy day."

Ivy greeted her customers, wondering if this was what it felt like to drift out of her lane.

"A TWO-EGG breakfast over easy and a short stack, coming right up." Cam ran a metal spatula back and forth across the grill, clearing it for a new set of orders.

"Hey." Ivy spun the ticket wheel around and snatched back the order. "You're not my cook. You're here to practice wedding-reception dishes. I'll fill these after I get their drinks."

"I got this." Cam cracked an egg and laid it on the grill. Had he kissed Ivy yesterday? Since her ex-husband left and the locals began pouring in, she'd regained some of her cockiness and her distance. "Don't worry about me cooking. After all, some people think I'm your new guy." He waggled his eyebrows suggestively.

She scoffed. "I also said you were Laurel's caterer."

"Neither of which is a lie exactly." He cracked another egg. "Notice how quickly I'm working."

She left the pass-through window and entered the kitchen. "Are you going to be trouble today?"

"Trouble? You said I needed to embrace a new path." He stirred the pancake batter quickly before pouring out two perfect rounds on the grill. "You said I needed to find happiness. And here I am." Searching for happiness with her.

"Apparently, I've been talking a lot more than I thought I was." Ivy crossed her arms. "What's the catch? Am I donating to your favorite charity when the day is through? Helping you on Laurel's wedding day? Come on. What is it?"

"Can't a guy just hang out and cook in a kitchen without there being an ulterior motive?" Like making sure the woman he wanted to kiss good-night wasn't harassed by her ex-husband during the day?

"Uh-huh." She wasn't buying it.

Think fast, chef. "You might make me something to eat later."

She gave him the stink eye. "Nacho tater tots?"

"Actually, I'm partial to Italian cuisine, and I don't mean frozen lasagna."

"Let me get this straight." Ivy's hands lowered to her hips, but she was none the happier. "You want to work for me today cooking plain eggs and burgers, and all I have to do is make you Italian food for dinner?"

Cam nodded, turning the eggs with finesse.

"Can't." Ivy began walking away. "There's an end of school year party at the lake by Shane's summer camp this afternoon."

"Rain check on that...*date*?"

"I'll have to think about it." But she smiled at him over her shoulder.

Oh, yeah. Rain check or not. They had a date.

CAM STAYED BUSY all morning.

The diner was nearly full by eleven thirty, what with various locals coming in to watch the end-of-the-school-year ceremony. The noise in the room rivalled that of a crowd in a high-school gymnasium.

It wasn't until a few minutes before the pomp and ceremony began that Shane showed up.

He looked road-weary with dark circles under his eyes. But his clothes were crisp and his smile broad as he led his fiancée to the rows of chairs set up for attendees. He beckoned Cam over, introducing him to Franny.

"How are you doing?" Shane checked his cell phone, barely paying attention to Cam. "Ivy just ignored me when I asked her about the bet."

"Um." Cam scratched his head. "There's been an adjustment."

Shane's head came up and his eyes narrowed. "You know I don't like surprises."

"Ivy forfeited." Cam hurried to explain. "Which I blame on you, because she panicked when she found out the doctor you were going to hire is pregnant. Ivy assumed she isn't going to want the job, but I'm not sure the doctor said as much."

"Hang on." Shane led Cam away from the parents taking their seats, disregarding Franny's inquisitive look. "Which doctor are we talking about?"

"I don't know." Cam shrugged. "The one who was out here the other day."

"And she's…" Shane's smile grew. "This is perfect."

"Please tell me the baby's not yours." Cam gave a significant glance toward Shane's fiancée. "Even you wouldn't sink that low."

"Of course not." Shane's eyebrows drew together. "Don't even go there."

"But you know whose it is." Otherwise, his clever brother wouldn't be so gleeful.

Shane nodded. "Maybe." That was a hard, end-of-discussion *maybe*.

Cam wasn't going to pry when he had other business on his mind. "So listen, we need to make a new deal. One that honors both parties." No way was he letting Ivy leave Second Chance.

Shane washed a hand over his face. "I've just spent two days on an airplane flying to South America and back for Laurel, surviving on coffee and airline pretzels. My head feels like a lead balloon. You've got to be clearer in your requests, bro, not to mention formulating an argument that sways me."

"I want Ivy to have that low lease, a guarantee regardless of whether or not we sell the land in town." Cam had tossed and turned last night thinking about it.

Shane pinched the bridge of his nose. "That's practically impossible, even for me."

"But not unfeasible," Cam said, pouncing on the opening. "You could do it. If Ivy upgrades her menu." She was a fantastic cook. It wouldn't be hard for her to add a few new items on the menu. All it would take was a little convincing.

Interest sparkled in Shane's eyes. "This sounds like a better deal for me."

"A sure thing." Cam nodded.

"What's the catch?"

"Besides getting her a doctor in town, I want your vote."

"To sell." Shane's gaze turned wary. "No." He looked around the room significantly, as if to say "I made promises to all these people."

Cam didn't care about anyone but Ivy and the boys. "Ivy forfeited, which means I have your vote, anyway."

"My head hurts. Do you need an answer now?" Shane gestured toward Nick and Adam, who wore men's black T-shirts that were supposed to be their graduation robes. "Did I mention my soon-to-be-adopted son is graduating from kindergarten in a few minutes and I can't get any sleep until this ceremony and the subsequent party are over?"

Cam knew if he gave Shane time to think about his proposition, his brother would come up with an alternative that Cam wouldn't like. He needed Shane's buy-in now. "Per your rules, I could walk away from Second Chance today. I've tried to influence the menu and failed. Do you want me to leave town? Or would you like me to get those menu changes you want implemented?"

"Nick, buddy!" Robert walked past them to give his son a shoulder rub, as if the boy was getting ready to go into a big game.

Cam's lip curled in a near snarl.

Shane noticed. He glanced from Ivy's ex to Cam. "The wheels in the old brain are turning slowly right now. With my vote, you could call a family meeting tomorrow. We'd sell Second Chance and you'd have your dream—a restaurant in San Francisco."

"If Ivy changes the menu for you and stays in Second Chance, I'll give you your vote back. And mine." Two for the price of one. Protecting Ivy was worth any price. Robert couldn't touch her here.

"You'd do that for her?" Shane's gaze sharpened and found Ivy sitting in the front row. "Does she know what you're doing? Does she know you love her?"

"No." Cam wasn't even sure he loved her that way. "And you're not going to tell her on both counts."

"Interesting." Shane grinned and waved at Adam, who was still with Nick. Their little arms were slung over each other's shoulders. "I think we have a new deal, bro."

They shook on it.

"You look happier, by the way." Shane clapped Cam on the back. "At least you did until you laid eyes on that guy." He nodded toward Robert, who took a seat in the back row next to his plastic-loving parents, Diane and Jarvis.

"That's Ivy's ex."

"That explains a lot." In usual Shane fashion, he didn't go into detail on just what it made clearer to him. Instead, he went to sit with Franny.

Sarah tapped Cam's shoulder, tossing her silver-streaked bangs in disapproval. "Ivy says you're working in the kitchen this afternoon during the end of school year party. I had plans to can today. Is that going to cramp your style, bub?"

"No, ma'am." Cam wasn't going to complain. "And you'll have ample time to watch me."

"There is that." She smirked and went into the kitchen.

The schoolteacher called for everyone to take their seats.

CHAPTER SEVENTEEN

THERE WAS SOMETHING about the kindergarten graduation that was silly and grand at the same time.

Ivy's baby was growing up, but he looked so adorable, Ivy couldn't be sad.

Eli had given Nick and Adam each a black cardboard graduation hat to match their robes. Adam chose to wear his straw cowboy hat instead. Not even his mother could persuade him to do otherwise.

The dining-room chairs had been organized into rows for the fifteen local children who attended independent study here, and into rows for the audience, which numbered twice as many. Shane sat in the next row back with his fiancée, Franny Clark, Adam's mom. Next to him was Laurel and her fiancé, Mitch, who were there to watch Mitch's daughter, Gabby.

Ivy chose a seat up front. Cam stood in the kitchen doorway, warm gaze upon her. Robert and her former in-laws sat in the back. Ivy heaved a sigh, relieved to be able to focus on the program and her children with the Parkers out of sight.

Eli stepped forward but before he could start the proceedings, Robert played musical chairs, coming to sit beside Ivy, which caused Cam to bookend her on the other side.

Ivy drew a calming breath.

"Ladies and gentlemen, thank you for coming to our annual promotion ceremony. I'm going to begin with our oldest students and then we'll have our milestone graduations at the end of our program. Let's start with Gabby Kincaid."

Gabby joined Eli, blushing furiously as Eli talked about her journey through the school year—"despite minor setbacks, like a broken nose"—along with what subjects she'd mastered and the highlights of her work.

Robert turned his head and made a fake snoring noise.

Ivy leaned away from him, shoulder connecting with Cam's. She caught R.J.'s eye and smirked, trying to send a clear message—being rude wasn't cool.

"Is your ex a classically trained chef?" Cam whispered. "He can't be. They teach manners at culinary school."

Ivy shushed him. Robert glared at him. And Shane gave Cam's shoulder a little shove from behind.

Things progressed, despite the two men on either side of Ivy huffing like bulls ready to charge out of the gate.

"R. J. Parker." Eli called up Ivy's oldest.

"That's my boy," Robert said, eliciting polite laughter. "Robert Junior. I bet he was best at everything."

Ivy pretended Robert wasn't sitting next to her. Her back was ramrod-straight and her smile would not be broken.

Eli discussed R.J.'s scholastic arc, from mastering multiplication up to his nines to his advanced reading level. "And he's started cooking snacks for us, which we greatly appreciate."

"A money-making chip off the old block." Robert's voice grated on Ivy.

"We don't charge the kids for snacks," Ivy said stiffly.

"Get out." Robert snorted. "You see? This is why you need to disappear, and I need to run this place. I could increase profits like that." He snapped his fingers.

Ivy's vision blurred around the edges.

From the kitchen, Sarah made a strangled

noise. She bought in to the seriousness of Robert's threat.

Threats aren't action. Ivy had to believe it or she couldn't sit next to him and remain calm.

"Ahem." Eli put a finger to his lips. "I didn't want you to miss R.J. receiving his third-grade certificate."

Robert waved a hand, like a king giving a serf permission to continue.

Ivy's shoulders tensed. She didn't hear the rest of Eli's presentation. Robert had no qualms threatening her in public. This took things to a new level.

"And now for our kindergarten graduates." Eli directed Nick and Adam to come forward. He spoke about their kindheartedness and enthusiasm for different subjects. And then he said, "We have a tradition at Second Chance Charter School. Graduates pick their favorite song or poem and give us their version. Nick and Adam chose the same song—the alphabet song. They've put together a little performance." He stepped back.

Nick and Adam shuffled forward, and then turned to face each other, grinning like kids who'd successfully stolen cookies from the cookie jar.

"One, two, three, four," Nick said, counting down, and then launched into the song. *"A-B-C-D-E-F-G."* He threw two finger guns at Adam.

"H-I-J-K-L-M-N-O-P." Adam pointed back at Nick.

"Q-R-S."

"T-U-V."

"W-X."

"Y and *Z."*

The pair of graduates faced the crowd and sang together. "Now I know my ABCs. Next time won't you sing with me?"

And then they started the song again, but this time they stomped their feet and slapped their palms together in coordinated high fives. For the third round of the alphabet, every student joined in. The performance brought a smile to Ivy's face. She gave the pair a standing ovation when they were through.

Adam and Nick removed their hats and bowed.

"When did they practice this?" Ivy asked R.J. afterward.

"When we did P.E. on Sled Hill." R.J. grinned. "Mr. Garland wanted to surprise you. Were you?"

"Yes."

A group entered the diner as Eli wrapped up

the ceremony. Ivy didn't pay much attention to them. She wanted to lavish some attention on her kids and encourage guests to eat Cam's cake before many of them headed over to the lake near the Bucking Bull Ranch.

"I need to talk to you, Ivy." Sarah glanced toward Robert. "In private."

"I can't right now." Ivy squeezed her hand, imagining she knew what Sarah wanted to warn her about—Robert. "It's Nick's first school graduation." She wanted everything to be perfect for him and perfectly normal. One of Sarah's lectures about Robert and safety, and she'd be a nervous wreck.

"But—"

"I'll be careful at the party. I promise." She nodded toward the order wheel. "You better help Cam with those orders or he'll be cranky all afternoon."

Sarah smiled and nodded.

A quick glance around revealed the Parkers had left. Another quick glance and she recognized who'd come in. It was Laurel's twin sister, Ashley, the famous redheaded actress, and her mother, she of the high gastronomic expectations. They were joined by Holden Monroe and a woman Ivy didn't recognize. They'd taken Shane's reserved booth—whether to annoy him or not wasn't clear. From what Ivy had noticed on their previous visits, Shane wasn't the biggest fan of Holden or Ashley's mother, and vice versa.

Although Ivy didn't want to, she swung by their table to greet them. They were Monroes, after all, and while she was in Second Chance, she needed as much Monroe goodwill as she could get. "Can I bring anyone water?"

"Sparkling?" Ashley's mother asked. At Ivy's shake of the head, she asked, "Bottled?"

"Tap." Ivy infused her answer with a warmth she didn't feel. She'd had go-rounds with Genevieve Monroe before. "Or we have tea or coffee."

"But no lattes," Ashley's mother said, continuing with her barbs.

Ivy didn't miss the implication. Genevieve was used to the finer things in life.

"We placed an order with Camden." Ashley's mother smiled at Holden. "Such a talent. Too bad he's cooking in this archaic place."

"I'll go check on chef Camden." Ivy told herself to resist but she couldn't. "Sometimes he can't get the woodstove we cook on to work properly."

"SARAH, YOU'RE HOGGING the burners." Cam's linguica was almost done. He'd been using the grill instead of the stovetop to cook it because Sarah had claimed every burner. "I want to make sauce."

Everyone and his brother—literally—had gone off to the end of the school year barbecue. There was no Roy drinking coffee and making small talk. No Nick playing with army men on his beanbag. No R.J. asking him twenty questions about what he was cooking. And no Ivy rushing around so fast she created her own breeze. All Cam had was the occasional milkshake-seeking customer passing through and Sarah.

Just the thought of Ivy out there somewhere with Robert made him nervous. That guy was up to no good.

"You want to make sauce. Well, I want to can." Sarah harrumphed. "My fruit is going to simmer until tomorrow morning. Keep out of my way." She tugged the bow of her old-school, frilly white apron. "I'm having a day."

If this had been his kitchen and he'd been the man he was two weeks ago, Cam would have fired her. He pushed his linguica around the grill. "Why don't you like me?"

She harrumphed again, fussing with her jars. Her cheeks turned a deeper shade of pink than the blush she'd stroked on. He was getting to her.

Cam tried a little harder to give her some good-natured suffering. "By the way, since you're watching me…watch me walk over to the pantry and get the Crock-Pot to cook my sauce." Cam strutted over to the pantry and disappeared inside, half expecting her to lock him in. When he made it out again, scot-free, he set the Crock-Pot near her precious jars. "Seriously, why don't you like me? I like you. I think the white streak in your black hair is interesting. It adds a kind of Cruella de Vil air to your persona."

Sarah turned to him, propping one hand on her hip. "Did your father teach you no manners?"

"He did not." This was the most fun Cam had had in a long time. He reached for his tomatoes. "But no one expects chefs to have good manners in the kitchen. And look—we're here in the kitchen."

Sarah shook her head in long, slow sweeps. "I don't see it."

"You see everything." He slid her a sly glance without breaking stride as he chopped tomatoes. "You're watching me, after all."

Sarah made a guttural sound, much as he

imagined a frustrated Cruella would. "I don't see why she likes you."

Cam nearly sliced off the tip of his finger. He gave Sarah his full attention. "Who?"

"Who?" She thrust her face forward and wobbled it like a bobblehead. *"Ivy."*

Cam blinked, trying to process what she was saying. And failing. "I'm sorry. It must be the high altitude. You think Ivy likes me." He was elated somebody aside from himself saw it. "Are you jealous? Is that why you've been *watching me?*" He put this last bit in air quotes.

Sarah wiped her hands on that formerly white apron, leaving purplish streaks from her raspberries. "I was here all those years ago when her car broke down. I saw the way Robert charmed her into staying. How could I not? I worked just a few doors down. I saw the way *he* changed *her.* And what could I do?" Her voice cracked. "Nothing. But not this time. I heard that excitement in her voice when she told me you'd be coming by to cook." She shook her finger at him. "I will not let that happen to her again."

The kitchen was silent except for his sizzling linguica and her simmering fruit.

Cam was almost afraid to ask… "What happened to her?" If it had anything to do with Robert… He set down the chef's knife. Thought about his question and whom he actually wanted to hear the answer from, and rephrased. "What happened to you?"

Sarah sucked in air and released a quivering sob that seemed to attack her by degrees.

Cam gathered her into his arms. Surprisingly, Sarah let him. And then he led her to a chair in the small office, kneeling in front of her and holding her hands.

She wiped her face with her apron. Her nose was red and her eyes were shiny with tears. "Do you know what? No one has ever asked me that question. Not when I was married. And not when I tried to tell folks in town what was happening to Ivy."

More than anything, Cam wanted to know what had happened to Ivy.

"The only person who listened to me was your grandfather." Sarah cradled his face in her hands. "You don't look a thing like him."

He took her hands and held them between his, as if they were praying together. "What happened to you?"

"In a nutshell? My husband had me convinced I was incompetent, maybe even crazy. It started so innocently. He felt uncomfortable around my family and friends. He felt they were unfairly judging him. He wanted proof of my love and loyalty, which meant it was him or them. Once I committed to him, I lost myself. He began to criticize everything I said and did, until I couldn't even do the simplest things without him, like choosing what to wear."

"How did you get away?"

"He died." She rocked back in the chair and gave a shout of laughter. "Can you believe it? While he was criticizing my weight and my hair and my cooking and the very way I drew in breath… A blood clot got him. One week, he was out hunting and fell over a log. The next week, he was dead."

There were several responses Cam could choose for a reply, ranging from condolences to snark. Given Sarah's laughter, he went with snark. "Did you dance on his grave?"

Sarah gave another shout of laughter. "No, but if you've got a mind to, I know where he's buried."

As if by mutual agreement, they both sobered.

"I'm not like Robert." Cam felt it needed to be said, because little R.J. had thought he'd scared Ivy. "I can be a jerk, but I'm not a manipulative jerk."

"Agreed." Sarah pushed herself to her feet and wiped her nose on her apron, which she then removed and tossed on top of her purse in the corner. "Robert crossed a line today. I tried to tell Ivy but she didn't want to listen."

"I have a feeling Robert crosses lines every day." Cam's linguica was in danger of overcooking. He hurried to the grill.

Sarah came to stand next to Cam, their shoulders touching as if in solidarity. "Robert told Ivy during the school festivities that he needed her gone. That's not just a verbal threat, it's a sign of escalation to violence."

Cam removed the linguica from the grill. "I remember him saying that. He was just being bitter."

"I'm not so sure."

Cam put his arm around her. "Hey, it's okay. Ivy's with a large crowd at the party. She knows to be careful around Robert." Did she? He'd encouraged her to stand up to him. Was that the right way to handle a guy like Robert? "Why don't you call her? We could both use some reassurance that she's okay."

Sarah hurried over to her extra large purse, rummaging around inside without finding anything until Cam joined her in the scavenger hunt. She had everything in that bag but the kitchen sink—foot powder, sunglasses, a ball of string, a melted chocolate bar. Her phone was black and on the bottom.

"Don't judge," she said.

"I don't know why people always tell me that. I'm very fair-minded." He stood close to Sarah as she dialed, ear angled for optimal eavesdropping.

"Sarah?" Ivy's tinny voice came out of the receiver. "Is everything okay?"

At the sound of her voice, Cam relaxed.

"Everything is fine except this deadweight in the kitchen you left me with," Sarah said, eliciting a chuckle from Ivy and a growl from Cam. "When are you coming back?"

"Not for a couple of hours. They just put the burgers on the grill."

Sarah told Ivy to have a great time and hung up. It was good to hear Ivy's voice, but Cam wanted to be standing next to her, arm looped over her shoulders and one eye tracking Robert. He should tell Shane about the guy. He'd know what to do.

Except this was all just talk at this point. Logic said Sarah was overreacting. Intuition said something else entirely. What had Ivy said about his intuition about the Parkers? She wished she'd had it.

Cam's stomach knotted. And not over worry about his career.

I've watched too much crime television.

Sarah tossed her phone in her gigantic purse—most likely it would never be found again. "I'm sorry, but even though I'm starting to trust you, you can't have a burner on the stove."

"You trust me? This is an unexpected turn of events." Cam welcomed the chance to make light of something. "Why aren't you using a pressure cooker for your fruit? You could cook each batch in an hour."

"I don't do newfangled." But there was a light of interest in Sarah's eyes.

"You don't do newfangled anything?" He went into the pantry and returned with a large, electric pressure cooker. Ivy was going to be fine but he needed a distraction to keep believing it until she got back to the diner. "Sarah, I'm going to teach you a cooking skill from this century."

"Not a chance." She spread her arms and legs in front of the stove, protective of her simmering fruit. "I have a lot of money invested here."

"I'll replace your fruit if it gets ruined." Cam plugged in the pressure cooker and removed the lid, letting her look inside six quarts of stainless steel.

Oh, Sarah looked, all right. Looked in and then looked away. "Aren't those dangerous?"

Cam gave her an up-and-down once-over. "Isn't all cooking dangerous?"

"Are you dangerous?" Sarah gave him a hard look. "To Ivy, I mean."

Hadn't they already covered this ground? "I'm more dangerous in the kitchen than to Ivy." He leaned in conspiratorially. "It being your first time with a pressure cooker, I promise to be gentle."

She grabbed a dish towel and swiped him with it. "And you'll be my dance partner on my no-account husband's grave."

He nodded.

An hour later, Sarah was sold on the pressure cooker. "Where did you learn how to do this? Tell me it wasn't in that fancy restaurant Sophie bragged you work in."

"I was curious and I tried it." Cam shrugged. "There's a lot of time to be saved. I can make black beans in less than an hour." Instead of soaking them all day and then cooking them for hours.

"You found a shortcut."

Cam paused before answering. He had

found a shortcut with his food, just like Ivy had done with her menu. What was it R.J. had told him? *Down here, it's short-order cooks and shortcuts.*

"Do you know what we should do?" Sarah asked.

"I'm afraid to ask."

"We should can your sauce." Sarah pointed to the simmering sauce in the Crock-Pot. "It smells fantastic."

"Oh, I don't think so." He'd rather be sentenced to years flipping burgers. It was blasphemy to can his sauce.

"Why not? Canning is great. You make it from scratch in large batches and then you only use what you need."

Cam shook his head.

She raised an eyebrow and swatted him with the dish towel. "You're so judgy. I tried something new. Now it's your turn."

Cam insisted, "Every time you cook sauce you steam away a little bit of flavor."

"So? Add more flavor when you start. Or you can add things when you open up a jar. You do that now, don't you? Ivy does. She adds a little something when she opens a jar of salsa."

"Why am I not surprised?" Cam would've

been before he'd explored her gourmet kitchen last night.

"Let's leave everything simmering. I want to show you something."

"The end of the school year party?" They could close up early and drive north.

"Oh, now you've got me worried again." Her eyes teared up.

"Hey, hey, let's reiterate. Robert is slime, but words are his weapon. Ivy will be okay." Cam's own words weren't making him feel better. Nerves skittered down his spine. "What did you want to show me?" Maybe it would keep his mind off Ivy. "Your husband's grave?"

"No. Something different." Something important to her by the sound of it.

CHAPTER EIGHTEEN

"OUR BABIES ARE first graders." Ivy raised her plastic glass of lemonade and clinked it against Franny Clark's.

They sat at the water's edge at Shane's soon-to-be-opened camp and watched kids swim in the lake. Franny's father was manning a massive grill. Robert sat on the mess-hall porch with his friends, drinking beer, always on the periphery of her vision.

He wants me gone.

Ivy forced herself to smile but inside her stomach was roiling.

"First grade is great news." Franny tilted her straw cowboy hat down to shade her face from the sun. "Except now that they're done with school, they're home all summer."

"Well, there is that." Ivy chuckled.

Their younger boys were kicking a beach ball back and forth to each other. Their older boys were waist-deep in water diving for quarters Shane had given them. Shane was asleep in a folding lounger a few feet away, a baseball cap over his face. There was nothing out of place about the day except for Robert being in attendance.

That man has got you so turned around, you don't know if you're coming or going.

How Ivy regretted not listening to her father on her wedding day. "How's your dad, Franny?" Recently, they'd worked out their differences after something like a decade of estrangement.

"He doesn't admit he needs a helping hand or that he's any different from the twenty-five-year-old he was when he took over the Silver Spur." The love in Franny's voice was clear. "Makes me regret not sitting down and knocking sense into him a long time ago."

"I envy you. I don't think my dad would sit down with me and break bread."

If you don't get into this car right now, you're dead to me.

Gabby ran past the boys and shot them with a water cannon. Nick's laughter filled the air.

Ivy bent her knees and wrapped her arms around them because she couldn't hold on to Nick's joy and she needed to latch on to something. "Do you ever worry that your boys are going to go into the family business because they feel a responsibility rather than because they love it?"

"I worry about that every day." Franny sat up, swung her booted feet around and stared at Ivy over the top of her sunglasses. Franny was a cowgirl through and through. She'd worn boots with shorts and a tank top to the lake, and she wrangled bulls for a living. She didn't care what people thought of her. She went about her business and expected others to do the same. "Ranching is a hard, dangerous life, not to mention they could get bit by the rodeo bug. Even if my boys decided to raise sheep instead of bucking bulls, it'd still be dangerous. Which one of your boys is interested in becoming a restaurateur?"

"R.J. He loves being in the kitchen, especially now that there's a 'real chef' there." Oh, there was no sarcasm in her voice.

"A real chef?" Franny put her sunglasses back on and readjusted her hat. "You mean Shane's brother? Can he actually cook? Has he cooked for you yet?"

"He has." Cam had skills to back up that ego. "And he's been so patient with R.J."

"What's the problem?" Franny cast a glance toward Shane, smiling at her sleeping fiancé.

"He sounds dreamy. Not as dreamy as Shane, but dreamy."

"The problem isn't Cam. It's the Bent Nickel. We have no backyard. No barn. No lake." Ivy gestured toward the boys. "The river is either too icy or too fast to play in. If the boys are looking for something to do, they look in the kitchen."

"There are worse places for them to look," Franny pointed out.

"But doesn't it send the wrong message? I mean, look at the Monroes." Ivy pitched her voice low for privacy. "They all had to work in the family businesses. The expectations of their parents defined them." Scarred some of them, too. Look at how Cam had been side-lined by adversity, second-guessing himself over the smallest thing.

"Yes, look at the Monroes. Harlan righted the ship." Franny gave Ivy a cool stare. "If you feel something is wrong, right the ship, Ivy, the way Harlan would have."

"The only way I can right this ship is to move away." Out of her lane. There were more and more reasons to go and fewer reasons to stay.

"Ivy, moving isn't the only answer." Franny had a way of looking at a person that made you want to straighten up and "get 'er done." "If what you want is a backyard, you could live in a house somewhere else in Second Chance and still run the diner. If you need a break from running the Bent Nickel, you could hire someone to take on the dinner shift or close it down altogether after three."

"I don't feel comfortable having someone living above the diner." But Ivy did like the idea of separation between work and home.

"I'll move back in." Robert came to stand next to Ivy.

"No." Ivy sat up with a barely contained shiver. "You won't. If you want to run a restaurant in Second Chance so bad, why don't you talk to Shane about it. There are plenty of empty buildings around." Ivy could not believe she'd just suggested a way for Robert to stay in town.

"Perfect. And when I put you out of business, I'll take over the Bent Nickel, too." He took a swig of beer and headed toward Shane.

Franny tugged Ivy up and dragged her in the opposite direction, stopping only to ask Deb Jones to watch the boys for a few minutes.

"Where are we going?" Not that Ivy was complaining. Anywhere was better than with Robert. She hurried after Franny.

"I want to show you my engagement present." Franny led Ivy to the row of cars and trucks parked along the fence. "There it is. My gas-guzzling engagement present."

A shiny silver truck sat beneath a pine tree.

"You have to see the inside. It's got air-conditioned seats and more gadgets than I'll ever learn to operate in the dash." Franny pressed a button on a key fob and the doors opened, and then she laughed. "Like I need help opening a door."

"You never know. You might have your arms full of groceries or be carrying a baby horse or..." Ivy gave up. "You really only wanted a truck with a good heater, snow tires and a towing package. Am I right?"

Franny nodded. "Climb in. It would hurt Shane's feelings if I didn't give you the nickel tour." She started the engine with another press of the fob.

Ivy sat in the passenger seat, which was plusher than anything she'd ever sat in before—in or out of a vehicle. Cold air blew on her face, on her toes and from the cushion to her backside. The air blew so hard out of the vents, it blew both women's brown hair back.

"When my dad sees this, he's going to flip."

Franny laughed. "He doesn't believe in extravagances."

"Mine, either." Suddenly, the hole in Ivy's heart where her parents used to be was a gaping wound that begged to be filled.

Robert's car was parked on the other side of the gravel road and he was walking toward them.

He wants me gone.

Parents forgotten, Ivy's heart started to pound.

"TELL ME AGAIN why we're taking a walk together," Cam asked Sarah as they headed toward the shops north of the Bent Nickel.

"You're a sourpuss, but you have a few redeeming qualities." Sarah swung her arms with verve, like this was her hour of exercise. "Keep up, will you? For some inexplicable reason, I feel the need to tell you something."

"Tell me now. Has my shirt been on inside out all day?" Cam glanced down but Ivy would have noticed if it was.

How was Ivy? He was dying to know.

"Come on." Sarah increased the pace, stopping in front of the empty insurance space. "This used to be mine."

Cam rubbed a spot on the pane clean with

his shirttail and bent down to peer inside. "You sold insurance?"

Sarah nodded. "Back before you could buy insurance on the internet." She took in his look of disbelief and frowned. "Don't look so surprised. I'm a widow. Health insurance ain't cheap."

Cam shaded his eyes, trying to get a better look inside. "What's that big piece of furniture back there? No, don't tell me. It's your trophy case for all your canned fruit." He forced out a laugh. It was getting harder and harder to relax. His worry for Ivy was increasing with each passing minute. But what could he do? Race out to the party and…what?

"Did you drink some of that wine you put in your sauce?" Sarah tapped the glass. "I ran a bakery *and* an insurance business."

"At the same time?" Cam frowned. Which of these two things didn't belong? "Was it successful?"

"It's closed, ain't it? For a smart man, you are rather thick sometimes."

"So my grandfather bought you out and you retired because ends still weren't being met." A guess, but that's what happened to a lot of folks in Second Chance. "Are you feeling guilty because you closed up shop?"

"Oh, you make my head hurt." Sarah ran her fingers through her hair, and then pressed them against her temples. "I think I liked you better when you didn't talk so much. Boy, I wanted to point out that this shop would be great for canning those sauces of yours, and maybe selling a few, too. Maybe you and I could go into business. There are a lot of tourists coming through lately, just looking for something to buy out of boredom. They could stop here, buy a jar of your sauce and my peaches. Maybe a cookie."

"Fudge. Brownies." Something decadent and chocolate to soothe a weary traveler's soul.

"Now you're on board. There's a kitchen in back. We wouldn't have to crowd Ivy."

She was serious? Cam took a step back. Sarah was moving too fast. It was like the time he'd befriended a girl at middle school and she'd started telling people they were dating. "I know we've been in this like-you phase, but I don't *like-you* like you."

"You lack your grandfather's vision."

"Oh, no. I can see fine. I'm not staying. I'm a Michelin-star chef." The words had a ring of finality. But the tune of those bells sounded like betrayal. He couldn't be a world-renowned chef and protect Ivy. And he really just wanted to protect Ivy.

Sarah rediscovered her sour face. "That's your loss." She turned on her heel and headed back to the diner.

"Hey." Cam easily caught up. "That doesn't mean you can't reopen this place."

"It does." But she wouldn't elaborate.

"Okay. You go back to canning." Cam was going to find Ivy, even if he made a fool of himself in doing so.

ROBERT LEANED ON his car and stared at Ivy in Franny's truck.

Franny's locked truck.

Gone.

Ivy had her knees drawn up tight against her chest, wishing she'd listened to Sarah, wishing she'd stayed home with the boys, wishing she had reported Robert to the authorities for making her feel afraid with just words.

"What do you want to do?" Franny asked, worry threading her question. "He's being creepy. Neither one of us has our phone. And my gun is back at the house. We can wait him out or..."

Ivy knew whatever she decided, Franny would do. If she was Franny, she'd hop down from the truck and face Robert head-on. And, jeez, what was she doing? Cowering. The boys were getting older. They needed their mother to be more like Franny.

"You go get Shane." Ivy straightened her legs. "I'll talk to him."

Franny looked from Ivy to Robert. "I don't like the look in his eye. Frankly, he looks like a feral bull. I wouldn't trust him."

Gone.

"I'll be fine." Ivy reached for false courage the way she reached for shredded cheese to sprinkle on nacho tater tots—a quick grab before some of it fell between her fingers. "There are fifty or sixty people out here. He's not going to do anything but toss nasty words at me." She hoped those weren't her soon-to-be-famous last words.

Ivy held her head high, trying to stand above Meek Ivy's maudlin thoughts.

Franny shut off the truck and they both got out.

"I'm going to get Shane," Franny said in a loud voice intended for Robert's ears, before threading her way through the rows of parked cars.

Gabby and a couple of the older kids were using cars as shields in their ongoing water-cannon battle. But they were on the other side of the makeshift parking lot. There was no one else on this end but Ivy and her ex.

Robert didn't take his eyes off Ivy. He waited for her to come around to his side of the truck. "And now, we're alone," he said.

It was the kind of statement made in the movies right before a feral bull charged out of the undergrowth and trampled the villain. Ivy hoped Jonah wrote something like that in his movie script. He'd been promising everyone who'd listen that he'd written a Western that was gritty and bloody.

Those types of movies didn't happen in real life. In reality, Ivy's life was too mundane.

Ivy thought of R.J.'s cut finger. She needed to limit his time in the kitchen the same way she limited his time with video games. And there was Nick, a barrel of pent-up energy at five. He was going to need space to run soon. And her parents… She really needed to get home to see them. To tell Dad he'd been right and ask his forgiveness for their estrangement.

"Ivy," Robert snapped.

"What?"

Robert smirked. "You never could keep a thought straight in your head."

He was right. Her mind had wandered, but her heart was racing and all she could think of were things she'd left undone. Like Robert. She needed to finish things with Robert.

"I think you should leave." Ivy drew a shaky breath. She'd never pass herself off as a tough ranch owner, but there was something to be said for the power of a well-defined lane. She was a short-order cook and single mom in Second Chance. She'd handled drunks and belligerent teenagers and kitchen fires all by herself. She could handle one pain-in-the-butt ex-husband.

Ivy tried to channel Franny's take-charge walk, just a few steps in Robert's direction to show she wasn't scared. But she quickly discovered the walk wasn't as take-charge in flip-flops as it was in cowboy boots. She planted her feet, propped her fists on her hips and said, "There is nothing you can say to me that you haven't already said. You need to leave."

He applauded. Three slow claps that managed to surprise Ivy.

Gone. Gone. Gone.

A fast glance in the direction of the party revealed no kids with water cannons and no Franny, either.

"Come over here." Robert patted the white door panel of his run-down car. "I've got something to show you."

Her father used to say "Once you put it in the sauce, the damage is done."

Well, she'd hopped out of that truck and tossed down a challenge to Robert. She'd thrown the pepper flakes in the sauce. There was no going back now.

Ivy walked forward.

Robert moved to the back door.

Ivy stopped. If there was such a thing as intuition, hers was swinging wildly, like the needle that measured earthquakes.

"I told you, I have something to show you." He put his hands on the back door of the car. "It's a surprise."

Her instinct was to flee, but she'd never had good instincts when it came to Robert. "You better not have bought Nick a puppy."

He smiled. It wasn't his slick smile. It wasn't his being-polite-to-strangers smile. It was his I'm-happy smile.

No bad words had ever been flung at her when he made that I'm-happy smile.

Ivy took a deep breath and took the four steps remaining between her and Robert. And as she came forward, he opened the back door, reached inside and turned, still smiling.

She didn't see what hit her.

Gone.

CHAPTER NINETEEN

GABBY WAS BEING HUNTED.

She hefted her water cannon and hid behind Zeke's truck, listening for the sounds of her pursuers—the three Clark boys and the two Brody kids.

The party was a welcome getaway from the continued guilt over the whole Wyatt Halford online-encyclopedia thing. She still hadn't confessed and the more time that passed, the harder it was to start the conversation.

I'd much rather douse kids with my water cannon and pretend the Wyatt thing never happened.

She'd just reloaded from the lake and was ready to fire. It was not the kind of toy her father would approve of. It packed a punch. She'd nailed Davey square in the chest and it had knocked him backward. She'd apologized but kept on going. They hadn't raised any white flag of surrender. Yet.

Gabby was twelve, after all, still a savage

kid at heart sometimes, not to mention it was the first day of summer.

She heard the murmur of voices somewhere to the right. Those kids should learn to use hand signals. She grinned and almost laughed, moving silently toward Zeke's truck bumper. This was almost too easy.

And then she heard feet crunch on gravel.

Gabby picked up her pace.

Just beyond Zeke's truck, on the other side of a white car, there was a thud, as if someone slipped and fell on the ground.

Gabby let out a battle cry and ran around the car's back bumper.

Nick and R.J.'s dad stood above Ivy. He held a small baseball bat and had his arm raised like he was going to pounce.

Gabby's eyes connected with Ivy's as they started to close and she said weakly, *"Help."*

Gabby didn't think. She hit that sucker with every ounce of water in her water cannon.

WHEN HE'D SAID everybody and their brother had gone to the end-of-the-school-year party, Cam was right. There was no parking. Cars, trucks and SUVs were parked in either direction along the highway and on either side of the gravel road leading to Shane's pet project and the Bucking Bull Ranch.

Cam pulled slowly around another tight corner and saw Gabby pump water from some humongous water gun into Robert's chest.

What the—?

Robert fell back into the open car door, dropped a billy club and then slid onto his butt on top of...

"Ivy?" Cam jammed the rental into Park, blew the horn and leaped out of the car. He sprinted to the woman he was now one-hundred-percent certain he loved.

Gabby dropped the empty weapon and started hopping up and down, and shaking her hands like they'd been burned. But all she could say was "OMG. OMG. OMG. OMG."

Robert was cursing and trying to get to his feet when Cam reached him.

Cam, who wasn't the violent Monroe, like Holden or Bo.

Cam, who'd never been in a fight in his life unless it involved food.

Cam, who grabbed Robert by the collar of his shirt and threw him as far away from Ivy as humanly possible and wished like he'd never wished for anything before that the guy would get up and beg him to throw a punch.

"Whoa, doggies." Zeke skidded to a halt on the gravel where Robert had landed. He was used to working with angry males, although of the four-footed variety, and undoubtedly made split-second decisions. He didn't ask questions. He just flipped over Robert, grabbed his wrists and put a knee in his back to hold him still. "Somebody get me a rope."

Cam didn't wait to see who among the oncoming rush of people had one handy. He hustled to Ivy's side. "Ivy. Honey. Are you okay?"

Someone was calling the sheriff.

Someone was crowding close, asking the same question Cam was. "Ivy, are you okay?" It was Shane's fiancée, Franny.

There was a lump forming on Ivy's temple and she was trying hard not to cry. "Once you put it in the sauce, the damage is done." And then she did start to cry, big wracking sobs that broke Cam's heart.

"We need an ambulance," Cam told Franny. "She's got a concussion." Because whatever she was saying made no sense.

Someone else was crying at the bumper of Robert's car.

Cam spared a glance toward the sound. It was Gabby. She sounded hysterical. "He was going to hit her again. He was going to hit her again. I ran out of water. He was going to hit her again." Shane slipped an arm around her shoulders.

"Gabby nailed Robert with that water gun. She saved Ivy's life." Cam kept Ivy close, stroking her hair, holding on. He had to hold on or he'd march over to where Robert's hands were being tied and… He knew he wasn't supposed to imagine beating the crap out of another person, but it was hard not to when that scumbag had hurt Ivy.

"Oh, honey." Laurel stepped in to replace Shane, drawing Gabby to her pregnant belly. "Listen, Gabby, sweetheart, you're safe. We're all safe."

Gabby sucked in air. "It was… It was…*life or death*." And then she started to wail like a siren, one of those keening cries that told you not just one thing was wrong. A lot of things were wrong.

Mitch joined Laurel in trying to comfort his daughter.

"You okay, bro?" Shane kneeled next to them, touched Cam's shoulder, squeezed Ivy's hand. "Ivy?"

"Once you put it in the sauce—"

Cam shushed her and found his older brother's gaze. "We need a doctor in town."

Ivy must have been listening. She cried harder. Or maybe she was in pain. Cam had never felt so helpless. All he could do was hold her and tell her everything was going to be all right.

"You two hang in there." Shane moved on to the crowd surrounding Robert.

Ivy's fingers dug into Cam's arm. "I don't want...the boys to see me. Not like this."

"Sophie rounded up all the kids." Franny leaned over them, smiling gently, so calm, so like Shane in a crisis. They really were meant for each other. "They're playing games in the dining hall. You don't have to worry about anything, Ivy. You're surrounded by friends and people who love you." Franny spared a smile to Cam.

He caught her arm. "Can you call Sarah Quill? She's running the Bent Nickel for Ivy. She'll be worried."

And she was never going to let Cam forget she'd been right.

WHEN IVY WOKE UP in the hospital, it was night and she was alone.

Her body felt thick, heavy and cold. Machines were beeping. Voices murmured somewhere else.

The events came back in degrees.

Robert's smile. The sting of the blow.

Gone.

He very nearly got his wish. After all she'd been through, Ivy felt stupid. The classic baby-sitter going down the stairs in the basement to investigate a noise, knowing full well there was a killer on the loose.

She shifted her hands, one so cold from the IV it ached. The blanket on her hospital bed was fuzzy. Nick's blue fuzzy blanket.

How am I going to explain this to the boys?

They expected their mother to be able to protect them, to be invincible. She couldn't even protect herself.

More memories returned.

Gabby's war cry. The moment their eyes met. And then being drenched with water.

That girl is never paying for food in my diner again.

Gabby was braver than Ivy was.

And then there was Cam throwing Robert off of her like her own personal superhero. She'd stared up at him, his face haloed by the sun, and she'd babbled something. She couldn't think what, though.

Soft footsteps approached. A nurse drew back the curtain that separated Ivy's bed from someone else's. "Good. You're awake. It's time for your vitals." The nurse was younger than Ivy and ten times more talkative.

"Where is everyone?" Ivy finally got a word in edgewise after she'd practically learned the nurse's life story.

"Everyone? You mean that man of yours?" She tsked, tucking Ivy in the covers so tight, she couldn't even roll over to ring the call button. "Visiting hours are over. He's sleeping in the waiting room."

The agony of being alone built like a tide that threatened to break. "Can I see him?"

"Nope. You have a neighbor in the next bed. Only family can be in here after visiting hours." The nurse fiddled with her bed linens again. "FYI. Don't even think about taking your IV for a walk to see him. You have a head injury. You're at risk of falling. And the doctor ordered a bed alarm. If you get up, the alarm will go off and Betty Ann in the next bed over will be upset."

"But—"

"Get some rest. You'll most likely go home in the morning."

But, even so, home would never be the same again.

CHAPTER TWENTY

"GOOD MORNING." CAM was sitting in the chair next to Ivy's bed when next she awoke. "I can't tell you how happy it makes me to see those beautiful brown eyes staring back at me." He kissed her forehead and adjusted Nick's fuzzy blanket. "How are you feeling?"

Gone.

Ivy swallowed thickly.

Perhaps sensing murky waters, Cam changed the subject. "I can't update you on your medical condition because of privacy laws—*they wouldn't tell me*—but I can tell you Robert was arrested." Something dark passed across his eyes. "And that's about all I know about that. On a brighter note, Sarah's at home with the kids, who send their love."

Ivy knew she should say something, but everything she wanted to say brought a flood of emotion. She stared at Cam and said nothing.

Her silence didn't seem to bother him. He'd come with a list of conversation starters for

use when visiting people with head injuries.
"I brought you coffee but you haven't been
cleared for caffeine. You can just smell it." He
adjusted her bed, bringing her head higher.
And then he moved the cup back and forth
beneath her nose. "Kona. Nice, huh?"

She nodded. Morning. Coffee. Cam. It was
so normal.

"And somehow in the midst of all the brou-
haha, Laurel and I settled on a wedding-
reception menu that centers on modern Italian
cuisine." He recited a very impressive list of
items that made Ivy's mouth water. "I might
just need some kitchen help at the prep table."
His gaze never left Ivy. He stopped talking.

Oh. Help prepping. He meant her. He had
no idea she'd made half those dishes growing up in her family's restaurant. He thought
she was just a short-order cook with a violent
ex-husband.

Gone.

Ivy looked away. It was all too much. Her
head hurt.

"I forgot how exhausting the world outside
of Second Chance is." Cam tilted his head
from side to side, cracking his neck. "Or
maybe it was the waiting-room couch. How
is your bed? Are you comfy? Can I fluff your

pillows or call the nurse to demand a lift of the caffeine ban?"

"I'm fine." Ivy sounded like she'd been shouting for help for days, when in fact she'd only been able to utter the word once.

"When we get back, we're going to bake a cake for Mack, Shane and Gabby," Cam said in that same semicheerful tone. "Mack was the one who ordered those mega water cannons, as well as other high-tech water guns. Shane bought them all and brought them to the party. And Gabby..." He pressed his lips together.

"She's great." Tears were building in Ivy's eyes and pressing at the back of her nose. "They were all great." And then softly, she added, "You were great." She, on the other hand...

I could have been gone.

Cam leaned forward, seeming to hesitate, and then lifted her blanket to find her hand, and took it in both of his. He stroked his thumbs over her fingers. "Don't blame yourself for something he who shall no longer be named did."

That would take time. But Cam's soft touch and tender way of referencing what happened helped.

"I don't think your grandfather would be proud of me now," Ivy said in a small voice.

"Because you stood up to a bully?"

She squirmed, curling her fingers. "Because I got hit."

"Listen to yourself." Cam pulled his chair closer, planted his elbows on the bed and held on tight to her IV-free hand. "You said, 'I got hit,' like you're to blame. *He hit you*, Ivy. Don't forget that. Don't be the victim."

"But I was." Suddenly, it was hard to breathe. The machine beeping on the other side of the bed let out a flatlining bonk. "I was a victim."

"No." Cam checked the machine's read-out and then loosened her fingers from the IV tube. "My grandfather would argue that you were a target. That's an entirely different thing. Victims lie down to die. And you…" He put his fingers beneath her chin. "You looked up and asked Gabby for help."

She had. Ivy was a bit amazed. She had.

Cam returned both hands to cradling hers. "Tell me how my grandfather helped you. He didn't just buy you out, did he?"

"No. He knew about Robert all along, I assume." Recognizing evil when Ivy didn't. Her shoulders curled, as if trying to protect her very essence. But those were old hurts, old wounds. They shouldn't have been so debilitating. Except everything about her time with Robert was like an open wound. "Harlan was always so supportive, so kind. He and Sarah managed to give me hints, subtly telling me I didn't deserve to be treated the way Robert was treating me."

"Grandpa Harlan was a good judge of people." Cam looked wistful. "He sure did like you."

Ivy smiled. "Five years. That's how long it took me to admit what was happening." Everything inside her clenched. "That's how long it took me to ask Sarah and Harlan for help."

"That took guts."

"R.J. was nearly three." Ivy wanted to stop there but she wanted Cam to know the truth. "I was about to give birth to Nick when I noticed Robert manipulating R.J." The same way he'd manipulated Ivy.

She'd been coming slowly down the stairwell, ungainly in her ninth month of pregnancy, all those years ago, when she had heard Robert speak.

"You're an idiot."

For a moment, Ivy thought her husband was

talking to her. She paused, one arm wrapping protectively around her belly.

"You made me burn the sauce. Look at that. It's ruined." Disgust sharpened every syllable. "What good are you? Sit in the corner and don't move. Don't speak."

They were familiar complaints, familiar put-downs. They were the words Robert used frequently on Ivy. The tone that made her feel insignificant and inept. The tactics he used to keep Ivy alone and isolated.

But she'd never heard him talk to R.J. like that before. She never dreamed that anyone else was the focus of Robert's unhappiness.

She'd wanted to run into the kitchen and scoop up her dear, sweet boy, and keep on running. But she was so big and awkward. And she hadn't asserted herself with him for years. Had she forgotten how?

She might have stayed in that stairwell, frozen in indecision, if not for Harlan and Sarah coming into the diner for a cup of coffee.

Robert greeted them, and then called for Ivy. Waitressing was beneath him.

Nothing was beneath Ivy. She'd entered the kitchen, swung a tearful R.J. into her arms and waddled into the dining room. She greeted her saviors and whispered, "You have to get me out of here."

Sarah nodded.

Harlan held his response until she'd filled a coffee mug for him. "I have something different in mind."

Back in the present, Ivy's fingers were in Cam's hair at the base of his neck. "Not only did Harlan buy us out a decade ago, but then five years later he paid Robert to leave."

She'd stood in the kitchen downstairs. Sarah had been upstairs with R.J. and baby Nick. Harlan had stood behind Ivy when she handed Robert a check and told him to leave. Harlan also had divorce papers drawn up with supervised visitation. Robert had been red-faced and livid.

"Robert couldn't just leave with the money." Oh, how his eyes had sparked when he'd read all those zeroes. "He had to tell me what a horrible wife I was, what a joke I was as a cook, how I'd come crawling back to him someday and how much he'd enjoy rejecting me when I did. And when that didn't make me cave, Robert accused me of using Harlan as a crutch and threatened to find me if I ever left Second Chance. He told me—" and now her voice got very small "—that if I ever left, he'd take the boys away. He'd take them somewhere I'd never find them." It had been the hardest day of her life—standing up to Robert, not crumpling at his feet and agreeing with everything he said. "I should go into witness protection."

"The Monroes and I are going to help you make sure Robert can never hurt you or the boys again," Cam said softly, stroking her hair, her cheek, her wounded pride. "You're safe now. You don't have to be afraid anymore."

Ivy held on to him tighter, wanting to sink into his goodness and believe. "After Robert left town, Sarah and Harlan sat me down. They told me I could be safe if I stayed in my lane, which was Second Chance and the Bent Nickel. Later, I added 'single mother' to the definition of my lane, out of distrust of confident, powerful men who might try to control me."

"Like the buffoons who try to change your menu?" Cam kissed the back of her hand. "I've heard you talk about your lane. Maybe there's room enough for two in there?"

Everything about Cam was different from Robert—from the way he carried himself to the heart that called to hers. Everything about him said he wasn't going to stay in Second Chance—from his style of cooking to his expensive chef's apron. They were at an intersection, lanes crossing, but not merging.

CAM WAS HUMBLED by Ivy's years of experience with abuse, and grateful that his grandfather had helped save her and the boys. He wanted to know everything about her—all the details—although in his heart he felt he knew enough.

Because I love her.

His arms came around Ivy more fully, cradling her carefully. Hospital beds and medical tubes weren't made for romance. Ivy was his equal in every way and yet was a better person than he could ever be.

She deserves to be loved by a strong, humble man.

Someone more patient, someone kinder. Someone who wouldn't snap when things weren't going his way. When batter wasn't the right consistency and sauce wasn't layered with flavor. But just the thought of someone else holding Ivy made Cam's fingers convulse, as if wanting not to let her go.

Love. It would take some getting used to.

Someone whispered out in the hallway.

Love shouldn't need getting used to.

"Tell me about growing up as a Monroe."

Ivy had just woken up, but she looked drained. "Tell me all about the decadence of being wealthy."

"Decadence?" Cam smoothed her hair from her face. "We didn't grow up flaunting a lavish lifestyle. My branch of the family is based in Las Vegas. I suppose the most important thing to know about Monroes is that everyone contributes something to the bottom line. It's how we're raised."

"And here I thought you were the spoiled rich kid."

"My father was Harlan's second son and probably the most competitive. The last thing he wanted us to be were spoiled brats."

"Which explains you and Shane, always striving to be in charge."

Cam liked that Ivy understood him, even if he wasn't always proud of his drive to be the best. "My father runs the hospitality branch of the Monroe Holding Company. His goal is world domination in the luxury market. And his plan for that was to have Shane run the domestic business while I ran the international side."

Ivy reached out to touch his cheek. "That's a very specific dream."

Cam shrugged, capturing her hand again,

hoping she couldn't see the hurt in his eyes. "Shane loved the idea, even if he had a rebellious streak that tested Dad to no end." And still did today. "But me..." Cam sighed. "I hid the fact that I loved cooking from him for years. Shane and Sophie were great, covering for me, at least until Shane was sent to live with Grandpa Harlan in high school."

Those had been the tortuous years. His father had tried to fit Cam into Shane's shoes. But as much as Shane was a pain in the butt, he was a good man. No one could fill his expensive Italian loafers.

"You didn't pay attention in that meeting," Dad said during spring break. He'd forced fourteen-year-old Cam to shadow him at the office all week. *"You're a Monroe. That means you have to work harder than everyone else in the room."*

"Why?" Cam asked, slowing to stare at the lunch plates being wheeled into a conference room.

"Because being successful means always having a bull's-eye on your back." His father's voice snapped with annoyance. *"Being successful means someone is always after what you have."*

"You didn't want to disappoint your father." Ivy snuggled closer. "I can relate to that."

"What about you? What was it like growing up in a restaurant?"

"I grew up very much like I live in Second Chance. Our home was an apartment above a downtown restaurant in southern Oregon. No backyard to play in. And no permission to play in it if there had been one. Afternoons and weekends were spent helping the family business."

"That prepared you for the long hours here."

She nodded. "I can't complain. I was never hungry and I was never bored. Sitting still wasn't allowed." Her fingers were warm against the back of his neck. "My parents were strict. I think that's how Robert drew me in. I was used to being told what to do, but my parents weren't effusive with their praise."

"Did you meet Robert in Oregon?"

"No. I was driving up to Montana to see my brother, who started a restaurant in Falcon Creek. My engine blew coming over the pass from Boise."

"And there was Robert."

"Not at first." She shook her finger. "At first, I saw the Bent Nickel. It was bright where my family restaurant was dark with white tablecloths. I always felt like I never saw the sun in there."

"And then you saw Robert."

"Nope." He could feel her smile, warm and glowing, like that sunshine she'd rarely seen growing up. "And then I met Robert's parents. Jarvis burned his hand on fryer oil as I came in."

"So you offered to help."

She nodded. "As they went across the road to the medical clinic."

"And then you saw Robert."

"And then Robert saw me. He praised my cooking. He told me I was beautiful. I'd never felt so appreciated." She sighed. "I only went back to Oregon once after we met."

"But you keep in touch with your parents."

"No." That was a very small no, but it was big on regret.

"Not even since Robert went away?"

"No." She sat up, face pinched. "How could I tell them what I'd let happen to me? My father was right all along, but I couldn't see it."

"You didn't *let* anything happen to you. It just happened." He eased her back into bed. "You should tell your parents what's been going on. Give Nick and R.J. much-needed grandparent time." Her parents had to be better than the Parkers. "And besides, you should be proud of you. You're a chef. And from what I can tell, a brilliant one. I can't wait to cook with you. I mean, not that we haven't cooked side by side, but we haven't collaborated on a dish. We could make such wonderful food together." He couldn't resist, so he added, "I think I love you, Ivy. We could be wonderful together, period."

Ivy's pained expression morphed into surprise. "Who told you I was a chef?"

CHAPTER TWENTY-ONE

"WHO TOLD YOU I was a chef?" Ivy asked a second time because he wasn't answering her.

Cam's eyebrows drew together. "Nobody told me. I mean, you told me you grew up in a kitchen."

The wheels of Ivy's brain were spinning. "When did you *suspect* I was a chef?"

"I don't know." He shrugged but didn't meet her gaze.

"When?"

"What does it matter as long as I believe it now?"

"Robert wanted me for my kitchen talent." He'd taken advantage of her. That happy smile of his. She wouldn't be fooled again.

"I'm not Robert," Cam insisted but with none of the gentle tone he'd used before.

"And you have been nothing but critical of my cooking skills up until...yesterday morning." Ivy clutched the fuzzy blue blanket.

"First off, I was never truly critical of your cooking skills."

"Oh, really." She rolled her eyes.

"Yes, really. I've always just taken issue with your food. That menu. It's lack of quality and personality."

"I cook it, therefore I am it." Ivy crossed her arms over her chest. "I've never claimed to be a chef." No matter how much she wanted to, she wouldn't. Not until her father gave her the title.

Ivy could tell the moment Cam lost his temper. His gaze hardened. It was like Chef High-and-Mighty was deigning to make an appearance in the hospital room.

"All right. Do you want to know the truth? I came up to your porch the night you made peach tarts and you were asleep. I tried to wake you, but you were out. So I carried you inside."

"*You* put me to bed?" No wonder she hadn't remembered.

"Yes. It's not like I stripped you naked and put you in your flannels." He scowled. "I carried you to bed, is all."

There was more to it than that. "You saw my kitchen." Her wonderful chef's kitchen.

The one Robert had never cooked in because he said gas burners were inferior to electric.

"Yes, I saw your kitchen." He sat ramrod-straight in the chair as if he was on trial. "I had a peach tart—which was exquisite, by the way."

"Is that all you did in my kitchen? You didn't cook in there, did you?" That space was hers and hers alone.

"I didn't sully your workspace, if that's what you mean. But, no, it's not all. R.J. and I had a conversation. He confessed to sabotaging my waffles." Cam didn't call them booger waffles, another sign he was upset. "I asked him to lock up when I left. That's it. Nothing weird or creepy happened."

Do I forgive him?

Should I have held a grudge in the first place?

Ivy hesitated, unsure. Part of her wanted to sigh with relief that Cam knew her true talent. Part of her was afraid he'd tell Shane, who'd expect more from her in the diner. And there was a third part, the wounded part, that was suspicious of a man whose positive regard had changed when he'd walked through her kitchen and learned of her skill.

"I finally passed inspection," she murmured, going with option number three because it had been trust of a man that had put her in the hospital in the first place.

"What?"

"You could never fall for a country cook." It was like Robert was feeding her lines but she couldn't stop, even if deep down a voice inside was crying out for her to stop talking. "Come on, Cam, you're a Michelin-star chef. What would people think if you fell in love with me?"

"Ivy." Cam sounded so put-upon, as if it wasn't a big deal. But he was a Monroe. He was a big deal everywhere but Second Chance. And there was no way he was staying there.

"Think about it, Cam. Your father would have a conniption. And all those dreams you have of becoming a celebrity chef with your name splashed across all kinds of products. What could I, a simple short-order cook, contribute to your bottom line?" It felt so wrong to say, but it was the truth and he needed to hear it. She couldn't fall for him only to have him realize he couldn't fit in her lane.

Cam crossed his arms and scowled harder. "It's not like that."

"Isn't it?" Ivy poked his puffed-out chest, trying to get a rise. "My kitchen doesn't inspire you. You were appalled by my freezer. You look down on my clientele. How could you not look down on me?"

In the hallway, the hospital announced a code blue. Somebody's heart was crashing.

News flash: *it was Ivy's.*

"And here I thought…" Cam shook his head. "You don't know me at all." He got up and walked away, past the occupant of the next bed and out the door.

Ivy held herself together by a thin thread. She couldn't believe a talented, successful man could love her, especially not a Monroe.

Fairy tales don't happen to me.

But a part of her wished they did.

CHAPTER TWENTY-TWO

"I DID NOT get up in the middle of the night to hear this." Sarah stood in a ratty gray pair of sweats in the Bent Nickel's kitchen in the pinkish light before dawn. "I'm going home. I suggest you go back to bed for a few hours."

"Sarah." Ivy latched on to her friend's arm. She'd come home from the hospital at midnight, but she'd known she couldn't stay. "I'm leaving. I need you to run the Bent Nickel."

Sarah pried herself free of Ivy's grip. "For how long?"

Ivy grimaced. "I can't say." Because she didn't know. All she knew for certain was that she couldn't stay in Second Chance with Cam in town. And Cam, surprisingly, hadn't left town. He was going to cater Laurel's wedding and cook that wonderful Italian-themed menu.

"Honey, you're forgetting who you're talking to." Sarah leaned an elbow on the counter. "Robert unsettled you. I get that. And then

Cam rocked your foundation. I get that, too. But you can't go running away."

"I have to go home."

"This is your home."

Ivy shook her head. "I have to go back to Oregon and see my parents. I've stayed away for more than eight years. I have to try and mend that bridge, like Franny did with her father."

Sarah tsked. "You're a runner."

Ivy rested both hands on the counter and hung her head, which made her bruise ache more. "Maybe I am. But maybe I can't work up the courage to trust a man again—" especially a take-charge man like Cam "—until I make peace with my parents. I can't hide who I am anymore. Or who I was. Not even to my kids. Everybody knows, except them. How can I move forward if every time I look back my heart clenches?"

"What you're saying makes sense," Sarah said slowly, running a hand through that silver streak in her black hair. "But that doesn't mean it isn't going to hurt that man of yours. Cam needs you."

"He's not my man. And he doesn't need me." Ivy would only hold Cam back. Nothing about a person's private life was private anymore. If she got involved with Cam, her history with Robert would come out. Combined with her being a cook in a diner, it would embarrass Cam and probably dim his Michelin star.

"All right," Sarah said, relenting. "I'll help you out. But only if you keep one thing in mind." Sarah gripped Ivy's shoulders and levered her upright. "Cam loves you. He may not be your man, but he could be."

"STOP OR I'LL SHOOT," a female voice ordered.

Cam froze in the open doorway of the Bent Nickel Diner.

Ivy and the boys.

Whoever was inside with a gun was a threat to three people he loved more than life itself. He dropped his groceries and stomped forward. "Show yourself, coward."

There was a pause. "Cam?" Sarah sat up in one of the booths, clutching a pillow and blanket. "What is it with you chefs and unholy hours?"

Cam's heartbeat peaked. He returned to the door and withdrew his key from the lock. "What is it with you canners and sleeping in restaurants? What have you got simmering on the stove? Sekai Ichi apples?" He gathered his grocery bags.

Sarah scooted to the end of the booth, rubbing her eyes. "I have no idea what those are, but I think you should gift me some."

"They're only the most expensive apples on the planet." He marched across the dining room.

"Put them on my Christmas wish list, Santa."

There was nothing bubbling on the stove, no sweet aroma of fruit in the air. The reason for Sarah's presence suddenly sank in. "Are the kids all right?" He set his bags of groceries on a table, ready to race upstairs and check on everyone. "Did Nick have another earache?"

"They're fine." The older woman yawned. "If you're going to make coffee, can you make me a cup?"

Cam marched over to her booth. "Why are you here?"

Instead of answering, Sarah asked a question of her own. "What did you say to Ivy in the hospital?"

"Nothing." Nothing that was any of Sarah's business. Or Shane's. Or Gabby's. Or anyone in Second Chance. Although it didn't stop them from asking.

Sarah got to her feet, straightening her twisted, baggy gray sweatpants. "Well, that nothing made Ivy bolt. She loaded up the boys about an hour ago and headed back to Oregon."

Cam was stunned. "For good?"

Sarah shrugged. "Do you know what it's like to survive an abusive relationship?"

Cam shook his head.

"For some, it leaves a deep mark of shame. Right here." Sarah tapped her chest over her heart. "And a bucketload of fear. Right here." She tapped her temple. "Fear that someone is going to take advantage of you again, because long-term abuse is like muscle memory. Someone snaps their fingers and your first instinct is to jump." She heaved a sigh. "Now, your second instinct is to bare your fangs, but there's this fear that you won't be quick enough, that someone will put something over on you."

Cam stated, "Ivy doesn't trust me."

"She wants to, but these feelings you two have…" Sarah tsked. "They came on so quick. Can you blame her for not trusting you? Or herself?"

"No."

"That's a start." Sarah did a series of joint-popping moves. "I'm going back to bed." She headed to the door.

"Hang on. Who's going to run the Bent Nickel?"

She didn't turn around to answer. "You are."

"NO TIME FOR breakfast since my summer camp officially opens for business today." Shane appeared in the doorway between the dining room and the kitchen. "But I hear you're in charge of the Bent Nickel."

"Had to tell him, sir." Roy saluted from his seat at the counter.

"I'm filling in." Cam had three two-egg orders on the grill next to a short stack of pancakes.

"The question is…for how long?" Shane asked, cutting right to the chase.

"For as long as I can stand it."

Three more families tumbled out of cars in the parking lot. The increase in business was due to Shane's summer camp. Parents were dropping off their kids, but not without one last family meal together.

"I'm not sure how much longer I can stand it," Cam admitted. Without Ivy, the diner was a thankless grind. And highly embarrassing. Two tables had stiffed him for tips and he'd only been open ninety minutes.

"Should I ask where Ivy is?" Shane had the decency to keep his voice down.

"On her way to Oregon." It was a ten-hour drive across several mountain passes. He'd Googled it. She'd have a grueling day and probably only stop for fast food.

"I need the diner open," Shane said, just as quietly. "Even if we have to hire someone to do so while she's gone."

Kudos to Shane for not asking if Cam had any part in Ivy's abrupt departure.

"Do you know who needs a summer job?" Cam was suddenly inspired.

Shane stole a piece of bacon. "Who?"

"Gabby."

"Oh, you don't know what you're suggesting." Shane crunched his bacon, chuckling softly. "She's twelve going on trouble."

"I just need someone to take orders and bus tables." And Gabby, Ivy's savior, was the perfect choice. He felt it in his unknotted gut.

The three families funneled through the front door.

Cam cleared his throat and yelled, "Bathrooms are in the back. Menus on the tables. Sit wherever you like." This was a new low. He flipped pancakes and eggs.

Shane stole another piece of bacon. "We've

got the wedding in a little less than a week, so you'll need to be here for that."

"If you're asking if I'm going to cook in the diner up until the wedding, the answer is unclear."

"Cam—"

"Shane," Cam interrupted. "I screwed up with everything—my dreams, my career and now Ivy. I don't need you to tippy-toe around me. I'll be here until I'm not."

Shane opened his mouth to say more but Cam cut him off.

"If you're going to hang around like my personal therapist, I'll leave for sure."

Without another word, Shane backed out of the kitchen. He stopped to say something to Roy and then left.

Criminy. Did Shane have no boundaries?

"Roy, if my brother just put you on duty to watch me, make yourself useful and take those drink orders."

"Can't." The old man tapped his chest. "Ticker."

"I'm not in the mood for fun and games, Roy. Slurp your peach cup and help a man out or you can forget about the roast-chicken dinner I was going to make for you."

"Oh." The town handyman drank his fruit

cup and then made the rounds, slowly, because he was a talker.

After the first rush was over, Roy left, muttering something about a stuck door at the general store.

Cam bused tables and checked inventory, and wondered how far Ivy had gone. He wished he had her cell-phone number. He wished he hadn't gotten his nose bent out of shape when she'd accused him of only liking her because she was a chef. "If that was the case, I'd have higher standards, like a *classically* trained chef."

Mack entered through the back door without knocking. "Hey, is Ivy around? She didn't give me her biweekly food order."

Cam stared at Mack long and hard before answering. There were two ways to play this—the wounded Michelin-star chef who was above running a diner and ordering frozen supplies, or the chef who was in love with the short-order cook and wanted to prove it. In the end, he didn't answer. He slid to the floor. "Whoa."

"Yes, indeedy." Mack kneeled to his level. "Low blood sugar?"

"Low self-esteem." He held his hands to his face. "I just realized not everything is about me."

"Huh." Mack didn't sound impressed. She handed Cam a tablet. "This is the food-distribution company I use. I need your order placed within the hour. And Ivy usually places her order with the restaurant-supply company at the same time."

Cam nodded stiffly.

Mack stood, turning to go.

"I don't even warrant a helping hand?" Cam held out one hand.

"That would imply something between us, such as liking or respect or the offer of a low lease."

Props to his grandfather. He'd left the town in the hands of intelligent people, at least the ones who'd stuck around in some capacity.

Cam continued to hold out his hand. "I feel a responsibility to keep the diner going, even if Ivy's absence was unplanned." And heart-breaking. "Would it help if I apologized for wearing my ego like a badge?"

"It would." Mack extended her hand and helped him up. "But do you know what would be better?"

"What?"

"Onion rings. I could never get Ivy to make onion rings." Mack was gone before he could weigh in on the issue.

Besides, he was too busy toggling through the dizzying options in frozen food.

"CAMDEN, ESPRESSO, PLEASE." Aunt Genevieve settled into Shane's booth like she owned the place, although she'd divorced Uncle Lincoln, so her claim to ownership was more tenuous than Robert's had been.

"Coming right up." Cam was grateful for the request. It broke apart the monotony of milkshake and French fry orders that made up weekday afternoon fare. A few minutes later, he brought his aunt her small cup.

"I've had a call about you." Aunt Genevieve had the polish of Beverly Hills and the self-importance that went along with a successful career as a talent agent.

"I can't imagine why." But it gave Cam pause, anyway.

"Brian Fortenay."

"Oh." Cam's agent. That was a loose end that needed to be tied up.

"I told him you were off the grid, where cell-phone service is spotty, at best." She sipped her espresso. "You can thank me later."

"Uh-huh."

Aunt Gen fixed Cam with a look that said

she was disappointed. "Brian told me he needs to talk to you."

"Uh-huh."

"I thought so." She sipped her espresso again. "Funny thing about agents. They can't make you any money if you don't answer their phone calls, texts or emails."

Cam glanced around the diner, making mental notes of what needed to be done—fill napkin holders, check salt and pepper shakers, run the dust mop beneath a couple tables where toddlers had eaten lunch. Gabby was supposed to come in later for a job interview, but he planned to just tell her she was hired.

"No confessions needed," Aunt Gen said cryptically. "But you do need to think about your career when your head hits your pillow tonight."

Cam wondered if Ivy would approve of a sign in the window that read, Now Serving Onion Rings and Espresso. She might approve of frozen onion rings being served, but espresso was a beverage that took a little time to make. A little too much time, which was why Cam hadn't told anyone but Aunt Gen that she could get one.

"We all go through a crisis of confidence." Aunt Gen set down her cup without so much as a clink. "But you're a Monroe. You'll figure it out."

Cam nodded, not trusting himself to speak. After all, Aunt Gen had a reputation not unlike the Wicked Witch of the West. One minute she could be cackling with you and the next casting aspersions on your character. He headed back to the kitchen.

"Brian will be here in the morning," Aunt Gen said in that regal voice of hers. "I told him I'd like to sit in on the meeting. Second Chance has a way of polluting Monroe headspace. You'll need an unbiased opinion."

"I won't need any opinion." Cam hadn't turned when she spoke. He didn't turn now. "Brian's coming to release me from my contract with him."

He needed a signature to do that.

What a year. Cam had lost two jobs, lost his confidence, fallen in love, found his confidence, lost the girl and now his career.

"You have no idea what he wants." And that was all his aunt had to say on the topic.

CHAPTER TWENTY-THREE

IT WAS TIME for the early-bird dinner service when Ivy pulled into the parking lot at Pastasciutta.

Her parents' restaurant looked almost the same as the last time she'd seen it—golden stucco walls, black trim, Pastasciutta painted on the side in large letters, accented with purple grape clusters. The trim was faded and the white parking lot lines needed touching up.

"Smell that?" R.J. stood at the bumper of their SUV and breathed deeply. "Fresh bread."

"Does Grandpa make raviolis?" Nick's hair stuck up on one side. "I like bread and raviolis."

"We'll know in a minute, but first, let's straighten up." Ivy poured water from a bottle onto her hands and slicked back Nick's hair. She straightened R.J.'s polo-shirt collar. She tugged down her rumpled T-shirt, caught sight of her sneakers and froze.

"What's wrong?" R.J. stared at her sneakers, too. "Do you have a hole in your shoe?"

Nick squatted next to her feet. "Nope. No hole."

"I think…" *This is a mistake.* She'd driven ten hours practicing what she'd say to her parents when she and the boys arrived. She'd forgotten Pastasciutta was a high-end restaurant. Sneakers were frowned upon.

"Don't be afraid." R.J. wrapped an arm around her waist. "We love you."

"Who's afraid of grandparents?" Not to be outdone by his brother, Nick clung to Ivy's leg. "We faced them all the time in the plastic palace."

"Ivy?"

Ivy barely had time to register the familiar timbre of the woman's voice before a delicate pair of arms encircled her. "Mom?" It was her mother. "Mom." Ivy hugged her back fiercely. And then there were introductions, tears and laughter, all in a span of a few minutes that didn't require words or explanations or whys or apologies.

Nick tugged on his grandmother's dress. "Do you make good ravioli? Not the can kind."

"Oh." Ivy's mother clapped her hands once, and then cradled Nick's cheeks in her palms.

"I taught your mother everything she knows about ravioli. And, yes, we serve it. You can have seconds if you like."

"Oh, boy." Nick shot his hands in the air.

"You may have taught Ivy how to make ravioli, Lydia, but I taught her everything she knows about pasta." Her father's booming voice stretched across the parking lot and immobilized Ivy once more.

"Don't be scared," R.J. whispered, but he stood in front of her like a guard whose trust her father would need to earn before being allowed to pass.

Her father was grayer around the temples than he'd been the last time she'd seen him. But he still carried himself with confidence, at least until his steps slowed as he realized R.J.'s intentions.

"Look, Sal. Look at our beautiful girl and our handsome grandchildren." Ivy's mother stepped forward and took his arm.

"Your hungry grandkids," Nick added with a sigh.

"We don't want fights." R.J.'s chin was raised.

Ivy held on to his shoulders and drew him back against her. "No one wants to fight, honey."

Her father's foreboding expression changed. He kneeled by R.J. "Do you know what's so good about Italian food?"

R.J. shook his head.

"No one walks away empty, not in their belly." He touched R.J.'s stomach. "And not in their heart." He touched R.J.'s chest. "You have come a long way. It's time to eat, not fight."

"There will be no fighting." Ivy's mother linked her arm through Ivy's.

Her father stood. He brushed Ivy's hair away from her forehead, revealing her bruise. He frowned, nodded and then gently pulled her into his arms.

Later, when they'd eaten their fill and the restaurant was closed for the night, when the boys were tucked in bed in her brother Matt's room and Ivy sat in the family kitchen upstairs, the first thing she did was apologize.

"I'm sorry," Ivy said in a shaky voice. "I'm sorry I let someone take hold of my life and come between us. I'm so ashamed."

"You don't need to apologize." Her mother squeezed Ivy's fingers. She'd barely let go of her all night.

"But I do need to explain." And she did. About Robert. About Sarah and Harlan. About her deep, enduring shame. And—unexpectedly—about Cam. Kind, warmhearted, sometimes self-centered Cam, whom she couldn't quite bring herself to trust.

She told them that, too.

Her mother's clasp tightened. "Do you know what my biggest fear in life was?"

Ivy shook her head.

"Trusting in the love I had for your father. Trusting that his idea for a restaurant wouldn't tear us apart."

"It all comes back to trust." Her father nodded, swirling red wine in a glass.

"What if I don't trust myself?" Ivy said, covering her mother's hand with her own. Because during all those miles of driving, many of them while the boys had slept, she'd realized that it wasn't Cam who'd betrayed her, it was her own broken self.

"What did I tell you when you were a girl first cooking in the kitchen?" her father demanded, leaning forward.

At first, Ivy couldn't remember. But then, in the ensuing silence, memory emerged. She'd been put in charge of the pasta station. "You told me to trust what I know."

Her father nodded. "Trust what we know in our head and what we feel in our heart. Because you can't be a chef without both."

Her mother reached for her husband's hand while still holding Ivy's. "The heart acts on instinct when the head is prepared."

Her father reached across the table for Ivy's other hand, and they made a small circle. "I prepared you for the kitchen, chef. Now you must prepare to love again, daughter, whether it is this man or another."

This man, her heart said.

But her head…

Her head wondered if she'd blown her chance.

CHAPTER TWENTY-FOUR

IVY'S UPSTAIRS KITCHEN was truly marvelous, a work of art.

But her downstairs kitchen was good, too. Everything functioned properly and there was enough space to create in. No, it wasn't new. And, no, it wasn't designed for a modern-day chef. But it wasn't a hardship to cook in.

And that was Cam's revelation on Day Two Without Ivy.

He wrote both revelations on the whiteboard, where they'd previously kept track of their cook-off standings.

Day One: It's not all about me.
Day Two: It's not a hardship to cook here.

Cam was developing a rhythm. Customers came in. Gabby helped some. Roy helped some. Neither one was destined for the restaurant life, but that was okay. When they weren't there, Cam channeled Ivy's warm welcome, took drink orders and made the rounds. He'd spend a few minutes cooking—mostly flipping burgers or taking things out of the fryer. And then it was another round where orders were taken, drinks were topped off—thank heavens for the community coffeepot—and checks were left.

Ivy would make fun of him logging so many steps in his fancy apron, but he was who he was—his traditional cooking roots weren't going to change just because of where he was cooking. He hoped Ivy would be equal parts surprised and proud when she returned, if she didn't kick him out of the diner the moment her eyes lit on him.

Brian and Aunt Gen entered the diner around eleven thirty. Brian looked around with interest and none of the derision Cam had used upon his first experience at the Bent Nickel. They sat in Shane's booth and Aunt Gen called for espressos.

Cam delivered their order without a word, and then waited, like a server lingering to hear if the wine selected was acceptable. Or in this case, whether *he* was acceptable.

"In case you haven't listened to my voice mail…" Brian paused, perhaps on the off chance that Cam would confess he hadn't. "I have offers for you."

"Several fine establishments in Los Angeles." Aunt Gen sipped her espresso.

While Brian laid out the offers—including an evaluation of each restaurant, their social-media presence and compensation structure—Cam's mind wandered to the quality of tomatoes Mack had delivered. He'd tried to reject them as tasteless—a waste even to add to a burger where most drowned out the tomato with condiments. She'd told him replacements would take two days to arrive. The diner's supply chain was hideous, based on cost, not quality. A survival strategy, like Ivy's lane. Something would have to change to take the diner to the next level, but it wasn't Cam's right to change anything. Ivy was the chef here.

"Cam?" Brian cast a worried glance at Aunt Gen.

"You have to get him out of Second Chance," she said, enunciating each word clearly. "I couldn't get my daughter Laurel out and look at the catastrophe. She gave up a career in fashion to live up here."

"Cam?" Brian asked again.

"I heard everything." Cam thanked him and promised to consider his offers carefully.

Sarah sauntered in with a basket of berries and a box of canning jars.

"You can't be serious." Cam tried to block her entry, dancing in her way near Aunt Gen. "The lunch rush will start anytime. You can't have my burners."

Sarah gave Aunt Gen a condescending once-over. "I'd like to use your pressure cooker." Without waiting for his permission—and who was Cam kidding, he had no authority here—she traipsed back to the kitchen.

"If it's not too much trouble, I'd like some lunch." Brian gave Cam a smile that indicated he thought Cam was a wounded animal. "Anything you like. Surprise me."

"I'll take a caprese salad." Aunt Gen stared out the window, practically daring Cam to tell her that wasn't on the menu.

"Two lunches coming right up."

Sarah marched around the kitchen, leaving a trail of items in her wake—berry baskets, bits of sugar, lime husks. "I know temptation when I see it. Those two want you to leave this town."

"As if Ivy doesn't want the same thing." He huffed, but it wasn't a very big one.

"She doesn't," Sarah said firmly. "You can't give up. Not yet. Ivy wants you to stay."

How Cam wanted to believe that. "How do you know?"

Sarah stomped over to the stairwell and opened the door. "Because if she hadn't wanted you to stay, she would have locked this."

Cam huffed once more.

Sarah pointed emphatically. "That is her sanctuary. She left the door open. It's up to you to decide what to do with that. No half measures."

Day Three, he thought. *Decide what you want and go for it. No half measures.*

THE DRIVE BACK to Second Chance seemed longer than the drive out.

Ivy and the boys left early, with hearty hugs and tearful promises to visit and call.

They lost an hour with the time change. Nick had to go to the bathroom every hour but he was pokey about getting in and out. R.J. was curious about every fast-food restaurant along the way. Did they prepare their food differently or did every burger taste the same? Why were some fries cut like waffles and others curly?

They played the white-horse game and counted thirty before hitting Boise.

They played the alphabet game with license plates, and then road signs, and then billboards.

They made up stories about people they passed on the highway.

And all the while, Ivy kept wondering if Cam would still be in Second Chance when they returned.

Could she assume he still planned to cater Laurel's wedding?

Was Shane going to be mad at her for leaving Sarah in charge of the Bent Nickel? She refused to feel sorry about that. She hadn't taken an official vacation in years.

They arrived in Second Chance before sunset. The Bent Nickel was locked up and dark. They went in the back door and up the stairs.

"What do we have to eat?" Nick went straight to the kitchen.

"Can I make cookies?" R.J. followed him. "Please, Mom."

"That sounds great." Because Ivy was exhausted, too tired to make dessert. "But I think we're out of milk and maybe eggs." It was still early enough they could knock on Mack's door and get some.

"Hey." Nick pointed at a canister in the middle of the island. He was too short to reach it. "What's that?"

"I don't know." Ivy opened it up for him. "It's tarts." She sniffed. "Strawberry-lemon tarts." They might have still been warm. She opened the oven. It was definitely still warm.

Cam. He'd used her kitchen. She felt…okay with that.

"Mom?" R.J. had the refrigerator open. "We have it."

"What?" Ivy couldn't stop smiling.

"Everything." R.J. pointed inside.

There was milk and eggs, a container of pasta with mushroom sauce, a fresh container of cream. The produce had been replaced. The freezer had a small container of caramel gelato. It was stocked. For her.

There was a knock on the slider.

Nick ran over, pulling the curtain back. "It's Mr. Cam!"

Ivy's heart pounded clear up into her throat. She ran with R.J. to the slider, unlocked it and slid it open. "I'm sorry." At the moment, she couldn't articulate precisely what she was apologizing for.

Cam was busy hugging the boys and might not have heard. They were shouting over each other, trying to tell him about their trip and the food they'd enjoyed, about the joy of ravioli and the fun of making pasta from scratch. He didn't huff. He didn't puff.

When the hubbub died down and the boys were settled in front of the television with strawberry-lemon tarts and tall glasses of milk, Cam drew Ivy out to the porch.

He didn't let go of her once they were outside. He led her to the railing. "You missed the sunset."

She wanted to say "I'd much rather see you right now." But she choked on the words.

Instead, they both said, "I'm sorry" at the same time.

They stood staring at each other and smiling.

This is my lane. He is my lane.

Deep in her heart, Ivy knew it was true. "I was wrong to say I doubted you. What I should have said was that I doubted myself. I was scared."

Cam nodded, understanding in his gaze. "I don't care what title you have or where you cook. It doesn't change who you are. You're special, Ivy Parker. I think I saw it and envied it from the moment you took my breakfast order all those months ago."

She laughed. "You've made me face up to Meek Ivy, who only wants to stay in one lane." Cam wouldn't be content in one lane, but that didn't seem as scary as it had been days ago. She could look in the rearview mirror now without her heart aching with regret.

"If you were ever Meek Ivy, you haven't been for years." Cam cupped her chin with one hand. "I didn't change your menu while you were gone."

He'd run the diner? "That must have been hard."

"Actually, it was quite easy. You see, I realized that the world doesn't revolve around chef Camden Monroe and his Michelin star."

She scoffed. "My world might just revolve around him. Although the star...*meh*." She watched him closely to see if her opinion upset him.

Seemingly not. He pressed a tender kiss to her forehead, careful of her bruise. "I also realized that it's not a hardship to cook in the Bent Nickel's kitchen. Your father would be proud of the way you've set it up."

"He's going to come visit over the Fourth of July weekend. He and my mother were planning out their travel itinerary around restaurants they wanted to stop at along the way."

Because that's how they rolled, and she loved them for it. "My brother and his wife are planning to come down from Montana."

"They welcomed you with open arms, didn't they?" His smile was so big and bright, it filled up Ivy in places she hadn't realized were empty.

"They met us in the parking lot with those open arms." She still teared up thinking about it. "I shouldn't have waited so long to reach out, but it was the right time."

He placed a kiss on the tip of her nose. "You took the time you needed. No regrets."

"No regrets." Except maybe wanting him to move his lips a little lower.

"Do you want to know what else I learned?" Cam asked, still flaunting that smile that made her heart flutter.

"Yes." Ivy made herself say it, knowing he'd tell her, anyway.

His chest swelled with pride. She liked how he would always be proud of his own accomplishments, if only because his father hadn't been when he was younger. "I learned that when you want something, you have to reach out and take it, on your own terms. No half measures."

"That sounds exactly like you." Ivy stretched

up on her tiptoes for a kiss. But then the meaning of his words sank in and she dropped back on her heels. "What is it you've decided you want?"

The sounds of the Idaho night surrounded them. Coyotes, wind, crickets.

She imagined she could hear her heart pounding in her chest like a drumroll heralding his forthcoming answer.

Cam's fingers laced with hers. His gaze danced on her face. "I decided I don't need a company to approach me with a product deal. Sarah's taught me a lot about canning and I'm going to start my own line of dinner sauces. I'll sell some in Sarah's store, too."

"Chef Saucier." Ivy drew back to look at him. "That's impressive."

"I'm not too proud to ask for help, either." There was a sparkle to his eyes that hadn't been there since she'd known him. An excitement. A passion. "My big brother agreed to lend his masterful brain toward the endeavor. Sarah agreed to be my production supervisor."

"You've really thought this through." How long had she been gone? It didn't matter. She was thrilled at his change in direction. She'd be thrilled at anything he was passionate about.

"But I don't want to get too far away from the kitchen."

"Of course not. You're a Michelin-star chef."

His smile broadened. "So I was wondering... I'd like to offer a dinner service here a few Saturdays a month. Mitch thought we could sell some wine-and-dine packages that included a stay at the Lodgepole Inn."

"My dinner service is nearly nonexistent. It's yours." Had he thought about her at all? The promise of kisses had stopped. He was all business.

"And..." Cam huffed. "And I made all these plans without consulting you, but I thought... That is, I wondered... I hoped..." He blew out his frustrations on a puff of air.

It was like watching him cook the first few days he'd been in the diner. Slow. Methodical. Starting and stopping and starting again.

"Whatever you're trying to say to me, Chef Big-and-Bad, it'll be perfect. Trust me." *Trust me.* It was as if her parents were right there with her, accepting Ivy, flaws and fears and all. "I know I'm not perfect. I know I don't have the polish and credentials you deserve. Or the confidence I always need."

"You're who I want, Ivy." Her strong, kind chef closed her in the safe circle of his arms.

"I love you. I know I'm not practiced at saying it. And I'm sure not an expert when it comes to relationships. I'm prickly and I get distracted when I'm in the kitchen. But given the chance… I would love to love you."

"You may not be a long-term, short-order cook." She raised up on her toes, intent upon getting that kiss. "But you've found the perfect recipe to win my love."

* * * * *

*Be sure to look for the next title in
The Mountain Monroes miniseries by
bestselling author Melinda Curtis,
coming soon!*